"Prepare to be terrified . . . Hair-raising."

—*Parade*

"Peter Benchley (with an assist from Spielberg) scared everyone out of the water with *Jaws*. Hitchcock showed us how terrifying birds can be. Michael Crichton's *Congo* went overboard on gorillas. . . . Add Boone to the list. He has given everyone more reason to fear spiders."

—*Men Reading Books*

"Globe-hopping, seriously creepy read."

—*Publishers Weekly*

"Building on the success of *The Hatching*, Ezekiel Boone's *Skitter* is scary-good fun that sets the stage for at least one more epic showdown between mankind and the terrifying eight-legged beasts hell-bent on destroying them. If you're not already reading this series, it's time to start!"

—The Real Book Spy

"The mark of a good series for me is that I'm ready for the next book as soon as I finish the current one, and sometimes even before I'm finished. As soon as I finished the last page of *Skitter*, I hopped on Goodreads to see if book three had been listed yet."

—*Michael Patrick Hicks Reviews*

Praise for The Hatching Series

"Guaranteed to do what *Jaws* did to millions of people."

—*Suspense Magazine*

"You know those people who claim spiders are more afraid of us than we are of them? When it comes to *The Hatching*, they lied. Great gory fun—and creepy, in every sense of the word."

—John Connolly, #1 internationally bestselling author
of *A Time of Torment*

"*The Hatching* takes an impressively terrible doomsday scenario and adds spiders, making it one of the creepiest books of all time."

—Tor.com

"It's an original plot, with a horrifying premise guaranteed to entertain and shock the reader . . . *The Hatching* is a page-turner."

—*New York Journal of Books*

"*The Hatching* is a hair-raising thriller that reads like the love ch of *Independence Day* and *World War Z*, but is creepier than both

—The Real Book S

"It's been too long since someone reminded us that spid not just to be feared, but also may well spell doom for m Fortunately, Ezekiel Boone has upped the ante on arachn This is a fresh take on classic horror, thoroughly enjo guaranteed to leave your skin crawling."

—Michael Koryta, *New York Times* bestsel
of *Those Who W*

ZERO DAY

ALSO BY EZEKIEL BOONE

The Hatching

Skitter

ZERO DAY

A Novel

EZEKIEL BOONE

EMILY BESTLER BOOKS
—
ATRIA

New York London Toronto Sydney New Delhi

EMILY BESTLER BOOKS

ATRIA

An Imprint of Simon & Schuster, Inc.
1230 Avenue of the Americas
New York, NY 10020

First Emily Bestler Books/Atria Books hardcover edition February 2018

EMILY BESTLER BOOKS / ATRIA BOOKS and colophon
are trademarks of Simon & Schuster, Inc.

For information about special discounts for bulk purchases, please contact Simon & Schuster Special Sales at 1-866-506-1949 or business@simonandschuster.com.

The Simon & Schuster Speakers Bureau can bring authors to your live event. For more information or to book an event, contact the Simon & Schuster Speakers Bureau at 1-866-248-3049 or visit our website at www.simonspeakers.com.

Manufactured in the United States of America

10 9 8 7 6 5 4 3 2 1

Library of Congress Cataloging-in-Publication Data is available.

ISBN 978-1-5011-2510-2
ISBN 978-1-5011-2513-3 (ebook)

For Zoey.
I'll try to write faster.

PROLOGUE

Mars Conquest Shuttle, Low Earth Orbit

Commander Reynard never used foul language, so pardon him, but this was some grade-A bullpoop. Where the heck was his parade?

Reynard was a born-and-bred Saskatchewan wheat farmer. Canola and lentils and peas, too, but durum wheat most of all. His mom had managed the farm with an iron fist. She was quick with a kiss or a kind word, but she could squeeze a nickel hard enough to make it weep two quarters. Reynard's dad was in charge of the actual physical work of farming—sowing and reaping, disking fields and tasking the hired help, soil testing and fertilizing—but it was his mom who ran the show. And one of the things she'd always told Reynard and his sister was that complaining about the weather neither makes it rain nor shine. If you can't change it, don't complain; and if you *can* change it, change it. And you still don't complain. For his entire childhood, he'd been taught that the worst accusation that could be leveled against another person was that they were a complainer. "A dog barking at the wind," his mother said. And if it held true when he was just a boy on a farm, his mother told him, it held doubly true now that he was an astronaut.

But still.

Bullpoop.

He'd left the farm for university at seventeen, and although he'd gone back for vacations and holidays, he'd never really looked back. Yes, in some ways he knew that the open skies of Saskatchewan and the red dirt roads of his childhood would always define him, but he'd spent his entire adult life working to trade that childhood in for the endless skies of space and the red dirt of an entire planet.

Commander Brian Reynard. The first man to set foot on Mars.

And *this* was what he was coming back to?

Forget the hours he'd spent studying—an engineering and biochemistry double major as an undergrad—or in flight simulators as part of the Royal Canadian Air Force. Forget the time he'd spent at Edwards Air Force Base during a joint program that allowed him to attend the US Air Force Test Pilot School, or the time he'd spent getting his master's in aeronautics. Forget the chunks of his life that were eaten by the basement offices at NASA and the meeting rooms of the Canadian Space Agency. Forget the time he'd spent running and working out at the gym, making sure he was in better shape than the younger and more polished astronauts who were trying to bump him out of the spot he'd earned. Forget, even, all the years he'd spent preparing specifically for this one single mission.

Just look at the mission itself: eight and a half months flying the *Mars Conquest* shuttle using a fuel-efficient but relatively slow Hohmann Transfer Orbit to Mars; one and a half years establishing the first research station on Mars itself and waiting for the window to align for the trip back; another eight and a half months flying the return. How about that? Almost three years of his life. Sure, humanity had reached the point where simply going to space was no longer enough to make you famous—the Wikipedia list of people who've been in space was absurdly long—and even walking on the moon was a crowded field. But to be the first person on Mars? The first man to set foot on the Red Planet? The first human to stride upon a giant, cold, dusty sphere floating among the stars? That had to count for something, didn't it?

When it was already old news, the black-and-white echo of Neil Armstrong's one small step on the moon gave him the shivers as a kid. And even as Reynard stepped down the ladder and let the weak gravity of Mars pull him to the surface—even as he said the words that had been so carefully prepared for him by the committee that represented all six of the countries on the *Mars Conquest* Shuttle team—Armstrong's voice, static and all, ran through him like lightning. It felt electric.

So Commander Reynard thought it was reasonable to want a hero's welcome when he landed back on Earth. He thought it was reasonable to believe that he'd take his place among the great explorers of human history. And, gosh darn it, he thought it was reasonable to expect a ticker-tape parade when he returned.

He knew he was being ridiculous. Even if he hadn't been raised by a mother who thought that complaining was a cardinal sin—followed closely by bragging and then using foul language—he would have recognized that it was crazy for him to be upset that there wasn't going to be a parade. There were bigger things to worry about.

Maybe that was why he was fixated on his disappointment about the lack of a parade. It gave him something to think about other than the unthinkable. He and the rest of the crew had followed along when the first news of the spiders started making the rounds—bandwidth was limited at times, but they did have Internet access—and they'd alternated between disbelief and horror. It had seemed bad enough as they'd gotten closer and closer to Earth: a nuclear accident in China that turned out to be no accident and was just a harbinger of things to come, followed by outbreaks of spiders around the globe. And then, suddenly, it seemed like it was over. The Earth was reeling, but it still turned as it always did. As they settled into low Earth orbit in preparation for landing the shuttle, Commander Reynard thought how easy it would have been for him and his crew to be oblivious to what had happened below.

From two hundred kilometers up, Earth was luminous and peaceful. So startling in its beauty that Reynard, who never tired of gazing upon the planet of his birth, sometimes doubted that what he was looking at was even real. If he hadn't been a man of science, he might have entertained the idea that this was all some sort of dream, or that Earth was the product of some great being beyond his comprehension. Despite a childhood of being a good Protestant, as an adult he'd become a member of the church of science. He worshipped at the altar of math and engineering, so it was difficult to think of the hand of God. And yet, as he watched the sun rise and set and rise and set over Earth as the shuttle sped around in orbit at a speed of more than seven kilometers per second, it was almost impossible for Reynard not to believe in a higher power. As he'd said when he first stepped foot on Mars, "Mankind's place is among the heavens."

And then there'd been the second round of outbreaks.

But in the days between the end of the first outbreak and the beginning of the second, the crew had spent a lot of time . . . Well, no matter what kind of a spin he wanted to put on it, probably the best way to say it was that they had spent a lot of time freaking out.

Science officers Ya Zhang and Vasily Sokolov had gotten extremely different information from the Chinese and Russian governments, respectively, which made everybody nervous. They were all scientists, and they were used to working with data. Ya was told not to worry despite the fact that China had basically nuked half of itself, and Vasily was told there was a spider menace but it was being contained because of Russian ingenuity.

Reynard had called a meeting to talk about it, and after hours and hours of comparing information, of going back and forth, they'd decided that there wasn't anything to do but wait for orders. So they'd done everything they could to prepare for landing the shuttle, which under normal conditions would have kept them busy and anxious enough as is.

But it quickly became clear that these were not normal conditions, and when the second round of outbreaks began, it was almost a relief; Reynard realized he'd been expecting it from the moment the first outbreak died out, and to have it finally happen felt like a release.

They watched President Pilgrim's address to America, listened to her explain her plan to try to break the country apart in order to save it. Out of respect, Reynard and the rest of the crew acted like they didn't see the flight engineer, Shimmie, crying. And then, as near as they could tell, all hell broke loose. Communications were sporadic from Earth, until suddenly, with great bursts of light, communications were no more. They had another argument—the kind that only overly educated people can have in a time of crisis—over whether they had lost touch with Earth because the nuclear weapons detonated across the face of America caused an electromagnetic pulse that fried satellites and circuits in a way that the Chinese nukes had not, or because society was simply unraveling. But after an hour or two Reynard cut it off.

"It doesn't matter," he said. By then they'd seen the pinprick glow of three dozen tactical nuclear weapons dot North America, and they'd talked and fought for long enough to see a pair of sunrises and sunsets, the *Mars Conquest* shuttle making a neat circle of Earth roughly every two hours. "We might as well make a decision. We have enough redundancy to stay up here another two months. So we can wait for orders until our margins are razor-thin, at which point, if we haven't heard anything, we'll have to act on our own anyway. Or, and maybe I'm posing the answer as a question, we can recognize that things are all messed up down there, that we're never going to actually get real orders, and we should just say screw it, and go ahead and land her."

Despite the trappings of a military expedition, Commander Reynard took a vote. One by one, Vasily, Ya, Shimmie, Turk, and even Jenny each voted to take the shuttle out of orbit.

"Okay," Reynard said. "Let's go home."

The reentry made the ship buck and rattle like two bullfrogs mating on a cymbal, but once things had smoothed out and his body no longer felt buffeted, Commander Reynard was surprised to find himself crying. Two years, eleven months, three days. That's how long he'd gone without stepping foot on Earth. No matter that he'd always be the first man to have stepped on Mars: Earth was his home. From the captain's chair, the view was stunning. Sunny skies over Florida. A blue so clear that the few wisps of clouds only served to make it more perfect. The Atlantic Ocean a sparkling jewel.

The landing itself was almost anticlimactic. They used the same runway at the Kennedy Space Center that had been used for the space shuttle, and even though the *Mars Conquest* shuttle flew more like a running shoe than an eagle, they touched down gently. Commander Reynard used fourteen thousand of the runway's fifteen thousand feet to bring the ship to a stop. They ran through all their checklists and procedures and finally they stepped outside, with Commander Reynard, as was his right as the first person to have set foot on Mars, being the first person to set foot back on Earth.

After nearly three years of canned and recycled air, the thick soup of a Florida afternoon felt wonderful and alive in his lungs. For a moment he was unaccountably happy, all thoughts of spiders and nuclear weapons and mayhem and death and the end of the world set aside at the simple joy of breathing in and out and in and out with Earth's gravity keeping his feet connected to the ground beneath him.

But it was so quiet.

Nobody there to greet them.

No parade.

There was never going to be a parade.

Commander Reynard sighed. Total, complete, grade-A bull-poop.

Bethesda, Maryland

It took less than five minutes for Lance Corporal Kim Bock to realize they were on their own. Just before the nukes fell, they'd watched a helicopter fly off with the five scientists and two civilian passengers, Amy Lightfoot and Fred Klosnicks, along with Amy's great, goofy chocolate Lab, Claymore, to the safety of an aircraft carrier. Amy's husband, Gordo, and Fred's husband, Shotgun, were left behind with Kim and the Marines. The helicopter pilot had promised that she'd come back for them, but despite Kim's desire to believe in salvation, she knew it was an empty promise. The helicopter had been overloaded as it was, and while Dr. Guyer and the other scientists might have been a critical priority, Kim and her fellow Marines certainly weren't. No. Kim was pretty realistic about it: they were on their own. Spiders were eating people, the United States government was using nukes on its own soil, and the cavalry was not coming to rescue them.

At first they kept busy. For a little while they worked to transform Professor Guyer's lab and the biocontainment unit at the National Institutes of Health into a place where they could hide from the spiders. They gave up on that endeavor once Shotgun pointed out to Staff Sergeant Rodriguez that the suburbs of Washington, DC, might not be a safe place even if they could keep away from the spiders.

"The whole reason I built a bunker in the first place was because of nuclear weapons," Shotgun said. "Obviously, I didn't expect to need shelter from nuclear weapons because they were being used to protect us from spiders. Well, theoretically protect us. I have to be honest, I'm not sure that this has been the best strategy. But the point still stands: there's a reasonable expectation that DC could be next. The risk of getting vaporized if we stay here is bigger than the risk of spiders. We're working with incomplete information, but, still, I wouldn't wait around for orders if I were you."

They *were* working with incomplete information. Everything was crumbling around them—power outages, cell phone circuits overloaded or down, the radio nothing but static, the Internet more of an idea than a reality—but they heard about the nukes: Denver, Minneapolis, Chicago, Kansas City, Cleveland, Memphis, Dallas, Las Vegas. Maybe thirty, the best they could tell, wiping out all the major metropolises that were known to be infested. Not to mention the hundreds of thousands of pounds, maybe millions of pounds, of conventional explosives that had already been dropped on highways and byways in an attempt to make America impassable. The theory being that the harder it was for people to travel, the harder it was for spiders to travel with them.

"Well," Private Sue Chirp said, "at least Disneyland was spared. I've always wanted to go."

Kim started to correct her and then stopped. What was the point of telling Sue that Disneyland was, in fact, destroyed, along with all of Los Angeles and a good chunk of the West Coast? Kim knew that Sue was talking just to talk, to try to make both of them feel better. Besides, Sue really meant Disney *World*. And as far as Kim could tell, Sue was probably right: Florida, at least so far, seemed to have remained untouched by the spiders.

For some reason, thinking about Florida and Disney World made Kim start thinking about the difference between the two cartoon dogs, Goofy and Pluto, wondering why one could talk and walk on two legs, while the other was a straight-up dog, which made her think of Amy's dog, Claymore, which made her start crying. Again. She'd been doing that a lot.

While Rodriguez did his best to give the platoon busywork, there was still a lot of downtime. Which meant Kim had the free time to keep thinking about that stupid dog. She'd always wanted a dog as a kid, but her dad was allergic. And wasn't that the craziest thing? As close as they were to the Woodley Park neighborhood where her parents lived only walking distance from her dad's job at the National Cathedral School, Kim had barely thought about them. But she couldn't stop crying at the thought of Claymore wagging his tail while she loaded him onto that helicopter.

Meanwhile, Teddie, who worked at CNN, walked around filming everything and seemed excited about the idea of making some sort of a documentary. While she did that, the other two civilians, Shotgun and Gordo, got busy tinkering with their machine, the ST11, which was supposed to be a spider killer but mostly just seemed to make the arachnids sleepy. However, that didn't stop Shotgun from periodically calling Rodriguez over and repeating his point, which was that if the United States government in all its glory and wisdom had decided to drop a few dozen nukes as a way of eradicating infested cities, Washington, DC, might not be that far behind. And while the National Institutes of Health were not, technically, in Washington, DC, a couple of miles didn't seem like sufficient distance where mushroom clouds were concerned.

Every time Shotgun said it, Kim could see Rodriguez struggle with it. Rodriguez wasn't exactly an independent thinker, and with everything messed up and the platoon essentially without orders, it was clear that the staff sergeant didn't know what to do.

To his credit, Rodriguez had maintained discipline, and he'd also had them keep their distance from the other armed forces set up in the NIH parking lots and surrounding areas. Still, Kim couldn't help noticing that as the time slipped away, it seemed like some of the men and women in uniform from the units around them were going missing.

"I'm not imagining it, am I?" she asked Honky Joe.

"Nope," Honky Joe said. "Not as many as you'd think, all things considered, but there have definitely been some desertions. Credit Rodriguez for keeping things tight in our platoon. But it's a matter of time before we start bleeding." He studied her and then shook his head. "Nah. You ain't thinking of it yourself. I'd know if you were. You're too smart for that. No point, really. Where you running to? I don't think anybody has a handle on this. If it was something else? Russians. North Koreans. Terrorists, even. We plan for that, don't we? But spiders?" He laughed and then handed her the bottle of Gatorade he was drinking from. It was warm, and the sickly green color of the sugary liquid made her teeth ache just looking at it, but that didn't stop her from drinking it. It reminded her of childhood, a sweet comfort. "Better off sticking together, aren't we? Isn't that the whole point of being a Marine?"

She thought so. It was one of the reasons she'd joined. Being a Marine meant being part of something bigger than herself.

She kept the bottle of Gatorade and did her best to drift close to where Shotgun, Gordo, and Teddie were huddled with Rodriguez without being too obvious about it. She got close enough to hear Shotgun telling Rodriguez, in no uncertain terms, that whatever the Marines chose to do, the civilians were getting the heck away from DC as soon as possible.

An hour later, when Rodriguez called them in, Kim noticed that for the first time their unit was a man short. Garvey or Harvey or something like that. He was a quiet kid, skin so pale he looked like all he'd ever had to drink was warm milk, and Kim had been thankful he wasn't in her fire team. But even though Kim saw Rodriguez register that roll call had fallen short, the absence was left unmentioned. If anything, Rodriguez seemed relieved, and as he started to talk, Kim realized it was because he no longer had to struggle with making a decision: his hand had been forced. He couldn't just keep marking time.

"The primary assets at the NIH"—by this, he meant the scientists who'd flown off in the helicopter—"are no longer here. Which means that our original orders—to bring our civilian guests to Professor Guyer—are our most current orders. We're not going to be able to get Shotgun or Gordo to the USS *Elsie Downs*."

Kim heard Honky Joe mutter "Not without a helicopter" under his breath.

"So our primary goal in the meantime will be to keep these civilians safe. They were assigned as high-value assets, and we will continue to act in that manner, putting their safety as the highest priority. And, given the concerns about Washington, DC, as a potential strike target, it's my decision that we're moving out."

As he claimed that it was his decision, Kim saw his eyes flicker in the direction of Shotgun and Gordo.

"Where to?"

Kim didn't know who asked the question, but she didn't care. What mattered was that they were moving.

"Chincoteague Island, Virginia," Rodriguez said. Not a place of any importance on any national scale, but it was a good place for them to wait. It was far away from Washington, DC, but right on the ocean. That way, if they did manage to reestablish contact and hitch a ride on a helicopter, they'd be a little closer to the safety of the aircraft carriers. As Rodriguez told them the plan, Kim could see her fellow Marines looking around at the other troops in the area, but none of the others seemed to be thinking about leaving. Kim didn't care. As long as they were out of there, she was good.

Rodriguez handled it about as well as he could. He gave them orders and was clear that even if Teddie wasn't part of the original group, she was now under the umbrella of "high-value assets" with Gordo and Shotgun and their silly little box. As the Marines started getting ready to hit the road, Kim tried to get a read on the platoon. As far as she could tell, Honky Joe was the only other Marine who'd realized that Shotgun and Gordo had made the decision for Rodriguez.

They didn't have Hummers or joint light tactical vehicles— JLTVs—so they commandeered civilian vehicles from the parking lots at NIH and surrounding areas. It turned out that between Private First Class Elroy Trotter's history as a juvenile delinquent and Gordo's and Shotgun's skill with electronics, hot-wiring a bunch of SUVs and pickup trucks wasn't that hard. A couple of the guys—all guys, no women—grumbled that it seemed a shame not to "borrow" the gleaming fire-orange Porsche 911 GT3 that was daintily angled across two parking spots.

"Come on. Look at her. That's sex on wheels," Private Hamitt Frank said to Kim. "You know how much one of those things goes for?" Mitts shook his head, his eyes drooping in sadness like a hound dog's. "Fully loaded like that? It's got ceramic composite brakes, all kinds of carbon fiber crap . . ." He trailed off as he ran his finger along the roofline. For a moment Kim thought he had actual tears in his eyes. "Two hundred thousand dollars. At least. And all it's doing is sitting here."

But Rodriguez had been explicit: only vehicles with four-wheel drive and high ground clearance. The air force had done a number on the roads and bridges of the western and central United States of America. So far, the East Coast had been largely unscathed, but that didn't mean it would be easy travels. Rodriguez wanted them to be able to cut across fields and drive over curbs, to go cross-country when needed. Even if it hadn't been an order from Rodriguez to stick to trucks and SUVs, it was, Kim thought, a good decision. Besides, what was it with boys and fancy cars? Personally, she'd take a kick-ass pickup truck over a sports car any day.

She ended up behind the wheel of a Nissan Titan. The truck was a beast, and either it was brand-new, or whoever owned it treated it with a tenderness that Kim had never gotten from any boyfriend. She wasn't sure exactly how it had shaken out the way it did, but she ended up with all three of the civilians in her truck: Teddie in the front seat with her camera, Gordo directly behind Kim, and Shotgun behind Teddie. Teddie had offered to let Shotgun sit in front, since he was so much taller than she was, but he'd waved her off and said it was fine as long as she scooted the seat up.

"That was neatly done. You backed Rodriguez into a corner without embarrassing him," Kim said to Shotgun as they pulled out of the lot. She glanced in the rearview mirror and met his eyes.

"I don't know what you're talking about," he said, but it was clear he knew exactly what Kim was talking about.

For the first hour or two, she mostly tuned out the men in the backseat. They were talking about gigahertz and megahertz and ionization and frequency and longwave and shortwave and even sky wave propagation, although at that point she had long lost the thread. Teddie plugged her digital video camera into one of the twelve-volt ports to charge—Kim didn't know much about cameras, but it looked expensive—and then promptly fell asleep. Which meant that Kim was free to sync her phone to the truck's Bluetooth system and listen to the old-school rap playlist her best friend from high school had made.

The driving itself almost drove her crazy. Rodriguez had ordered his eight vehicles to stay in tight formation, which probably wouldn't have been a big deal if it weren't for the traffic. The roads were clogged. It seemed like everybody was trying to either get to DC or leave DC at the same time. They'd creep along for a few minutes and then drive a hundred yards at speed and then come to a complete stop for five full minutes. When a gap did open up, trying to get all eight trucks and SUVs through together was maddening. By the time Kim was singing along to the Sugarhill Gang's "Rapper's Delight," two hours after they'd left the NIH, they'd barely traveled four miles.

Which made her particularly cranky about Shotgun's request.

"Or a Walmart," he said. "Honestly, a Radio Shack would be ideal, but unless your cell phone is magically working and we can figure out where the nearest Radio Shack is, we're better off just finding a big-box computer store."

"But a Walmart really would be fine if we can't find a tech store or a Radio Shack," Gordo piped up.

"But I'd prefer a Radio Shack."

"Do you happen to know where the closest Radio Shack is? Or a Walmart?" she asked.

"No." Shotgun sounded doleful. "We've both got satellite phones, but no dice on Internet. Texts, sure. And I think probably voice calls would go through. But Google has deserted us."

Almost as a joke, Kim tried her own cell phone. She couldn't remember the last time she'd been able to get a connection, whether because circuits were overloaded or because of the whole terrifying nuking-the-spiders thing, she didn't know. But when she opened her maps app and typed in *Radio Shack*, a location just a few streets over immediately popped up. Teddie, who had just woken up, grabbed at the phone, but before she could make a call, the signal disappeared.

"It doesn't matter," Shotgun said. "I got a good enough look at the map. I can get us there."

Kim stole a glance at Teddie, worried that she was going to start crying, but the girl looked steady. She seemed pretty tough for a rich white kid from Oberlin College, Kim thought, although she realized she wasn't one to judge. She might look tough to some people because she was black and in shape, but her mom was a pediatric oncologist and her dad taught history at a posh private school. She hadn't exactly had a rough childhood.

"I'm under orders to stay with the platoon," Kim said. "We can't just go running off to Radio Shack."

"We have to," Shotgun said.

"Sorry. Orders."

She felt Gordo's hand on the shoulder of her seat, and then he was leaning forward so he was close to her. His voice was quiet and friendly, and she had to give him a little credit for not being dumb enough to think that raising his voice was a good rhetorical strategy.

"Kim," he said, "think about it this way. The whole reason we're here, in this truck, is because somebody very, very important thinks that we—okay, really, Shotgun—is very, very important. Important enough to have your whole platoon come find us all the way out in Desperation, California, and then babysit us from there all the way to the East Coast. Important enough to divert soldiers—"

"Marines."

"Sorry. Marines. Important enough, in a time of a national emergency, to divert Marines, to divert planes and helicopters and make all kinds of effort, to put Shotgun in touch with Professor Guyer, who, near as I can tell, is the woman that President Pilgrim has personally put in charge of figuring out what the heck is going on with these spiders. And when we decided we needed to leave the DC area, your whole platoon came along to make sure we stayed safe." He touched her gently on the arm. "So think about all of that, and then think that this same guy is saying that he needs to make a slight detour. We're just talking a few minutes. This isn't some sort of candy run. We don't *want* to make a stop, we *need* to make a stop."

"We need to go to a Radio Shack?"

Shotgun's voice was less gentle. Not angry but impatient. Urgent. "I've got to get some parts so I can make some important modifications to the ST11."

"Your weapon thing?"

"Yes. Well, no. Those are the modifications. It won't be a weapon, exactly. It will be a tool. But the tool can be a weapon."

The traffic had stopped again. They had skipped 495 thinking that city streets would be faster, but it was still an unholy mess. Her Nissan Titan was at the front of the convoy, but that didn't make things seem like they were moving any faster. Kim turned to look out the back window at the SUV behind her, some sort of Ford that Sue Chirp was driving. She raised her hand in greeting, and Sue waved back. Behind Sue, Kim saw the silver body of Honky Joe's pickup truck. She couldn't get a good look at the other vehicles, but she knew Rodriguez was in the last SUV, taking up the rear.

Crap.

"Okay," she said, angling herself so that she could look first at Shotgun and then Gordo. "Fine. We'll go to Radio Shack."

"Really?" Gordo sounded so surprised that Kim actually laughed. "That's it? We'll go?"

"If you're telling me that this is necessary, that we *need* to do this . . ." She turned around to face forward again. The car in front of her hadn't moved an inch. She hunched over and rested her head on the steering wheel. "God. Anything to get out of this traffic for a minute. Besides," she said, "I might be a Marine, but I've still got the bladder of a civilian, and it's been two hours."

"Great," Shotgun said, clapping his hands together. "Take a hard right here. We can cut through this parking lot and then it should be just a couple of blocks over. I think I can see the mall from here."

Kim shook her head, but she cranked the wheel to the right and goosed the engine so that the tires of the truck jumped the curb. They rocked back and forth inside the cab as the Nissan rolled across the grass and over the sidewalk, then lurched into the parking lot. She checked the mirror and, sure enough, the line of SUVs and pickups followed her lead, all the Marines behaving like good little ducklings.

Gordo spoke up again. "Aren't you even going to ask why we need to go to Radio Shack specifically? What the modifications are for the ST11?"

Kim thought for a second, trying to remember the snatches of conversation she'd overheard between the two men. "Does it have anything to do with sky wave propagation?"

Gordo was so excited that the words came blurting out of his mouth. "Yes! I mean, not exactly, but all we need to do is to solder in—"

"Gordo," she said, cutting him off. "To answer your question:

no, I'm not going to ask what the modifications are. Look, I'm a smart girl. I did well in school and my parents were extraordinarily pissed I joined the Marines instead of going to Vassar—"

"You got into Vassar?"

"I got into Vassar. I got into Colgate and Hamilton College, too. Do you know how hard it was to persuade my parents that the right choice for me was to join the Marines? Oh, for goodness' sake. That's not the point. The point is I'm smart. While I'm pretty sure that if you take the time to explain to me what 'sky wave propagation' means and why it's important, I'll understand it, right now my goal is simply going to be to get you to Radio Shack. Okay?"

She stopped at the exit of the parking lot, checking to make sure they were good to turn. The street here was breathtakingly clear, as if every person in the area were busy clogging up the highways and the street they'd just left behind. She knew it was an illusion—that once they were back on their way out of the city, things would slow down again—but for that moment it felt good to drive at something approximating a normal speed.

"Why don't we get in and out of Radio Shack and back on the road? Even without our little detour, it's about another hundred and seventy miles to Chincoteague Island," she said. "You can explain what you're planning to do with your little toy along the way."

USS *Elsie Downs*, Atlantic Ocean

The sailors were unfailingly polite. Manny supposed you had to be to live in close quarters on an aircraft carrier. An officer had given him a brief rundown of facts and figures—the aircraft carrier was something like 1,100 feet, more than three football fields long—but the numbers didn't do it justice. The USS *Elsie Downs* was a floating city. The older *Nimitz*-class aircraft carriers required larger crews, but the new *Ford*-class supercarriers normally got by with smaller numbers. Under normal conditions, however, that still meant nearly 4,500 members of the United States Navy. Even on a behemoth like this, that was a lot of sailors in close quarters. Not as bad as being on a submarine, Manny figured, but it made politeness seem like a good survival strategy.

Of course, these weren't normal conditions. The USS *Elsie Downs* was functioning as the White House. In a conventional war, President Pilgrim would have been whisked away to a bunker somewhere, but a floating fortress seemed like a wise decision. Or maybe not, Manny thought. If the spiders hatched here, there'd be nowhere to run.

He shook his head. He was overthinking things. For now, this was the safest place they could be. He stopped walking and stood in front of the president's cabin. There were two Secret Service agents flanking the door, which made Manny smile. Were they really expecting an attempt on her life here, on an aircraft carrier?

"Morning, fellows," he said. He didn't know the name of the white guy, but it was hard to forget the other man, Special Agent Tommy Riggs. Particularly here, he seemed outsized. Manny wondered how many times Riggs had hit his head on a doorway since they'd arrived on the USS *Elsie Downs*. "She awake?"

"Fair warning," Riggs said, "she's in a mood."

Manny nodded, took a breath, and then knocked.

George Hitchens, the first hubby, opened the door a crack and peeked out. He was a good guy, and Manny genuinely liked him. George was gregarious and charming when the occasion called for it, but he didn't need to be the center of attention the way most politicians did. He was the perfect political spouse: polished and polite and yet somehow undeniably bland. He was only ever in the news for ribbon-cutting ceremonies and charity work, for visiting orphanages and VA hospitals. The closest he ever got to controversial was insisting, as a born-and-bred Texan, on wearing a cowboy hat whenever he could get away with it.

But it had been a long while since George and President Stephanie Pilgrim had been in love. Which wasn't to say that they didn't love each other. They got along wonderfully. They just weren't *in* love. Manny, who was closer to the president than anybody alive—including her husband—had never seen them fight or heard Steph say a bad word about him. And though he was sure George must have known that Manny and Steph had been carrying on an on-again, off-again decades-long romance ever since

Manny had split from his wife, Melanie, George never let it show. For a while, one of Manny's big political worries had been that George would get tired of the marriage, but the man had been stalwart. Amazingly so.

"Manny," George said, shaking his head. He opened the door wide. It was the captain's quarters, and big by the standards of a ship's accommodations. Much bigger than Manny's, which would have been considered small even by the standards of a New York City bathroom. Of course, Steph was the president and he was only the White House chief of staff, and they were on an aircraft carrier, and spiders were eating people and nukes were falling, so Manny was trying not to be precious about it.

George glanced at Special Agent Riggs and then whispered, "Did Tommy tell you?"

Manny lowered his voice, too. "He said she's in a bit of a mood."

George grimaced. "That's one way of putting it. I'm sure that if I drew upon my Texas roots I could come up with a great colloquial expression having to do with rattlesnakes or something, but yeah. Be forewarned."

"Unfortunately, we've got work to do," Manny said, and stepped in.

Manny was shocked. He'd expected Steph to be hopped up and angry, but she was sitting on the bed. Her elbows were on her knees and she had her head resting on her hands. She was staring at the floor. She looked, Manny thought, defeated.

He turned to George. "Uh, hey, do you mind—"

"No worries," George said. "I was thinking maybe I'd head down to the mess and see about getting some breakfast. Half an hour enough time?"

Manny nodded and then closed the door as George left the room. He walked across the room, stood in front of Steph, hesitated, and then sat down next to her. He put his arm around her shoulder but she stayed rigid, and it worried him.

This wasn't the Stephanie he knew. She'd been miserable after the one election she'd lost, when she'd fallen short in her Senate bid by barely fifteen hundred votes. Worse still, the saddest he'd ever seen her had been after her second miscarriage, when the doctors told her that she and George should stop trying, which was the moment, he thought, when her marriage to George had truly stopped being about love. But even though she'd been devastated by both events—she'd cried and cried in private, no matter how well she held up in public—he'd never seen her like this. Defeated.

Broken.

Her voice was hollow. "I can't do it. I can't go to the meeting. My entire life I've had to push back against the assumption that, because I was a woman, I wasn't strong enough to be the president. And I've done it. I've stared down all the double standards and all the crap that came from the old boys who thought talking down to me was a good strategy. I made the hard decisions when I was a governor and when I was a senator, and I've made the hard decisions since I've become president. But I can't do it, Manny. My god, it was bad enough ordering the Spanish Protocol, to bomb our own roads and bridges, to tear the whole country apart. But bombing our own cities? The uniforms can throw around the word 'tactical' all they want, but at the end of the day? I ordered nuclear weapons to be used on our own soil. Denver. Chicago. Minneapolis. How many millions of people died because of my orders? How many millions of people did I save? Did I make the right decision, Manny? I don't know. What I know is that I pretty much maxed out that card."

Manny was quiet. She was right. The damage from the nuclear

weapons was incalculable. It had been an almost impossible decision. It was like treating an aggressive cancer. If you did nothing,
you'd die. But if you used heavy-duty chemotherapy, the chem-
icals in the chemo regime might kill you faster than they killed
the cancer. Same thing for the nukes. It was the quickest way of
destroying and containing spiders in the places where they knew
of—or suspected—infestations and outbreaks, but the costs were
so high.

They'd tried to be careful. They had. There were ways to use
nuclear weapons to cause maximum long-term damage—you
could irradiate an area beyond redemption—but they'd tried to
avoid that. The strikes had been tactical. Although there was no real
"safe" use of nuclear weapons, the military had done everything
to minimize fallout and radiation. Still, the scientific consensus
was that they were already pushing their luck. To *keep* using nukes
was to push America past the point of no return. If the spiders
were the cancer, well, they were going to have to let the cancer run
its course. There were some members of the military who were
pushing Steph hard to pursue a scorched-earth policy—the goddamned chairman of the Joint Chiefs of Staff, Ben Broussard, was
back to being a pushy son of a bitch—and destroy all the spiders,
whatever the cost.

"What was the point of it, Manny? Do you think Broussard's
right?" Steph asked. "Too little, too late?"

They were both quiet then. He knew she didn't really want an
answer. Broussard had been pressing his case over and over again.
He'd backed off a little last week when they authorized the Spanish Protocol, making nice with Steph so he could have the win.
But he was trying to lay blame. He was now claiming that much of
the damage from the spiders could have been averted if Steph had
acted more aggressively in the first place. If she'd gone nuclear the

minute the spiders hit the shore in Los Angeles. If she'd done that, Broussard kept saying, then America would have been safe.

They were quiet, because there was a chance Broussard was right.

The idea had been consuming Manny since they'd landed on the USS *Elsie Downs*. What if the moment that cargo ship had crashed into the port of Los Angeles—what if the moment they knew those spiders were loose in LA—they'd just wiped the whole city off the map? It was a terrible exercise, to second-guess like this. Monday-morning quarterbacking. It was crazy. It was impossible. At that point there'd been no way for them to understand how bad it was going to be, no way for them to know in that moment what needed to be done.

Steph broke the silence. "It's too late to change anything. Broussard can talk all he wants. It's just talk. I get that. He's maneuvering himself to make sure he doesn't take the blame." She gave a short, hard, bitter laugh. "Always with the politics, isn't it? Even now, in the middle of an existential crisis, there's politics."

Manny said, "You've got to give us humans that, at least. Nothing can save us from ourselves. Maybe, given enough time—"

"Time!" She barked the word out, interrupting him, and then her voice grew quiet again. "God. I wish there were enough time. Your ex-wife is telling me that if I can just give her three days, four days, she thinks she's got an answer. Or, and I'm quoting Melanie now, 'something close to an answer.' Something that is going to help us figure out how to survive without killing ourselves. Otherwise, what's the point? What's the point of fighting back if it just means we're killing ourselves quicker than the spiders can? Three or four days. Do you think we have three or four days to spare, Manny? Do you?"

He wanted to tell her that of course they did, that all she had to do was trust Melanie—brilliant, hardworking Melanie—and everything was going to be okay; but he didn't know, and that's what he said.

"Yeah, me neither." Steph shifted a little. "But I've got to go into that conference room and try to sell that idea to a bunch of gold stars, try to convince the whole lot of them that the best thing we can do right now is to wait. I'm going to have to beat back Broussard, who thinks that the only thing to do is to keep bombing, and I'm going to have to say 'Trust me.' I don't even know if I trust myself, Manny. They are all waiting for me in that conference room, and when I walk in, they're all going to stand up and call me Madam President, and they are going to expect me to know what I'm doing. But I don't know anymore. I don't. Maybe Broussard is right. Why don't we just go ahead and drop all of the bombs? Humanity won't survive, but at least we'll take those beasts with us."

"You don't really believe that, do you?"

"No. No, I don't. I think we've got to have hope. We've got to give ourselves a chance to survive. We've . . ."

She stopped. The room was as quiet as anywhere on the aircraft carrier, which was to say that there was still a solid thrum of energy under and around them. The USS *Elsie Downs* was not under way, but it never truly stopped moving on the great scything ocean, and that meant there was never a true silence anywhere on board. It was the same sort of hum you could hear in places that were out in nature but still wired for electricity. The static of human ingenuity.

Manny had kept his arm around her shoulder, and at last she relaxed into him. She was crying, he realized. Nothing dramatic. That wasn't her style. Just a soft whimper and her chest shaking. She let her head tuck against his chest.

There were times when he wondered if the two of them should have gotten married. Even though she was three years older than he was, they'd dated in college and off and on again—well, perhaps *dated* wasn't the right word, but they spent a lot of time together—in all the years since.

Did she know that he'd thought about it—that he'd considered proposing to her? She might have laughed if he'd gotten down on one knee and presented her with a ring in a velvet-covered box, but there were a few months, before she started dating George, before Manny met Melanie, when it seemed like a good idea to him. And maybe if they had been different people, if they hadn't both been so driven by politics, if they didn't have their eyes on their prize, maybe then he would have asked her and maybe then she would have said yes. Maybe then it would have been enough for the two of them simply to have each other, for their whole worlds and lives to be about a life together. Maybe they could have done without the power and the politics, without the trade-offs they'd made to keep climbing all the way to the White House. Maybe they would have been happy with smaller lives, smaller dreams, with their love filling all the gaps. Except, he knew, even back then, even when he was in his twenties, that the idea was a mirage: if they'd been different people, if they'd been the kind of people who could find happiness in something so simple, they wouldn't have been together in the first place.

But here they were, after so many years together, and what he needed to do wasn't about power. It wasn't about Stephanie being the president. It was about one man, one woman. It was about the love he had for her filling the gaps.

So he just held her for a few more minutes. His body turned toward her, his arms wrapped around her like a blanket, letting her cry against his chest, rocking together just a little bit.

And then, as her crying eased, he did what the two of them had been doing together for so long. He made sure she remembered that she wasn't just the girl from his dorm.

"Okay," he said. "That's enough now. You're going to wash your face and you're going to fix your makeup, and then you are going to walk into that room and you are going to be Stephanie Pilgrim, the president of the United States of America."

She wiped her eyes and then she actually managed to laugh.

"I know. I know. You don't have to tell me. But you're the only person I can do this in front of. I can't start crying in front of Billy Cannon or, god forbid, Ben Broussard, can I? Broussard already thinks I'm not up to the job. He's waiting, looking for any sign of weakness, any opening to pounce. It doesn't matter what I do. No action I take is ever going to be enough for him and the rest of the uniforms. And if I start crying? They want to act, even if it means destroying our chance to survive. All they can think about is winning, no matter what the cost. What the hell is it with those military guys? Some of them understand there's another way. Billy Cannon gets it. But for most of them? What's that saying? To somebody with a hammer, everything looks like a nail." She laughed again, and under it was the ghost of a sob. She stood up and pulled her skirt smooth, tucked her blouse back in. "Nobody said it would be easy, did they? Nobody said being the president would be easy."

"No," Manny said. He stood up, too, and walked over to the desk and picked up her tablet. "Nobody said it would be easy. If you haven't read the briefings yet, I'll give you the rundown on the way up to the meeting."

She stepped into the bathroom and started touching up her makeup. "Nobody said it would be easy, but I'm pretty sure nobody said I'd have to contend with spiders running amok. What the hell are we supposed to do, Manny?"

"I don't know," he said. "I don't. But I do know that you were born to be president."

"Do the job," she said.

"Do the job." Manny started to open the door and then stopped. "Listen, if you feel like you might break in there, just look at me. Just look at me and know I've got your back."

The president stepped out of the bathroom and stared at him. Whatever hollowness she'd had, whatever fragility she'd shown, was gone. "Manny, the second we step out of this room, you aren't going to have to worry about me. Who am I, Manny?"

Manny straightened. "You're the president of the United States of America."

"I'm the goddamned president," she said. "Now let's go to work."

He could practically feel his heels click together as he said, "Yes, ma'am."

Now *that* was the Stephanie Pilgrim he loved working for.

Osaka University, Osaka, Japan

Koji was sure that he would have been much more comfortable if he was wearing his normal lab outfit: a pair of khakis and a button-down shirt topped with a lab coat. The isolation suit was miserable, and it made it difficult to manipulate the specimens, but he wasn't going to risk it. He'd traipsed through a spider-infested Buddhist temple in Shinjin Prefecture, but he'd made it out alive. The scientists who'd tried going in wearing normal clothing hadn't. Hence, the isolation suit was staying on as long as he was in the same room as these monsters.

It meant, however, that he could spend only so long in the lab before having to go through the series of doors and procedures that had been installed to ensure that there was no chance of any of the spiders getting out. It was a little ridiculous, the lengths to which he had to go to get in and out of the lab, which he knew was an odd thing to hear from a scientist who was still having nightmares about the twenty minutes he'd spent in the temple and who insisted on wearing an isolation suit even though all the spiders were in insectariums, safely behind glass. Even when he did take a single spider out, there were so many precautions that the chances of anything going wrong were so slim . . .

It didn't matter. One mistake was one mistake too many. All you had to do was look at a map and think about how many cities could be scratched out to know that was true.

He'd been in the lab for nearly an hour, and he figured he had about five more minutes before he needed to take a break. The suit was so hot that by the end of each of the last few days, he'd sweated out more than three kilograms of water weight. He'd taken to eating as much salty food as he could in the hope that he'd retain some fluid. Five minutes was enough time for him to clean up, though. He was done with the vivisection, and all that was left was to put the remains in the incinerator and clean up his instruments.

Not that he was any closer to an understanding. He'd been against burning the temple in the first place. Yes, of course it made sense to contain the menace, but it also meant there was no hope of his understanding what was happening. No hope of figuring out how to stop it. He was sure that if they'd only given him a little more time . . .

Still, at least he'd been allowed to take thirty spiders with him back to his lab. He had to obey all the restrictions placed on him, including allowing the military to wire his lab with explosives so they could blow up the whole thing at a moment's notice if there was some sort of breach. That didn't make him happy, but what could he do? He simply agreed to all of the conditions, put on his isolation suit, and did his work as best he could. The misery was just something to be endured.

The misery was worth it. The spiders hadn't acted the way he had expected at all. He had no doubt that they were still dangerous—hence the isolation suit and all the precautionary measures—but there was none of the savagery. They appeared completely uninterested in feeding. It made more sense once he realized that his samples had begun ecdysis. Like most spiders, they fasted in the time immediately prior to molting. What worried him, however, was what it meant. Given that these spiders were nothing like anything he'd seen before, was this simply a case of their shedding their exoskeletons so they could increase in size, or was it something worse?

He hated that he was essentially working blind. He'd been able to share some information with the lead American scientist, but he hadn't been able to get in touch with Dr. Guyer for more than forty-eight hours. He didn't know if it was because communications were down or if something worse had happened. News was just one more thing that had become unreliable since the onset of this crisis.

He scraped what was left of the spider he'd been working on into the incinerator and then placed his tools in the autoclave. Laboriously he went through every checkpoint and inspection, and it was another ten minutes before he was able to take off the isolation suit. His hair was matted with sweat, and he'd soaked through his clothes. He was spent, and he couldn't decide what he needed more, a shower or a nap. He thought for a moment about trying to get through to the Americans again, but he was too tired. In the morning, he thought.

Soot Lake, Minnesota

Mike looked at the ladder skeptically. His ex-wife's husband, Rich Dawson, wasn't the kind of guy who did his own maintenance. That was probably the worst thing Mike could say about him—well, that and the fact that the guy was a criminal defense lawyer—but it meant the old shed out back was full of cast-off tools and bits and pieces that dated from the construction of Dawson's cottage. After last night's storm, somebody had to fix the gutter. Unfortunately, that somebody ended up being Mike. He wasn't particularly handy himself, but his partner, Leshaun, begged off on account of the fact that he'd been shot relatively recently. The meat of his arm, where the bullet had gone clean through, was healing just fine, but he'd also broken a couple of ribs where his vest stopped a round, and those were nagging.

Which meant Mike was the one staring at the old, rickety aluminum extension ladder. It had been hanging on a pair of rusty hooks on the outside of the shed. The ladder was splattered with paint, and when he'd pulled it down it rained dirt and pine needles on him. He'd expected it to feel more substantial, but it was weirdly light, and when he jammed the feet into the dirt next to the cottage, it gave an ominous, tinny rattle. He leaned it carefully against the roof and looked at Leshaun.

"You keep hold of this ladder."

"Come on dude. Let's go. We don't want to be out here longer than we need to. You were the one who said we want to try to minimize our exposure to radiation by staying inside. Hurry it up."

"Hurry it up?" Mike shook his head. "Easy for you to say. I don't see your black ass getting ready to climb a ladder."

Leshaun laughed. "Now, now. As if nuclear war wasn't bad enough, now you're bringing race politics into things?"

"Tactical nuclear strikes," Mike said. "Not nuclear war."

"Does it matter?"

Mike ignored the question and stuck three screws between his lips for safekeeping and then shoved the screwdriver in his back pocket. He put his foot on the first step and then, experimentally, his other foot. The ladder shook a little, but it seemed like it wasn't in imminent danger of collapsing.

Ugh.

He kept his eyes on the rungs in front of him, trying hard not to look down as he climbed. A mist of rain had made the metal cold and slippery, so he stepped carefully. When he got up to the roofline, he reached out to where the section of gutter was hanging down. He pulled it up and held it in place with one hand as he reached with the other for the screwdriver and then pulled one of the screws from between his lips. It made him feel horribly exposed, up on the ladder, both hands occupied with something other than holding on. He jammed the screw through a hole that was already in the gutter, pushing it far enough into the wood that it held for the second or two it took him to get the screwdriver seated.

He felt the ladder vibrate and almost dropped the screwdriver.

"Huhawn!"

That was as close as he could come to saying his partner's name while keeping the extra screws between his lips.

"Sorry, sorry. Just getting my feet set."

Mike glanced down and immediately wished he hadn't. He was only ten feet off the ground or so, but he wasn't great with heights. And, okay, so Dawson wasn't the kind of guy who could fix a gutter, and Leshaun had a pretty good excuse himself, but it wasn't like Mike was 100 percent. There was the lack of sleep and all that, but his hand was still sore. He'd cut the heck out of it on the jagged metal of the downed jet that had been, near as he could tell, the first real sign that things were about to become monumentally messed up.

He'd lost track of the days. It had been only a couple of weeks, but it could have been merely a day ago or it could have been a lifetime ago that he stood in the burned tube of metal, watching a spider eat its way out of the face of one of the richest men in the world. And since then? Oh, nothing much. Just mayhem. Panic. And, most recently, the brilliant second sun of a nuclear explosion wiping Minneapolis off the map.

He'd been outside with his daughter, Annie, when Minneapolis was turned into a sea of glass. He'd known immediately what it was. He didn't want to believe it, but he'd known. From the moment he'd gotten the message from his boss at the agency that he and Leshaun were on their own—they'd been trying to pick Annie and his ex-wife and Dawson up from the cottage and then get back to Minneapolis to get on a government plane headed east—he'd known that things were going to get worse. And they had, with the president ordering the highways and byways, the veins that carried America's lifeblood, bombed into the Stone Age. But it was clear pretty quickly that conventional weapons and explosives weren't going to be enough to stop the swarms of spiders marauding across the country. So when he saw the stunning flash to the south, he'd hustled Annie inside.

Since then, since Minneapolis had been nuked, they'd been hunkered down inside the cottage. Dawson had a slick setup with solar power, but Mike figured that would start to be a problem. He didn't know enough about what caused a nuclear winter, but the best they'd been able to tell, most of the major cities from Chicago on west had gotten the gift of fusion. Or fission. Mike couldn't remember. Maybe it was both. Physics hadn't been his strong suit in high school. Either way, he figured there'd be enough dust and smoke in the air to cripple the solar cells. In the short term, it was okay, however. They'd used duct tape to seal seams as much as possible, taped up garbage bags, filled every available container with water. Anything they could think of to keep the outside out, which was why he was bothering to fix the gutter; because of the broken gutter and the rain, water was streaming through the seam where the roof met the wall, a line of dampness working its way inside the cottage.

Fixing the gutter, taping the windows—all of that was short-term, though. He was pretty sure that staying hunkered down inside the cottage wasn't a good long-term solution. How long could they stay where they were? How much radiation was too much? For him? For his ex-wife, who was pregnant? For Annie? And even if he knew the answers, he didn't have a way to measure their exposure.

He finished screwing the gutter in place and realized that maybe not knowing was an answer in and of itself. He didn't have a Geiger counter, he didn't have an expert he could consult. All he had was his gut to go by, and his gut was telling him it was time to get out of Dodge. Fixing the gutter on Dawson's beautiful cottage, with its mullioned glass and cedar shakes, its deck that cascaded in multiple levels until it met the dock, had been a waste of time. All of it had been a waste of time. There was no way to keep safe if they stayed in place.

There weren't any good answers, not with the spiders, not with the deliberate destruction of America as a defensive measure, but they couldn't stay. The moment Minneapolis bloomed radioactive was the moment he needed to get his daughter—get all of them— to a safe distance.

If there even was such a thing. Was anywhere safe?

But they could go east. The roads were destroyed, the world on fire—and who knew if the spiders were coming out for another round of feasting—but they could go east. The best they could tell, the East Coast was still untouched. If they could get from Minneapolis to the East Coast, they'd be safe, Mike thought.

Or as safe as he could make them.

Now all he had to do was figure out how to get them there.

Boothton, South Dakota

She could feel herself growing stronger, which was good. But there was not enough food here to sustain her in this place. The little ones had almost exhausted what was available nearby. Soon enough, she would have to move. There was food elsewhere.

Although she knew that some of her sisters were no longer communicating, there were still many out there. She could feel them like the pulse of her body, could feel them as clearly as if they were her own little ones, and through them she could feel their little ones.

There was food elsewhere. All she had to do was go find it.

Kearney High School, Kearney, Nebraska

The flock of pilgrims had swelled to more than five thousand. Which sounded impressive, but it was a headache for the Prophet Bobby Higgs. Interstate 80 was impassable by vehicle, and trying to keep that many people walking together wasn't easy. Worse, however, was the weather. Since they'd seen the twin nuclear suns of Denver and Lincoln, one behind them, one in front of them, the unseasonably warm weather they'd been enjoying had turned. The sun disappeared behind the gray decay of clouds and rain. Sheets of water drenched them. And when the rain slowed, it was replaced with an inescapable mist that crept through the seams of jackets and shirts and left people shivering and feverish. Perhaps they should have been worried about fallout, but that seemed like something that was a long way off. The worry right in front of them was exposure. They'd lost nine pilgrims already on the march.

It weighed on him. As the Prophet, Bobby rated one of the eleven tents that the horde of pilgrims had among them, and at night he could have been warmed by any one of the many women who were eager to spend time with him. But he chose to sleep alone. There was a time, before he was the Prophet Bobby Higgs, back when he was just Bobby Higgs, street hustler, when he would have availed himself of the flesh, when he would have tried to use his power to fleece his flock. But Bobby found himself in the curious position of feeling responsible. These five thousand men, women, and children were looking to him for salvation, and, by god, he wanted to give it to them.

When they approached the outskirts of Kearney, after nearly fifty miles of walking, he'd decided to give his followers a day or two of respite. They took over the high school, setting up volunteers in the cafeteria to cook, people eating in shifts. Bobby had tasked his disciples—the people in the first twelve vehicles that had joined his caravan had taken to calling themselves his twelve disciples—with organizing scavenging parties to gather clothes and food. They'd stripped the Walmart and the Hy-Vee almost bare. Kearney had been a welcome relief, but there was no more solace to be found here. No solace, no sustenance, just the promise of a slow misery if they stayed. And perhaps it would be a slow misery for them if they kept moving, but at least that would come with the hope of finding something good. Didn't the Israelites wander in the desert for forty years before they reached the promised land? And wasn't the Prophet Bobby Higgs a kind of Moses?

He had just come to the decision that it was time for them to head out the next morning, marching who knew where, but forward, forward, forward, when he heard the voice on the shortwave radio: Macer Dickson.

Macer.

The man who, in the aftermath of the first wave of spiders eating their way through Los Angeles, had helped transform Bobby into the Prophet Bobby Higgs. The man who had orchestrated the break through the quarantine lines. The man who had left Bobby standing on the side of the road. Stranded. Alone.

Macer's voice was so clear through the headphones that if Bobby had closed his eyes he would have believed he could reach out and touch him.

And what was Macer doing on the radio? He was offering sanctuary to any person who was willing to work and who brought supplies—food or gas or anything else of use—to where he was holed up, at some sort of a rest stop on the interstate.

Bobby called to one of the disciples to bring a map.

Huh. Near as he could tell, Macer was broadcasting from less than fifteen miles away.

Bobby smiled.

And then he organized work crews to go out and bring back something even more useful than food or clothes or camping gear: guns and ammunition.

He was going to war.

Our Lady of Mercy Catholic Church, Pistol Gap, Ohio

There had been many, many days when Father Thomas resented living in Pistol Gap. He'd long since reconciled himself to the idea that he wasn't going to be part of the Catholic Church's elite. For a very short time, when he first entered the priesthood, he had fantasies about the Vatican, but at heart he was a Pittsburgh kid who loved the more pedestrian parts of his calling. Even in his early fifties, being a priest still felt that way to him: like a calling. But, honestly, how had he ended up in Pistol Gap?

His first posting had been in the Bronx, and he'd loved it. This was back when the city was still gritty, and his church was in a neighborhood that hadn't been desirable in decades. He was twenty-five and newly ordained and every morning he woke up full of God's grace. He threw himself into the community, reinvigorating programs that had gone stale, fully immersed in God's work. Even though he knew it was coming, it was jarring when he was reassigned after six years. But that was to Phoenix, Arizona, and when it was January and sunny and in the mid-sixties, it was just fine that the Bronx seemed far away. He was there long enough to learn Spanish to go along with his Latin. He conducted Mass in both languages, and grew the parish by embracing the location and doing things like celebrating the Feast of Our Lady of Guadalupe. So it made complete sense to him that his next posting was Laredo, Texas. He was happy enough there, but he was more than ready to move on after five years of dealing with a small group of female parishioners who thought volunteering gave them the right to meddle in church business. He assumed that he would be reassigned near the border. But then, just after he turned forty-three—Father Thomas was not blind to the fact that forty-three was ten more years than Jesus had been given on earth—he was moved to Pistol Gap.

He couldn't complain about the church itself. Our Lady of Mercy was surprisingly beautiful and well maintained. The parish had been consolidated in the late 1990s, so there were enough parishioners and resources to keep the church and its grounds in fine condition. Nor could he complain about the numbers. If not every pew was filled on Sunday, it was close enough. And the people? They were every wonderful stereotype ever made about midwesterners. Friendly, solid, thoughtful, polite, conscientious. But the town itself?

In the triangle that could be drawn linking Pittsburgh, Cleveland, and Columbus, Pistol Gap was almost directly in the middle. Far enough away from all of those cities so that Pistol Gap was convenient to none. And while the church itself was a testament to the glory of God, he could not, in all honesty, find another single building in all of Pistol Gap with any charm. It was a town of strip malls full of discount stores and restaurants with apostrophes. When his parishioners took him out to dinner, they brought him to places where you could get an appetizer, dinner, and dessert for less than twenty dollars, and the portions were so big that he'd go home with enough leftovers to provide him with lunch for days.

He'd resigned himself to making the best of it, knowing that it was only for a few years. But after three years, and then six years, his posting was extended again. He had been told, however, that this coming fall he would finally, finally, finally be moved, and he'd gotten hints that it was somewhere that was going to make him happy. Perhaps, he thought, San Diego.

And then the spiders came, and for the very first time Father Thomas was thrilled to be in Pistol Gap.

He knew that it was shameful, that he shouldn't be delighted to be kept safe from earthly harm when so many innocent people had died, and yet he was. It was not uncommon for laypeople to forget that priests like him were also men. Flesh and blood. No matter how much faith he had, he still didn't relish the idea of being eaten by spiders. Nor, if he was continuing to be honest, was he particularly interested in dying in the hot, quick whiteness of a nuclear bomb or, for that matter, of the slower, insidious corruption of nuclear radiation. Everything else being equal, he was quite content to stay alive. But he needed to believe there was a *reason* he had stayed alive, a reason tens of millions of people had perished but he, Father Thomas, was still here in Pistol Gap, Ohio, still holding Mass at Our Lady of Mercy, still taking confessions, and still visiting the sick and the elderly in the community.

Which was why it filled him with such guilt that his first reaction had been to recoil from the homeless man.

He'd spent his entire life in the priesthood serving in places where ministering to the homeless was a substantial part of his week. And though the populations of homeless men and women and, yes, children, were so much greater in the Bronx and Phoenix and even Laredo, Pistol Gap was not immune. He'd coordinated with Pastor Grace at the Unitarian Church to start a food pantry, and at times, when the weather was severe, he'd opened the church's recreation center as an emergency shelter. So this was certainly not the first time he had encountered somebody used to sleeping in the rough.

He'd gone for a walk on the trails in the preserve behind the Pistol Gap library, hoping to find some clarity. Mrs. Hounslow, who had been the secretary at Our Lady of Mercy for nearly forty years, was the one who'd forced him to go. She insisted that he needed to take a break—that even a priest could benefit from some time away from the church. Father Thomas hadn't wanted to admit how good the idea sounded, taking an hour to himself, free from the parishioners who were coming to the church in droves seeking comfort, seeking safety, seeking something he couldn't give: the promise that God would protect them. Oh, he was clear that God had not deserted them, that everything happened for a reason, that God's eternal love never wavered. But that's not what they wanted to hear. At this particular moment, most of his parishioners were uninterested in eternity. They were worried about the here and now.

The preserve itself was not large, perhaps twenty acres at most, but a network of trails wove in and out and around the land, so that at a modest pace he was able to walk aimlessly and allow his thoughts to drift away. As was his wont, when he was trying to relax, he said the Hail Mary, first in English, then in Latin, and then finally in Spanish before repeating the series. It was, he supposed, a form of meditation, and he found that it helped center him in God's grace. He said the prayer slowly and evenly in a quiet voice: "... *in hora mortis nostrae. Amen. Dios te salve—*"

"Help me. Please."

A man came out from behind a tree, lurching at him. His hair was matted and his clothing disheveled from sleeping outside.

Father Thomas stumbled back with a small, childlike shriek that embarrassed him. He was so startled that he almost ran, but the homeless man fell to his knees and stared up at him beseechingly.

"Please, Father. Help me."

Father Thomas reflexively touched his collar. He could feel the jackhammer of his heart, but it was already passing. He simply hadn't expected to have somebody leap out at him from behind a tree.

"Do you need something to eat? I can take you to . . ." He trailed off, watching the man closely. It was rare for him to feel physically endangered, but the sad truth was that the scourge of drugs left no man untouched. This man didn't look high, however; he looked sick. "Do you need a doctor?"

The man sat back on his heels. His knees pushed the mulch forward a bit, and at the same time that he was leaning back his head dropped forward. He started pulling up his shirt.

"They're inside me."

The words came out in a low, wailing moan, like a ghost chased through a keyhole on a night full of storms, like the creak of rusty hinges being opened. When he spoke, he bared his midriff: Father Thomas could see the bloody smear.

He recoiled, taking several steps back. As he did so, he caught his heel on a root and fell backward heavily. He felt a sharp pain as his elbow smacked something hard, but even greater was his panic at losing sight of the man. But then, almost immediately, he felt himself filled with a great calmness. He allowed himself to lie there for a moment and consider. Wasn't all flesh the flesh of God? Hadn't he felt that he was here, in Pistol Gap, for a reason?

Slowly he sat up and then got to his feet. He brushed himself clean and moved closer.

The homeless man was crying now, a deep guttural shaking that moved his whole body, but he was still holding his shirt up. Father Thomas could see something lumpy under the skin. It almost seemed as if the man's flesh was rippling with movement.

He felt . . . detached. He knew there was a part of him that was still shrieking. A part of him that wanted to run as fast as he could, to leave this man in the preserve and get as far away from him as he could, even though there was nowhere truly safe to go. And yet that part of him that was panicked seemed as if it were thousands of miles away. It was as if he were standing outside himself, watching his own hand make the sign of the cross and hearing his own mouth say the words, *"In nomine Patris, et Filii, et Spiritus Sancti. Amen."*

Invercargill, New Zealand

Felicia Belling understood conceptually that this whole thing with the spiders was bad, but she was only eleven, so there was a limit to how far intellectualizing a disaster took her. Her parents had been exceedingly careful to make sure she didn't see any of the videos or the news. One of her school friends, Crystal, had come over to hang out, and she had a short, grainy clip on her phone, but there was no sound and it mostly just looked like a person covered in black dots running around. That didn't stop the two of them from discussing it endlessly, and it was clear from the way her parents were acting and what they told her—school had been canceled for weeks now, and she'd been made a virtual shut-in!—that things were not good. But still. Was it really that bad? There was no indication that any of those spiders had made it to New Zealand. Wasn't everybody overreacting just a bit?

No, for Felicia Belling, this was all just a great nuisance.

USS *Elsie Downs*,
Atlantic Ocean

Melanie banged her head on the doorway. Again.

Normally she didn't mind being tall. When she shot up in height, in fifth grade, she had been self-conscious. Her father was firm about it, though: stand straight, stand tall, stand proud. By the time she hit six feet, in high school, she liked having the height. She was athletic, and on the basketball court the combination of size and speed worked to her advantage. Until the world went to hell, she had played basketball a couple of times a week. And being tall meant she could rock a pair of heels. The kind of man who was intimidated by her height was never the kind of man she was interested in anyway.

But being tall was not an advantage on a ship. Or a boat. Or an aircraft carrier, or whatever she was supposed to call it. She'd noticed that the taller sailors perpetually ducked their heads as they passed through doorways even when there was plenty of clearance. If she spent much longer on this floating city, she was sure she'd be doing the same thing.

In the meantime she would keep rubbing her head where she

banged it and make the best of things. And it could have been worse. Forget even the hundreds of millions of people who'd been killed in the past couple of weeks, and forget even the hundreds of millions more who'd been displaced. She knew there were people out there scrounging for food, people who were newly homeless, people suffering in all the countless ways that people suffered when society collapsed. Forget all that. Even on the USS *Elsie Downs*, it could have been worse for her and her colleagues. Because of the work they were doing, they had the unimaginable luxury of having their own beds. Well, *luxury* might be overstating it. The sleeping quarters were essentially bunk beds stacked three high. She'd gotten the bottom bunk, with Laura Nieder in the second and her graduate student, Julie Yoo, stuck on top. With the aircraft carrier well over capacity, most of the people on board, soldiers and civilians alike, were sleeping in shifts, taking turns using the bunks, slipping between sheets that were still warm from somebody else's body.

In the same way that she'd been afforded her own bed, a lab had been carved out for her and the other scientists. It was smaller than she was used to, and it was clearly makeshift. Still, it was well equipped. She'd been asked to provide a list of required equipment, and somebody had taken care of it. She had no idea who exactly that had been, but—given that they were on an aircraft carrier somewhere in the Atlantic Ocean, in a room that had clearly been intended as a recreation space—that person had done a good job. She felt kind of bad about it, however: much of the lab equipment bore the kind of inventory stickers that were common at universities; there was some poor professor at Johns Hopkins University who was going to have to suffer through a denuded lab. In the scheme of things, it wasn't a big concern for her, however. She had greater worries. They all did. Will Dichtel, an entomological toxicologist, was quite snippy about the close quarters of the lab, but it seemed like a coping mechanism; he was the kind of solid midwesterner who couldn't admit that he was terrified.

There was, simply, the weight of the entire world upon them. Earlier, her ex-husband, Manny Walchuck, had left a meeting with the president and the uniforms and come to the lab to lay it out for her: Come up with a way to stop the spiders or it was game over.

No pressure there.

She'd told him she was close but that she needed a few more days, but he was clear that time was not on her side. Because of their history, he was up front with her. The president was under immense pressure to order more nuclear strikes, which was a lose-lose proposition. Sure, maybe they'd kill all the spiders, but they'd kill all the people, too. Given their personal history, and Manny being Manny, he'd been honest about the political reality of the situation.

"But she's the president," Melanie had said.

Manny had looked at her in such a way that it was clear that, once again, she was being naïve about politics.

She'd promised to do what she could, but it felt like an empty promise. You could hurry your research only so much. That had been a few hours ago, and when he'd left the lab, she'd been glum. The good thing, however, was that she and her team were able to lose themselves in their work. They were all scared—Melanie, Julie, Laura, Will, and Mike Haaf—but they were also focused on solving a puzzle. There were times when Melanie forgot *why* she was doing this research and got excited about the sheer intellectual curiosity of it all. How did the spiders breed so quickly? How did they seem to coordinate their hatching cycles? Why was it that some people were stripped to the bone by the swarms of spiders and others were left alone? How was it that when a spider ate its way into a person's body to lay eggs, the wound almost zipped itself closed? And how, above all else, were humans supposed to fight back?

The amazing thing, and what she loved about being a scientist, was that for all of the pressure, all of the fear, they were starting to hit on real answers. Solutions. Hope. In the lab, Laura and Mike were in the air lock—the makeshift glass room within the room that would, in theory, keep things contained if somebody made a mistake with one of the eleven insectariums—getting ready to pull a single spider out for study. They'd noticed that one of the spiders had isolated itself, and they wanted to dissect it to see if there was something biologically unique about it compared to its brethren. In the far corner of the lab, Will had managed to extract venom from both the standard black spiders and the version with the red stripes across their backs. He was using a pipette to test both kinds of venom on samples of rubber, to confirm the efficacy of using hazmat suits safely in spider-infested environments.

She turned to look out in the hallway to see if the sailor who'd been tasked with bringing them lunch—or was it dinner? she'd lost track of time—was returning, and banged her head on the doorway. Again.

But it did nothing to dampen that jubilant feeling. They were onto something. Rubbing her head, she sat down on a stool next to Julie. Julie swiveled her laptop so Melanie could take a look.

"Basically," Julie said, jumping right in, "the trade-off is life expectancy."

"Like a Bernese or a Newfoundland or something?"

Julie narrowed her eyes, confused.

"Sorry," Melanie said. "Dogs. They're dog breeds. Big dogs. My parents had Bernese mountain dogs, but they live only, like, seven or eight years. They're huge balls of fur. Beautiful, sweet dogs. We almost always had two of them at any one time, sometimes three, but that meant that every couple of years we were putting one of them down. Honestly, it's one of the reasons I never got a dog of my own. My memory of having dogs as a kid is of crying all the time." She tapped the counter. "But it's the same point. The bigger the dog, the lower the life expectancy."

Julie nodded. "Except that's not what we've generally seen in spiders. Also, I'm more of a cat person."

"I like both. But that's beside the point." Melanie rubbed her eyes. "Good Lord, I could use a nap. Okay, you're right. More or less, the bigger the spider, the longer the life expectancy. What's the life span of the Goliath birdeater? Twenty years?"

"For the females," Julie said. "Across the board, females in the Theraphosidae family? Yeah, easily fifteen or twenty years. There are plenty of tarantulas hitting thirty and even forty years. The smaller spiders are the ones that go quick."

"Well," Melanie said, gesturing toward the glass and Mike and Laura, "these sure as hell aren't part of the Theraphosidae family."

"Technically, you're probably in line to name them," Julie said.

"Right now that's not at the top of my priority list. Writing a paper and—"

"Whoa, whoa. You're taking that a little too seriously, Melanie. I wasn't thinking of an actual taxonomic name. I'm not worried about proper biological nomenclature. We don't need Latin. But it would help if we had something to call them."

Melanie was taken aback. "I *like* the name Swarm X. I think—"

"Melanie. Please. Honestly." Julie reached out and put her hand over Melanie's. "You're the only one who thinks Swarm X is a good name."

Melanie fidgeted on the stool, narrowed her eyes at Julie, and then, finally, sighed and smiled. "Fine. You know, a couple of weeks ago, when you and Bark and Patrick . . ." She took a deep breath and they were both quiet for a moment, thinking about how Bark, one of the other graduate students who'd been working for Melanie, had been infested. A surgeon had him on the operating table and was trying to remove the eggs that were threaded through his body when the spiders hatched. And Patrick was in the operating room. Wrong place, wrong time. It wasn't that Melanie had forgotten about what happened to her two other graduate students, but saying their names aloud hurt.

She continued: "When the three of you came to my classroom, when this all started. Do you know one of the things I didn't understand? I didn't understand how somebody as smart as you could be so lacking in confidence. Well, silly me. Here I am a few weeks later with Ms. Julie Yoo, who now has the gumption to tell me that the name I came up with for these spiders is dumb."

"I didn't say dumb."

"Hell Spiders? I mean, I said they're sure as hell not part of the Theraphosidae family."

Julie considered. "Hell Spiders. Yeah. Actually, that's not bad. It's a lot better than Swarm X spiders."

"Okay. It's official. They're Hell Spiders," Melanie said. "Now, what were we talking about?"

"Uh, size?"

Melanie laughed and got off her stool. "We're all a little punch-drunk." She walked over to the door and, carefully bending to make sure she didn't bang her head this time, stepped out into the hallway. She turned to one of the sailors standing in the hall. There were always five or six sailors out there. It wasn't clear if they were supposed to be standing guard or not, but the scientists had taken to treating them as glorified gofers. "Can somebody please check on our food? And I need somebody to get coffees for me and . . .

Dr. Yoo. And don't get them from the mess. Get them from that fancy place. They know what we like."

One of the sailors took off at a brisk clip, and Melanie stepped back inside the lab. Julie was staring at her.

"*Dr.* Yoo? Did you just call me *Dr.* Yoo? You called me *Ms.* Julie Yoo, like, thirty seconds ago."

Melanie shrugged. "Screw it. I figure after everything that's happened, you've earned your PhD." She sat back down and pulled Julie's laptop closer. "So we've got three different kinds of Hell Spiders. The black ones. They breed and grow at an astronomical rate, and they burn out just as quickly. Then there are the ones with the red stripes, which also hatch and grow crazy fast. And then we've got the jumbo ones."

"The queens," Julie said.

"What?"

Julie glanced away, blushing. "Sorry. I've been thinking of them as the queens. Silly."

"Yeah. No. Maybe," Melanie said. "I don't know. Why have you been calling them that?"

Julie pulled the elastic out of her hair, swept it back into a ponytail again, and then secured it with the same elastic. As far as Melanie could tell, it looked exactly the same.

"I don't know. It's just, well, they're all the same species, right? If you didn't know better, you'd think they were really three different spiders, but they're all the same. I mean, the original spiders laid the eggs that hatched the red-striped ones and, as far as we can tell, the queens, too. Have you ever seen one of those photos that puts the tallest and biggest Olympic athletes with the smallest?"

Melanie nodded. They were always amusing. You'd get some seven-foot center on a basketball team standing next to some gymnast pixie who barely reached the basketball player's waistband.

"If you were an alien, you'd never look at those two people and think they were from the same species. And it's the same thing with the Hell Spiders. They don't look the same, but they really are. So I've been thinking about that and about what you said when this first happened: that we've got feeders and breeders."

"Well," Melanie said, "that was a crude way of thinking about it."

"Sure, but you weren't wrong." Julie pulled the laptop back and switched over to a spreadsheet. She ran her finger down one of the columns. "It's borne out in the data, right?"

Melanie was distracted for a moment by shouting. She'd left the door to the hallway open when she asked for coffee, and even though the voices were far away, she could sense the urgency. And then the sailors outside the door started shifting and ran off. Whatever it was, she thought, it didn't have anything to do with them.

"So the simple version is that we've got the first wave, the black ones. They come out, well, like a wave. They wash over everything in their path. It's so overwhelming, just the sheer numbers, that anything that could be a threat is neutralized. Even if the spiders had natural predators, there wouldn't be enough of them left to be a real danger. And whatever they don't eat is either available as food for later consumption or serves as an incubator for the second round of black spiders. Then, once they've spread out far enough, they pull back and lay more eggs. They're the breeders. So this is all the first wave. But then we get to the second wave."

"The red stripes."

"Right. The second wave are the feeders, because, near as we can tell, that's what they do. They wrap up whatever prey they catch—"

"Whatever or whomever is left from the first wave," Melanie interrupted.

"Right. Near as we can tell, the spiders don't eat one out of every five people—"

"Or goats or rats."

Julie stopped and waited.

It took Melanie a second. "Sorry," she said. "I'll stop interrupting."

"Or goats or rats," Julie said, nodding. "One out of every five. But we're clear, they don't leave one out of five alone. They leave one out of five *alive*. Of those, about one in ten gets used as a sort of surrogate." She hesitated. "God. Bark. And poor Patrick."

Out in the hallway, there was the sound of thumping boots, and then ten or fifteen sailors went past at a dead run.

"That's weird," Julie said.

"Yeah, yeah." Melanie was impatient. "Just keep going."

"So the question isn't why do they lay eggs in about ten percent of the survivors, but why do the other ninety percent get left completely alone? And the answer is: to feed the big spiders."

Julie shifted to a picture they'd gotten from an infestation in a rural village in Japan. Without context, it wouldn't have meant much. The picture showed a silky cocoon that was dotted with black specks. But the context was everything: the scientist who'd snapped the photo had been able to take fairly accurate measurements. The black specks were actually the spiders with red stripes on their backs—each one the size of a small grapefruit—and the cocoon was huge. The size of a pickup truck. The video also seemed to show that the reason the spiders were crawling on the cocoon was to *feed* it: the spiders grazed on the silk-wrapped bodies of men and women unfortunate enough to have been bitten, paralyzed, and wrapped up, and then delivered nutrients to the giant cocoon.

Julie gently closed the lid of the laptop. "Anyway, I was thinking about the order of things. We've spent so much time just figuring out *what* they were doing that we haven't really had the bandwidth to focus on *why* they were doing it. But I kind of thought, okay, they seem coordinated, and even the way they clear the area surrounding their infestations shows that the cocoons are of supreme importance. I mean, maybe it doesn't make much sense from a modern perspective, when four or five miles isn't that far, but back in the day, if you could clear a swath four or five miles around something, that was a pretty effective buffer."

Melanie could feel it clicking. She was following along with Julie and jumping forward. The key, she realized, and what Julie was getting to, was that there was a reason the spiders seemed like they worked together. She was just about to say that, breaking her promise to stop interrupting, when Julie spoke again.

"Do you hear that?"

"What?" Melanie listened for a second. She heard tapping and something muffled from the glass enclosure, and she saw that Laura was waving to her excitedly. "Guess they found something."

"No," Julie said. "Outside."

"Oh. The shouting. Yeah, seems like something has the military folks in a tizzy."

"Not the shouting," Julie said. "Listen."

So Melanie did. And after a moment her eyes widened. "Are those gunshots?"

USS *Elsie Downs*, Atlantic Ocean

Amy sighed. "You really want to start watching *Breaking Bad*?"

"*I'm* not the one who insisted we take the last two seats on the evacuation helicopter. Besides, I've never seen it, and you and Shotgun and Gordo always talk about how it was the best show ever on television and blah, blah, blah." Fred was sitting on the floor with Gordo and Amy's chocolate Lab, Claymore, curled up next to him, his head on Fred's lap. Fred was massaging the great lunk's ears, and every so often Claymore would let out a deep, throaty sigh of contentment.

They'd been given a private cabin to share. No matter that it was clearly designed to have one occupant; Amy was smart enough to realize just how precarious their position was here aboard the aircraft carrier. She and Fred were civilians with no special skills. Her husband and, more important, Shotgun might have value, and the scientists whom they'd shared the helicopter ride with certainly had value, but if push came to shove, she and Fred—and Claymore—were expendable.

Because of that, other than their popping out for meals, she'd insisted to Fred that they lie low. It was not something that came naturally to Fred, and it meant that they'd spent a lot of time watching movies and television shows. Fortunately, the carrier had a seemingly inexhaustible media library.

"But *Breaking Bad*?" Amy said. "You don't want to watch something lighter?" She looked down at her lap. She had her satellite phone on but hadn't gotten a text from Gordo yet that day. She was pretty sure that Fred hadn't gotten a text from Shotgun on his satellite phone either. Neither of their husbands was of the "Just checking in" variety. It didn't stop her from worrying, though. Reluctantly, she powered it off. She'd check again before she went to sleep.

"You've been telling me for years that I need to watch it, and this seems as good a time as any," Fred said, sounding pouty. "It's not like there's anything more exciting going on."

"Why don't we go pop into the lab and see if we can do anything helpful?"

"Please, girl. Like what? I mean, if Melanie needs somebody to throw a party, well, then. But what kind of real help are we going to be?"

"Please?" Amy could hear that she sounded a little whiny. She didn't like it, but she was stressed-out. Being stuck in this tiny cabin, watching television for hours on end, didn't help. "It would be good for Claymore to get some exercise."

"Really?" Fred raised an eyebrow skeptically. "The lab is just around the corner. It's, like, a hundred feet." But he was already getting to his feet.

She threw her sat phone into her purse, slipped the purse over her shoulder, and grabbed Claymore's leash. "Who's the best dog in the whole world?"

Claymore, who'd stood up when Fred did, wagged his tail as an answer. Amy stepped out into the hallway and was immediately bumped into by a young woman running full tilt. It was a glancing blow, barely anything, but it startled her. More surprising was the soldier's reaction: the woman didn't slow down. Didn't apologize. Nothing.

Amy watched her disappear around the corner and then let it go. Whatever.

She and Fred and the dog walked to the corner and for a second she was convinced she'd gone the wrong way. The lab should have been three doors down, but there were no guards. There were always guards standing outside the lab. As she was thinking this, a pair of sailors carrying rifles ran past her and she heard something like popcorn popping.

Oh.

She walked quickly to the lab door and knocked urgently. Claymore stood next to her, panting and happy to be out of the room, apparently not worried about whatever was happening.

"Was that—"

"Not now, Fred," she said.

The door opened cautiously, and Amy was relieved to see Dr. Nieder's face. "Laura," she said. "I think we better come in."

USS *Elsie Downs*, Atlantic Ocean

For a guy who prided himself on being able to read the room, to figure out the political winds so that he was ahead of the pack, Manny had sure missed this one. And it hurt. Literally. As in: he was on a helicopter, winging out over the Atlantic Ocean, on the run, and getting medical attention because he'd been shot. Aside from the injury to his pride from not having seen it coming, the actual physical injury was pretty unpleasant.

The Secret Service agent tending to him, a woman named Agent Cutbert, assured him that, as far as gunshot wounds went, it was minor—but it was still a gunshot wound, and in Manny's very limited experience, which was limited to this particular gunshot wound, even a minor gunshot wound hurt a lot.

Things had gone from normal to tense to everything turned completely upside down in what felt like a very, very short time.

He *had* noticed that there seemed to be more aides than normal in the conference room, but that hadn't been his main preoccupation. The meeting that morning had been really rough. A *lot* of yelling. It wasn't that unusual to have heated disagreements. There was a certain amount of observed decorum at any meeting with the president, but there was also a certain amount of fiery rhetoric. You didn't have the kind of career that let you attend meetings with the president if you weren't willing to argue for what you wanted. The first meeting of the day, however, had been spectacularly uncivil. After putting up with it for nearly an hour, Steph had essentially needed to shout over everybody to restore order. She'd adjourned the meeting at least partially to give Manny time to go talk to Melanie and see if she had anything new.

Time. There was never enough of it.

The plan for the most recent meeting was to try to stall. Melanie had told him that if he could give her just a little more time—time they didn't have—she thought she would have something. She *was* making progress, she insisted.

To that end, he and Steph had decided to start the meeting with a brief on civilian casualties both short-term and long-term directly related to the thirty-one strikes on major infestation points. They were going to put a particular emphasis on the damage caused by nukes, on what they'd destroyed. The hope, of course, was that it would serve as a proactive measure to blunt Broussard and his crew. But as Manny stood to call the room to order, Ben Broussard hijacked everything. Broussard was at the far end of the conference room, with a huddle of aides surrounding him. No, not a huddle, Manny thought. A posse.

"We've run out of time. You're not doing enough," Broussard accused. He was pointing his finger across the room at Steph in what seemed like an inappropriate way to address the president.

"You missed the opportunity to contain this when it first hit our shores," he said. "That was the moment when you should have acted. If you'd taken Los Angeles off the map, none of the rest of this would have happened."

Alexandra Harris, the national security advisor, spoke up, her voice dry. "It wouldn't have helped Europe or Asia or Africa."

She was sitting at the far end of the room, too, near Broussard, and he wheeled on her. "Screw Europe, and screw Asia and Africa. I'm talking about the goddamned United States. And you," he said, turning back toward Steph, "you own this. Even if the Spanish Protocol was the right decision, it came too late, as did the decision to use every tool at our disposal."

"You think I waited too long to use nuclear weapons on American soil?" The president did not appear to be particularly fazed by Broussard's aggression. She'd had a breather that afternoon, between the two meetings, but Manny knew she was seething.

"Darn right," he said. "You waited too long. As it is, I had to twist your arm to get you to buy into the Spanish Protocol. Better than nothing, but not by much. Typical." He was almost spitting the words out. The anger he was showing toward Steph was astounding. Sure, Manny had seen people furious at Steph, but you didn't act like this in front of the president. He didn't understand why none of Broussard's aides were attempting to calm him down.

Broussard continued. "This has gone on too long. You're going to do what you should have done in the first place. You're going to order the air force to turn everything, and I mean absolutely everything, west of minus seventy-four degrees, into rubble." Manny watched Steph motion to an aide, who whispered in her ear, while Broussard kept going. "Those things can't spread more than a few miles on their own. The mistake you keep making, over and over, is being too soft. Trying to save too many people. It's a typical civilian mistake, thinking that patience always pays off. Maybe in diplomacy, but you can't negotiate with these critters. They're like a damn tumor. The only solution is to cut it out. If you lose some good with the bad, that's the price you have to pay to contain it. If you want to save the patient, you need to order the surgery."

Broussard's face had turned red, and by the end, he was nearly yelling.

Manny was not surprised to see Steph stand up like the president she was. She had never been the kind of woman to roll over.

"How dare you?" Her voice was dark and dangerous. For an instant Manny actually felt sorry for Broussard. But only an instant.

"How dare you say that so glibly? So casually? That's the price you have to pay? You're talking about American citizens here. You're talking about hundreds of millions of souls. You can dress it up however you like, call it a tumor, try to make yourself feel better by saying minus seventy-four degrees, but my god!" She turned and pointed at one of the aides. "Pull up a map. Pull up a map of the entire country with longitude and latitude. Pull up a damn map!" And if Broussard had nearly been yelling, Steph had gone fully past nearly. She was shouting at Broussard.

Manny could feel an unpleasant spark of static start through the room while they waited for the frantic aide to get a map up on the screen. Something was off, but he couldn't quite put his finger on it. Why didn't Broussard seem cowed by having his commander in chief screaming at him?

"There," the president said, stabbing a finger at the screen. "That's what you're talking about. New York City. *That's* minus seventy-four degrees. You're proposing we destroy everything west of New York City. Look at that map. What the hell is left of America if we do that? Enough is enough. We need to take the information from Dr. Guyer—"

Broussard cut her off, an act that in normal times would have been almost unthinkable. "You mean Manny's wife."

"My ex-wife," Manny said, "who happens to be a brilliant scientist who has spent her entire career studying spiders, and who is working with several other PhDs who have spent their careers studying spiders; so unless it's too hard for you to imagine a woman being smart, how about you listen for a second?"

Broussard glowered at him. The rage on his face was so transparent, it made Manny suddenly thankful that there were other people in the room. Not that Manny was a coward, but he *was* a realist. He was good at politics and throwing verbal punches, not physical ones. Although, judging by the way Broussard kept looking at him, it was quite possible Broussard was thinking knives and guns rather than fisticuffs. That was not the problem of the moment, however, so Manny continued.

"Look, the point that the president is making is that we have already sacrificed nearly two-thirds of the country. It's the same point she made—a bunch of us made—this morning. We're having the same argument over and over again. You need to listen, Ben. We can't just keep bombing the heck out of stuff in the hopes that maybe the spiders take the hint and head on home. Sure, the nuclear strikes so far have been, quote, unquote, 'clean,' but give me a break. The truth—"

"The truth," Broussard shouted, "is that you're a goddamned politician. Both of you are goddamned politicians," he yelled, pointing at Manny and Steph, "and you need to let the military do its job! And its job is to win or die trying!"

The room was deathly quiet.

Stephanie leaned forward, her palms on the table. "It is up to *me* to tell *you* what your job is, Chairman. Your job is not to *win or die trying*, as you seem to think. Your job is to do as you are told by your commander in chief. Our goal is not to win, and it sure as hell doesn't include 'die trying.' Our job, and the order I am giving, is to *survive*. The priority isn't wiping out the spiders—the priority is ensuring the ongoing survival of the human race; and if we can't do that, then we've lost, no matter what you think. And since you seem incapable of understanding that, you are relieved of your command. We've already lost too much to these monsters as it is. I am the president of the United States of America, and I give the orders. As long as I am the president, we are not going to cede another inch. We are going to fight, but we aren't going to die trying."

Broussard looked around the room quickly, seeming to count.

It gave Manny a sick feeling in his stomach. Like he was falling off a building.

Broussard nodded. "The key thing that you said there, ma'am, is, 'as long as I am the president.' That's a fixable problem."

Behind Broussard, two men, one white and no older than twenty-five, the other black and middle-aged, pulled out their pistols. Manny felt, rather than saw, movement around him. Heard shouting.

Broussard had his sidearm out now, and maybe another eight or ten people with pistols seemed to be with him. As swiftly as they drew their weapons, however, the three Secret Service agents drew theirs.

One of the agents, a Latino man Manny didn't recognize, swept his arm across Steph's body, moving her behind the agents, and then Billy Cannon, the secretary of defense, who'd been sitting near Manny, drew his own gun and stood shoulder to shoulder with the Secret Service agents. The members of the military who recognized what was happening but were not part of Broussard's group, another half dozen people, formed up with Billy and the Secret Service agents. There were maybe fifty or sixty people in the room all told, and at least half of them had no clue that a coup was under way.

The room suddenly felt small.

It certainly felt dangerous.

Manny did the math and couldn't figure out how they were going to get out of there without bloodshed. He didn't understand. Was Broussard really so arrogant that he thought he could pull this off? Did he really believe that as soon as he made his move everybody would come to his side?

Would they?

Manny wanted to throw up. Had he missed the way the wind was blowing? Was this just Broussard losing his mind, or was it something more? Was the military so against Steph now, so deeply committed to the idea of a scorched earth, that Broussard knew he'd already won?

He didn't know. But, looking at Broussard, Manny could tell that the man thought he could pull this whole thing off without firing a shot.

Broussard was wrong.

Alexandra Harris pushed her chair back and stood up. She took a step forward until she was directly in front of Broussard.

"What the hell are you doing, Ben?" Alex said, reaching toward his gun. "You need to respect—"

Manny wondered if the gun would have sounded as loud if the room hadn't contained the shot so that it echoed and echoed. Somehow he suspected it would have sounded just as loud even outdoors. It was loud enough that he wasn't even sure he heard the gunfire that followed.

He saw it, though.

As Alex's head snapped back, a red mist opening like an umbrella in the middle of the room, there was a bloom of light from the muzzle of one of the pistols held by the woman standing next to Broussard. One of the Secret Service agents to Manny's right stumbled backward, and then the spark of gunfire returned.

Chaos.

The men and women surrounding Broussard scrambled to find cover. Manny was knocked back in his chair, spinning away from Broussard. There was screaming and the noise of gunfire. He saw three bright blooms of blood on the chest of a short black sailor wearing her dress uniform. She had close-cropped hair and a look of surprise on her face, as if the red on her chest were a bouquet of flowers instead of the end of her life.

He banged against a desk and then spun around again just in time to see an arm reach out and grab Steph by the back of her collar, dragging her out the door, and then he himself was being manhandled. If they hadn't been seated near the exit, he wondered if they would have gotten out. He wanted to believe that Broussard wasn't intent on killing the president, but he was sure Broussard wouldn't shed any tears if Manny caught a bullet.

As it turned out, he *had* caught a bullet. He hadn't realized it as they ran down the corridor or as they sprinted across the flight deck to the president's helicopter, *Marine One*. It was only when he was already aboard the Sikorsky VH-92A, when Agent Cutbert told him he was bleeding, that he even understood he'd been shot. He pulled up his shirt to see a neat line across his right side. It was a few inches above his hip, through the part of his body that had the most padding. While Cutbert pulled on a pair of nitrile gloves, Manny unbuttoned his shirt. It was covered in blood, although he wasn't sure how much of it was his own.

Cutbert poked and prodded in a way that made Manny wince, and then pressed a gauze pad on the wound. "Here," she said, "just hold this tight. Barely a scratch. A quick in and out. Basically just a shot across the bow. Almost more like a cut than a real bullet wound."

Manny was too distracted to feel insulted by how dismissive

she was. A phalanx of Secret Service agents stood on the flight deck in a rough semicircle around the helicopter, guns out. Several of them were holding compact machine guns. Just a few seats over from Manny, Steph was almost completely hidden behind a wall of three agents. Manny was glad to see that one of them was Tommy Riggs, who alone was big enough to make Steph invisible.

The heavy rotors of the helicopter began to slice through the air, and Steph began struggling to get to him.

"No!" she yelled. "We're not going!"

"Are you out of your mind?" Manny yelled back over the sound of the helicopter powering up.

Outside, they saw Billy Cannon with his hands up, talking to the line of agents.

"Let him through!" Steph shouted.

"Madam President," Billy said, hoisting himself up into the helicopter. "You've got to get out of here now. Right now. Broussard wouldn't have done this if he didn't think he could pull it off. I think we can hold him off for a few more minutes, but it wasn't just the men in the room. He's got the ship's captain on his side, and that means he's going to have the whole ship soon enough. Without you and without the football, it's going to be a little while before he can use nuclear weapons. He knows about Operation SAFEGUARD, and he'll start working on that immediately, but it's going to be at least seventy-two hours, maybe longer, before he can shut it down. But if he gets his hands on you, he'll be able to act almost immediately."

"We're not going without Melanie," Steph said.

"My ex-wife?" Manny kept his hand pressed to his side. He was aware that he probably looked ridiculous—his shirt wide-open, blood all over himself, his tie still around his neck.

"Not everything is about you, Manny," the president said evenly, and in another time or place Manny would have laughed.

She turned back to Billy. "It's either my way, where we try to save what's left of the United States—what's left of the world—or Broussard's way. And if we leave here without Melanie and the other scientists, we're giving up. Without them, there's no chance. We might as well just give ourselves up. We can only stop Broussard from using nukes for, what, seventy-two hours? Seventy-two hours until they undermine Operation SAFEGUARD and all bets are off."

"Ma'am, you could always exercise Matthew 5:45."

Manny wasn't sure what surprised him more: that he didn't have any idea what Cannon was talking about, or the look of surprise on Steph's face. Very, very few people knew about Operation SAFEGUARD, perhaps fewer than a thousand. It had been enacted during the second Bush's presidency and served, essentially, a gatekeeping function. When a nuclear strike was ordered, Operation SAFEGUARD had to provide a second confirmation before the weapon could work. It was technically complicated and very secure, but it had been designed to stop a rogue officer or a mistake, not a coup. As long as the officers inside stayed loyal to the president, the arsenal was worthless to a single bad actor. Unfortunately, since it had never been conceived of as a way to protect against the entire military, there were ways to work around it. Manny figured that Billy's estimate of seventy-two hours was probably accurate. But what the heck was Matthew 5:45?

"How the hell do you know about Matthew— No," Steph said. "Never mind. I don't care how you know. I don't think we're there yet. I hope we're not there yet. That's an extreme step. Right now we need to get Melanie and the other scientists. She promised me an answer, and I want an answer."

Manny looked at her and then out over the flight deck. There were sailors all over the place, but they didn't move with anything more than their usual urgency. Aside from the sailors close enough to do double takes at the line of Secret Service agents with their weapons drawn, there was no real indication that anything was out of the ordinary.

"Crap." He turned to Billy Cannon. "She's right. We can't leave without them."

"You can and you will."

The voice, deep and full, was Special Agent Tommy Riggs's. He hovered over Steph and put his hand firmly on Manny's shoulder. "Our first priority is the president's safety. You might need those scientists, but you don't need to be here."

Manny felt paralyzed. Steph was right, and Tommy was right. What was the point of running from Broussard if they didn't have a better plan? But if they stayed, what were the chances that they'd be able to get Melanie and the other scientists out before Broussard hunted them all down?

Maybe solving one problem solved the other.

"Okay. We're taking off!" he yelled over the rotor wash.

"No, Manny—"

He cut Steph off. "Broussard will let us go. He doesn't need you. And it will buy us time. You know as well as I do that with Operation SAFEGUARD it's not actually that easy to order unauthorized nuclear strikes. With you off this tub, we'll have a chance to get Melanie out. But if we stay and try to do it now? Well, you'd be asking a bunch of good men and women to commit suicide. There's something like four or five thousand members of the armed forces on this aircraft carrier, and we've got maybe twenty Secret Service agents."

Stephanie hesitated and then looked at Billy. "I want to know how you found out about Matthew 5:45. Not now—after we've gotten through this. You really think that's the right thing to do? That I should exercise it? Because if you know what Matthew 5:45 is, you know we can't walk back from it."

"I do, ma'am."

"Even though you're a military man and—"

"You're right about not using any more nukes. It's that simple. Mutually assured destruction is only a good strategy if it never comes to pass. It was true with the Soviet Union and it's true with these spiders."

Steph nodded. "Okay. I'll consider it. In the meantime, if I'm leaving, that means I'm counting on the two of you," she said, looking first at Billy and then at Riggs. "You better follow through. You get me Melanie and the other scientists. You get me my answer."

She reached out and solemnly shook the hands of both men. They got off the helicopter, and everything after that was a blur. He and Steph were buckled in, and *Marine One* practically jumped off the flight deck, the pilot angling the helicopter hard, the engines screaming. When they traveled in DC, they usually flew in a convoy of four helicopters rotating in a sort of shell game to try to confuse potential attackers, but today it was just the one.

It took Manny a while to realize he was holding his breath, that he was waiting to see if they were going to be shot down. But after five or ten minutes he knew Broussard was going to let them go. It was one thing to get support for a mutiny, Manny figured, and another thing entirely if he blew the president out of the sky. No, he thought, they were safe.

And then, immediately after having the thought, he laughed. Safe.

As the helicopter's shadow skipped across the waves, Manny leaned back and closed his eyes. He wanted to ask Steph what the heck Cannon had been talking about with Matthew 5:45—he recognized that it was a Bible verse—but the adrenaline had left his body. What he needed at that exact moment was just to close his eyes.

Delhi, India

She surveyed the world before her. Around her, the little ones skittered and danced, emptying the cobwebbed packages and bringing her food.

There were pinpricks of fire, entire blocks in flames, made to look small by their distance. The little ones gave a wide berth to fire. There was plenty to eat here without risking the hot crackle of death.

She moved forward, to the edge of the tall building. It was a slow, laborious process. She preferred to rely on the little ones, but the great pulsing hunger drove her to where she could see the feast spread out below.

Oxford, Mississippi

Santiago's hands were the worst. He'd also burned off his eyebrows, and he felt raw everywhere, but it was his hands that were killing him. The burn on his forearm was probably more serious—he'd bandaged it because it kept weeping some sort of clear liquid—but all he had to do was be a little careful to avoid bumping it and it was fine. With his hands, however, there wasn't much he could do to protect them. He had work to do.

The fire in the moat he'd dug around his property still burned, and periodically he slid a pair of work gloves over his pink and swollen hands and loaded more wood or charcoal into the trench. With any luck, if he was careful to marshal what was left, he could keep the ditch burning for another day, perhaps two. After that? Who knew?

The fire was much smaller now, almost restrained, but still enough to keep the spiders at bay. When he'd first lit it in a great whooping explosion that must have been bright enough to see from space, he thought all he had to do was hold the spiders off for a short period; the first wave of spiders in Los Angeles and around the world had died off so quickly. But these spiders seemed differ-

ent. They seemed built for the long haul. There were not many of
them—at least, not after the initial onslaught of the first night—
but they did not seem to be dying off. Worse, they seemed to be
learning.

That first night, there had been thousands—tens of thousands—
of them, countless numbers throwing themselves against the great
ring of fire that lit the heavens around his convenience-store-cum-
gas-station-and-house. His neighbor, Mrs. Fine, who was feisty despite being nearly eighty, summed it up perfectly.

"They're like demons," she said. "An inexhaustible supply
crawling up from the depths of hell to drag us down."

Through the dancing flames, he'd seen the black shapes skittering and dancing, but the spiders couldn't get past the fire. Oh,
there were a few scares that night. Some of the spiders released
streamers of silk that caught the rising air and lifted them up and
over the moat of fire, but they were either carried past in the whirls
of wind created by Santiago's inferno, or the heat was enough to
kill them even from a distance, the black shells bouncing hollow
and lifeless on the ground. He deployed his son, Oscar, to smash
any of those that landed in the yard, just in case, but every last one
was barbecued. Another big fright came around four or five in the
morning, after he thought the worst was done: he'd missed a flying
ember that had landed on the roof of his house and started to smol-
der and burn. But he'd planned ahead for that as well, donning a
backpack-style water tank, climbing up a ladder, and extinguishing
the blaze on his roof.

Since then, it was as if the spiders had been deliberately avoid-
ing his property. The numbers were substantially less—that was
one thing—but whereas, before, they'd thrown themselves at the
fire, seemingly consumed by a bloodlust to get at Santiago and his
family, the dozens of spider clusters—they seemed to travel only

in groups, scuttling and skittering past each day—had kept their distance from his property.

He didn't understand how it was that the spiders that first night had burned themselves to a crisp in their attempts to get at him, and yet these other spiders seemed to understand that fire was bad.

Santiago flexed his fingers and then poked at the blisters on his right hand with his left index finger. Fire was bad indeed, he thought, wincing, but why hadn't the spiders feared the flames the first night while the subsequent swarms steered clear? The only plausible explanation to Santiago was that they'd somehow *learned*. Somehow, in the shriveled and charred bodies of the thousands and thousands of spiders that had not been able to overcome Santiago's resourcefulness, there'd been a lesson for the survivors.

But the question, Santiago realized, was that if they were smart enough to learn, were they also smart enough to understand that the moat of fire would not burn forever? Would they begin to test and prod and eventually find their way through his fortifications? He had a reserve of fuel in the large holding tanks buried beneath the gas station, but that would burn quickly and fiercely. It would be good as a last resort, as a measure of desperation, but it would not serve to protect his family for any length of time. And if these spiders did not seem intent on dying out as quickly as the first wave had in Los Angeles and around the world—the image of hundreds of thousands of weightless, almost empty black shells mounded up and being swept away in the streets by men with brooms would haunt him as long as he lived—then it was just a question of time.

Time.

Santiago understood that the longer things went, the worse his odds were. He'd been counting on a ticking clock, on the spiders melting like a nightmare held up to the daylight; but if that wasn't the case, then he was in trouble, because that meant it came down to a numbers game: the spiders could die by the thousands without it seeming to matter, but to Santiago any loss was unbearable. No, a numbers game was not a game that he wanted to play.

He sighed and then pulled his work gloves back on. He pushed the wheelbarrow to the southwest corner of his property, where he carefully sprinkled two shovelfuls of charcoal into the trench, his hands smarting the whole time. When he was done with that, he pushed the wheelbarrow as close to the middle of the yard as possible and covered it with a partial sheet of plywood so that no errant sparks would set the pitiful amount of remaining charcoal ablaze.

Inside the house, he walked over to the couch to watch his son sleeping. Oscar was a good boy. A beautiful boy. He looked more like his mother than like Santiago, and for that, Santiago was thankful. In his marriage only one side brought good looks. He knew that he was a decent man, and he had incredible fortitude and stamina—as long as he could close his eyes for ten or fifteen minutes in the afternoon, he needed no more than four hours of sleep a night—but the mirror did not lie. His wife insisted that he was a handsome man. She liked his rugged face, she said, but he joked that the jagged peak of his nose was attractive only to a mountaineer.

Gently, he reached down and tapped Oscar on the shoulder. The boy woke up quickly and took the work gloves from his father. Neither of them spoke, but they didn't need to, and that was another thing Santiago was thankful for. To have a boy who listened to his father's words? A boy who didn't complain? A boy who took on the unfair mantle of responsibility, who understood that there were things that needed to be done? To have a boy like that, Santiago thought, was to be living in an age of miracles. No matter what was going on around him, he knew that to have a boy like that meant he was still living in a world in which he needed to give thanks to God.

He watched Oscar open the back door and then close it behind him, and then he stared down at his hands. He could feel them throbbing with each beat of his heart. The generator was necessary to keep the fridge running so his daughter's medicine wouldn't go bad, but that didn't mean only his daughter could enjoy the spoils of electricity, and in the kitchen he cupped his hands together and scooped out as much ice as he could hold into a large plastic bowl full of water. He let the ice sit for a few seconds, cracking and bobbing, and then he thrust his hands into the water.

Pain.

And then bliss.

After ten minutes he took his hands back out and carefully blotted them on a kitchen towel, trying to be gentle, and then he went upstairs.

His wife was asleep on the reclining chair in the corner of Juliet's bedroom. The shades were down, but the reading lamp spilled light over her face. He turned the knob to cut the light. There was still enough light for him to see Juliet's face, however. She was awake, her eyes open. His wife had turned Juliet's wheelchair to face the small aquarium. It could be difficult to tell what Juliet was thinking, but she always seemed calmer when she could watch the fish tracing patterns through the water. Today, however, she was bobbing her head and letting out small grunts.

He inspected her oxygen and then her urine bag, making sure all of her lines were clear. If his wife had been awake, she would have scolded him for fussing over details that she had already checked, but they both knew he couldn't stop himself. One of the first things they had learned in caring for their daughter was that since Juliet couldn't tell them what was wrong, they needed to check her physical well-being before anything else. Nothing obvious seemed to explain what was bothering her, so he crouched in

front of her, putting one of his stinging hands on the wheelchair's
arm to steady himself.

Quietly, so that he wouldn't wake his wife, he sang to her:

La linda manita
que tiene el bebé
qué linda, qué bella
qué preciosa es

What a lovely tiny hand, he sang. How pretty, how lovely, how
fine. And then he sang of her fingers, her toes, her arms and her
legs, her mouth, her ears, her nose, her eyes.

By the time he was finished, he was crying.

Juliet was still staring at the fish tank, but her head had stilled
and she'd stopped grunting. Her breathing had relaxed into a regu-
lar rhythm. Santiago stood up, smoothed her hair, and then kissed
her on the forehead.

He stopped in the hallway to look out the window. He could
see Oscar walking the perimeter. His son was moving slowly, at-
tentive, careful. He checked his watch and decided he could steal
a quick shower.

First, though, he stopped in front of Mrs. Fine's bedroom.

She'd been their neighbor for long enough that Oscar called
her *abuela*. When Santiago had first suggested his plan to survive
the spiders—a plan that involved knocking down the house she'd
lived in for nearly sixty years—she didn't hesitate. He knew that
there were plenty of people in Oxford who were at the university who wouldn't have welcomed a blue-collar family like the
Garcias as neighbors, but Mrs. Fine, and Mr. Fine when he'd still
been alive, had treated them like family. Which, Santiago, realized,
was the truth. Mrs. Fine *was* family. His own mother died when
he was still a teenager, and his wife's parents had never taken to

him. Twenty years after the wedding, and they still acted like he'd somehow tricked Elizabeth into marrying him and then bullied her across the border.

He knocked once and then, after a few seconds, again. When there was no answer, he slowly opened the door, thinking he would just check to make sure all was well. Her bedroom was a hastily converted home office, and he expected to see her sitting at the desk, playing cards on the computer, but the room was empty.

Her bed was neatly made, and a note, written in longhand on a piece of computer paper, rested daintily on the pillow. Her writing was immaculate, in the looping style of a woman who'd learned to write in cursive when that was still a valued skill.

Santiago,

I used to wonder why God didn't see fit to allow me to have children, but, well, as they say, God works in mysterious ways. I've been lucky to have two great loves in my life: my husband, of course, is the first, but the second has been your family. I've seen the way that you and Elizabeth work so hard and sacrifice so much to take care of Juliet without in any way doing any less for Oscar. Having a sick child can bring out the best or the worst in people, and for you and Elizabeth, it's brought out the best. It's been a wonderful privilege to be part of that. You've always been so sweet and thankful whenever I've babysat or cooked or when you started celebrating Christmas at my house, but the truth is that you've given me far more than I could ever give you.

And so.

It's time.

You've done an amazing job preparing so quickly, but at best, you have six months of food. There are no good choices here.

While I do not eat much, I do eat, and we do not know when—or if—things will return to normal. In the meantime, every day that I am here is a day's worth of food. The sooner I am gone, the better. Without me, you will be able to stretch perhaps an extra month, and that may make all the difference in the world.

It has been years since I have been in a classroom teaching anthropology, but I'd be doing a disservice if I didn't point out that the idea of the Inuit sending their elderly off on ice floes to die was a bit overblown. Did it happen? Yes. Was it common? No. Certainly not in the last hundred years or so. But I'm still an academic at heart, so it's hard not to love a beautiful idea. If you look at it one way, it can seem heartless: sending an old woman off to die alone? But looked at another way, it's a generous act of love: that old woman choosing to go off to die alone because she knows that resources are scarce. What could be a more glorious final action than to release the people you love from the burden of taking care of you?

The last thing I want is to be a burden to you. I can't stand the idea that I might be taking food out of the mouths of your family.

I hope you see it the way I do, Santiago.

I'm sorry I wasn't brave enough to say good-bye in person, but I knew you and Elizabeth would try to talk me out of it. It is enough that you have to keep Juliet safe without having to worry about an old lady.

I've had a good life, Santiago. No regrets.

My love to all of you,
Abuela Diana

He sat on the edge of her bed and reread the letter. When he looked up, he realized his wife was standing in the doorway.

He shook his head.

"No," he said.

"No? No what?"

"No," he said. He stood up and handed her the letter and then walked downstairs.

"Wait, Santiago!" He heard his wife following him, and he waited for her out on the porch. He looked down at his hands again, tapping his fingers together, testing to see if they had somehow become less sore in the last half hour. He kicked the heel of one work boot against the other, shifting back and forth impatiently. Across the yard, Oscar flicked his wrist in a wave. Santiago nodded back.

Elizabeth stepped out on the porch, one hand holding the letter and the other covering her mouth in horror. She was trying not to cry. She was unsuccessful.

"What . . ." She stopped and caught her breath, tamping down her tears. "What are you going to do?"

Santiago cupped the back of his wife's neck. "The only thing I can," he said. He kissed her gently and then tipped his head forward so their foreheads were touching. "I'm going to go rescue that damned old fool."

When there wasn't just static, there'd been sketchy reports on the radio that spiders didn't seem to recognize you as prey if you were wearing a hazmat suit. While Santiago didn't have a proper hazmat suit, he had a full-face respirator, and that—combined with a rubber rain suit, a little duct tape, and a lot of faith—seemed like it might do the trick.

Oscar wanted to come along, but Santiago stared his son in the eyes and told him the truth, which was that if he didn't come home, it was going to be up to Oscar and Elizabeth to keep Juliet safe.

He scanned the yard until he figured out how Mrs. Fine had crossed the moat. There was an extension ladder on the asphalt next to an old truck on the other side of the moat; it looked like she must have rested the ladder on the hood of the truck and then either walked or crawled across. Like walking the plank, Santiago thought. The heat would have been uncomfortable, and it couldn't have been easy. Not for an old lady like Mrs. Fine. But old ladies were always tougher than they looked. Unfortunately, she'd pulled the ladder across after her. It was a smart move, because it stopped the spiders from using it, but it meant there was no easy way for Santiago to get across. The only option was to jump.

He took a few minutes to psych himself up, and then, finally, with a deep breath, he took a running start and leapt across the moat.

He landed heavily, stumbling and then falling to his hands and knees. His hands stung, but thankfully he hadn't torn the rubber pants or the dishwashing gloves. He double-checked that the duct tape still held around his wrists and ankles, gave one last wave to his son and wife, and then turned toward town.

All he had to do now was find Mrs. Fine's ice floe.

Chincoteague Island, Virginia

Gordo took another bite of his frozen yogurt. Somewhere between Bethesda and Chincoteague Island, four Marines had disappeared. After their little shopping trip to Radio Shack— okay, a smash and grab, which had included about twenty of those Motorola Talkabout radios, since there weren't enough military radios for every vehicle, as well as all the bits and bobs that Gordo and Shotgun needed—they'd hit the road again. Traffic was still brutal, but, four hours in, the road cleared enough for them to drive at something approximating a reasonable speed. However, when they finally came to a stop on Chincoteague Island, in front of a small strip mall with a gourmet grocery store, a wine store, a bakery, and a frozen-yogurt store, they were down one vehicle.

Lance Corporal Bock had tried raising the missing Marines, but after a few minutes Staff Sergeant Rodriguez stopped her.

"Don't bother, Bock," Rodriguez said.

Kim held up the little yellow radio. "Sir, they weren't equipped with a JTRS. They only had one of these suckers, and Family Radio Service has a limited range. They may just be out of range."

Even as she was saying it, Gordo could see that she didn't believe it. She knew as well as Rodriguez did—as all of them did—that the SUV hadn't just gone missing. The four Marines in the vehicle were AWOL.

There was a moment of glum silence, and then Rodriguez did something that Gordo thought was brilliant: he took all of them to the frozen-yogurt store.

Amazingly, Yogurt Wonderland was open for business. The boy working behind the counter, a teenager with a pierced ear and shoulder-length hair that had been dyed cherry red, didn't seem particularly surprised to see most of a platoon of Marines plus the three civilians—Gordo, Shotgun, and Teddie—come inside.

"Listen, kid," Rodriguez said. "You total all this up and then send a bill to the Marines, care of the US government."

The boy blew a small bubble and then shook his head. "Don't think so. Cash or credit."

Gordo had to admire the boy's cojones. With Gordo and Shotgun and Teddie and all of the Marines inside Yogurt Wonderland, the store was crowded, and every Marine was packing. Although Gordo wasn't sure why they were even bothering when it was clear that guns weren't the most effective weapons against spiders.

Rodriguez tensed, but before he could respond, Shotgun stepped forward.

"I've got this," he said, and he slapped down a credit card. It hit the counter with a solid thunk.

The kid rolled his eyes and pointed to the sticker next to the cash register. "No AmEx."

Shotgun pursed his lips, pinched them in, and then spat out a word. "Fine." He pulled his wallet back out, slid the metal card away, and then dug out a flimsier plastic credit card. "I'm assuming Visa is acceptable?"

The boy shrugged his assent.

Shotgun told the Marines to go nuts, and boy, did they listen. They filled their tubs with yogurt and then added toppings
until the M&M's and sprinkles and Butterfinger bits rained onto
the counter; they drizzled caramel syrup and scooped Oreo pieces
and chocolate-covered waffle-cone bits with the enthusiasm of the
young. It was all Gordo could do not to laugh. And then he caught
Teddie's eye and did laugh.

"What?" she said, hefting her own overflowing container. "So
I like frozen yogurt."

Which seemed fair enough. Gordo's own frozen yogurt tasted
like sweet relief. His choice was simple—plain tart with a healthy
dose of fresh strawberry slices and chocolate chips—but there was
something soothing about sitting out in the parking lot and spoon-
ing it into his mouth.

After they finished eating, Rodriguez told them they were staying put, so the Marines sorted gear and tended to personal hygiene.
While that happened, and Teddie went from Marine to Marine
asking questions on camera, Gordo and Shotgun pulled out the
ST11.

He and Shotgun had been able to do a lot of the work in the
truck on the way from Bethesda. It hadn't been ideal, but aside
from a brief adventure with a lost screw, they had managed to be
productive. Still, they'd left the soldering until now, not wanting
to risk an errant pothole ruining the whole endeavor. They set
up on the asphalt of the parking lot and ran the soldering iron off
an inverter they'd scrounged from Radio Shack and plugged into
the truck that Kim had been driving. Shotgun double-checked his
notes and then gave Gordo the go-ahead.

He cradled the wand gingerly. Both he and Shotgun were
snobs about tools, and the soldering iron in stock at the Radio
Shack wouldn't have been Gordo's first choice. But his hand was

steady, and after a few minutes they were done. While Gordo put the cover back in place and secured the Torx screws, Shotgun unplugged the soldering iron from the inverter, plugged the ST11's cord in place, and then ran a cable from the ST11 to a laptop.

They had to spend a few more minutes debugging, but then the screen lit up.

"Holy crap," Shotgun said.

"It works?" Gordo asked, and then he repeated himself, but as a statement: "It works." The asphalt wasn't the most comfortable place to sit, but in that moment he didn't care.

He felt Kim's presence before she said anything, and when he looked up at her he knew he had an idiot's grin on his face.

"Told you it was worth stopping at Radio Shack."

She didn't look as impressed as he had expected.

"That's it? That's the whole thing?"

"Well," Shotgun said defensively, "it's not like we've spent any real time on the end-user interface. I mean, you're used to slickly made apps with great graphics and all sorts of things that are fundamentally useless but are designed to create perceived value. Sure, it doesn't look like much, but it works."

"You ready for me to get Rodriguez?"

Shotgun hesitated, perhaps thinking of the underwhelming performance of the first iteration of the ST11—the way the spiders had simply gotten lethargic instead of keeling over dead as intended—but after Gordo gave him a reassuring nod, he told Kim to go ahead.

Rodriguez hadn't asked for an explanation when they'd stopped at the Radio Shack, so now they gave him the nickel version: essentially, Gordo said, the ST11 was designed to use extremely low-frequency sound waves that were tightly funneled at their target. In theory it should have been lethal. In practice, not so much.

But they realized there was something about the ST11 that altered the behavior of the spiders, and, working backward, they figured that maybe the spiders were using similar frequencies as the ST11 to communicate.

"Or, well, maybe not communicate," Gordo said. "There's a lot we don't understand, but think of the ST11 like a jammer— you know, messing up the radio. And then we—well, mostly Shotgun—thought if we're jamming something, that particular something has to be coming from somewhere, and instead of *jamming* the signal, we could track it."

"So," Rodriguez said, "like radar?"

The greater point, Gordo said, was that it worked like they'd hoped, and as soon as they turned on the ST11, it was clear that there was a specific something, or multiple somethings, communicating with the spiders.

"What?" Rodriguez said, raising one eyebrow, clearly skeptical. "Like radio broadcasts?"

"Not exactly but, yeah, close enough. And the thing is, with this," he said, patting the ST11 fondly, "we can figure out where the broadcasts are coming from."

"The command center?"

Shotgun got up. He put a hand on one hip and then stretched a bit. "Honestly? I don't know. But for the first time I think we have a way to figure out where those things are before they pop out and start eating people."

Rodriguez scratched his jaw and then stared at the row of shops. The teenage boy came out of the yogurt place, locked the door, and then walked away. Rodriguez sighed. "Holy crap. Okay. That's good. You sure?"

Both Shotgun and Gordo were sure.

Rodriguez pulled the yellow Motorola radio from where it was clipped to his waistband. "We're going to need something with better range than this, though I'm not sure who the heck I'm supposed to tell."

"Yo! Yo!"

Gordo looked across the parking lot. The Marine they called Honky Joe was waving and yelling at them. A number of Marines huddled around him. As he, Shotgun, Kim, and Rodriguez walked toward Honky Joe, Gordo could see that the Marines were all staring at the radio in his hand: one of the military ones, not the bright yellow kind they'd gotten from Radio Shack. It had been silent the whole trip, but now it was broadcasting.

When Gordo got closer, he recognized the voice coming through the speaker. "Is that the—"

"It's on a loop," Honky Joe said.

He was surprised at how good the sound quality was. Even if they hadn't been in the midst of a complete collapse of, well, everything—even if he hadn't known that Denver, Minneapolis, Chicago, Milwaukee, Houston, and so many more cities had been vaporized—he would have been impressed with the sound quality. President Pilgrim sounded like she was right there next to them.

"—scientists are working on a way to fight back. I am your president, and I am with you. Please rebroadcast this message."

There was a slight delay, and then it started again:

"Attention: This is President Stephanie Pilgrim. A few moments ago, a small faction of men and women in the armed forces attempted to forcibly overthrow the United States government. Their aim was to seize control of our nuclear arsenal and destroy most of the continental United States. Any and all members of the military who assist these cowards who are attempting to subvert the democratically elected government, know that you are traitors to your country and will be treated as such. This is a time of great crisis, and we must work together, not tear ourselves apart. We must fight our common enemy. To that end, I have established a new, temporary seat of government in New York City. If you are hearing this, this is a direct order from the president of the United States of America: you are *not* authorized to use nuclear weapons of any kind. I repeat, you are *not* authorized to use nuclear weapons. Earlier, I authorized tactical nuclear strikes on approximately thirty targets that were overrun with spiders, with the intention of containing the threat against us. I believed this was a necessary action, but enough is enough. We will not turn our country into a wasteland. For now, I beseech you, stay the course. As I speak, our top scientists are working on a way to fight back. I am your president, and I am with you. Please rebroadcast this message." And again the slight pause before the message looped. "Attention: This is—"

And then it suddenly cut off, leaving only dead air. After a few seconds a new voice came on the air.

"This is General Ben Broussard, chairman of the Joint Chiefs of Staff. I have assumed command of all branches of the United States military. We will respond to the threat against our country with each and every weapon available to us. To all members of the armed services: Stand by for further orders."

And then that message started to loop. They listened to it four or five times before Rodriguez reached out and turned off the radio.

All of them, including Gordo, Shotgun, and Teddie, stared at Rodriguez.

"You heard the man," Rodriguez said, "we're standing by for further orders."

White House Manhattan, New York, New York

New York City. Shining. Eternal. Untouched.

Well, not completely untouched. The air force and the Army Corps of Engineers had turned more than a thousand yards north of 122nd Street into rubble, creating an impassible no-man's-land protected by a hodgepodge of National Guard, army, and Marines. The men and women were armed with a mix of flamethrowers and machine guns: the guns for anybody who tried to enter, and the flamethrowers for any unwanted eight-legged guests that might be hitchhiking their way in. They didn't have as many flamethrowers as they needed, but an engineer out in California had designed a kick-ass homemade version that could be turned out in any well-equipped metal shop or by anybody with a 3-D printer that worked in metal instead of plastic. For once, Manny was thankful for the whole hipster idea of "makerspaces." They'd turned out nearly two hundred of the flamethrower nozzles yesterday, and the guy in charge of manufacturing them—a dude with a topknot who was so ridiculously good-looking that it actually made Manny angry—said they'd be able to make closer to

five hundred a day going forward. The best thing was that whoever designed the flamethrowers had made them so they worked
equally well with gasoline and with those barbecue propane tanks.
It wasn't perfect, but it beat a can of Raid any day.

They'd have been able to make even more of the flamethrowers if New York City was still one unified, glorious beast, but the
entire island of Manhattan had been turned into a no-go zone:
tunnels and bridges destroyed with explosives, the Hudson and
East Rivers natural barriers. Fortress Manhattan. Along with the
thousands of soldiers, there were also private citizens, all making
sure that Manhattan stayed untouched. The Bronx and Brooklyn
and Queens were on their own, but Manhattan was free of spiders.

So far, it was working, although Manny knew it was just luck:
all it would take was one infected person, one lousy unseen spider,
and the whole thing would fall apart. On top of which, Manny
was now worried about the fealty of the entire armed forces. The
coup on the USS *Elsie Downs* was a done deal. Was the rest of the
military far behind?

Judging by the reaction to their appearance in New York City,
it was something to worry about. Stephanie needed to deliver
something better than just a line in the sand. He happened to agree
with her: If the only way to annihilate these eight-legged monsters
was to also annihilate the human race, what was the point? It was
smarter to take their chances that the spiders would go back into hibernation or return to whatever hell they came from. But in times
like these, the rhetoric of inaction was always defeated by the rah-
rah-rah of destruction. The intellectual argument usually fell in the
face of somebody who could make smashing stuff sound exciting.

All of this was made worse by the scale of what had happened
on the USS *Elsie Downs*. This wasn't just a few dozen sailors dis-
obeying orders. This was the chairman of the Joint Chiefs of Staff

in conjunction with the senior officers of a *Ford*-class aircraft carrier. Broussard's message of fighting back whatever the costs resonated.

What he needed, Manny knew, was something concrete from Melanie.

Which was a problem, because Melanie was still on the carrier and he had no way of getting in touch with her. All his faith rested in the idea that Melanie had an answer and that Billy Cannon and Special Agent Riggs were going to be able to get his ex-wife and her colleagues off that tub. In the meantime he was keeping pretty busy trying to help Steph make sure that the rest of what was left of America didn't go down the drain, and trying to figure out how long they could stall before Broussard was able to Dr. Strangelove the country into oblivion.

God, he missed normal politics. He missed the way it could be grand at times, how there were moments when everybody came together to do the right thing. That wasn't where he excelled, though. What he loved, and what he was aching for, was the petty horse-trading, the maneuvering, the way he could count votes and twist arms and engage in backroom quid pro quos and emerge the winner.

He realized he'd completely missed whatever it was the woman in front of him had been talking about. She was a city engineer and had come in with some plan involving . . . the sewers? He nodded and dismissed her, and she left the room with a walk that was positively jaunty. At least somebody was happy, he thought.

He looked at his watch. Nearly eleven o'clock at night. Late. But there was still work to do. He got up from his desk and poked his head out the door into the small antechamber where his administrative assistant was typing on a laptop. The admin, a soldier named Champ Jones, was on loan, but in the few hours since

Manny had acquired Champ, he'd already decided to poach him permanently.

"Yes, sir?"

"Nothing, really. Just stretching my legs. Who's up next?"

He knew there was a line out in the hallway. Even at this time of night, there was a line. Part of his job was to lighten the president's load, and even though all the standard parts of the job had been stripped away—nobody was waiting to corral him to get their cousin's nephew a White House internship—the state of emergency and the coup meant a new can of worms.

"Cathy Silverberg."

"From the mayor's office? How long has she been waiting? You should have bumped her to the front." He could hear that his tone was too harsh. Scolding.

"She just arrived, sir. After your last appointment was already in the office."

And now he felt like a dick.

"Okay. Send her in. And get me a Diet Coke, please." He turned, stopped, and then looked at Champ. "You're doing a good job. Keep it up."

"Thank you, sir."

Manny went back into his office and sat down. They were operating out of an immense town house on the Upper East Side, just a block from Central Park. There were official offices they could have occupied, but given that they were in the middle of a coup, it had made more sense to pick something a little more difficult to find. There were nearly a dozen properties like this spread throughout New York City—buildings that looked like private residences but were actually property of good old Uncle Sam. He didn't even want to think about what the open-market value of a property like this would be. Forty, fifty million?

It was close to ten thousand square feet, with a dozen bedrooms—ten of which had been converted into offices—multiple living rooms and a grand dining room, and had enough glitz and gilt to make even the tackiest president happy. And that was just aboveground. After purchasing the building through a series of shell corporations during the economic crash of the aughts, the Secret Service dug out the basement and added three lower levels. Two levels of conference rooms and offices, and the very deepest level a bomb shelter. As it was, the entire building had been hardened: windows capable of withstanding a bazooka blast, reinforced concrete, all that sort of crap that got the Secret Service folks excited. If you were upstairs, you were probably safe from any conventional terrorist attack, and on the lower levels you were safe from anything within reason—the caveat being *within reason*. Manny knew that if Broussard decided the only course of action was to remove President Pilgrim from the face of the earth, the phrase *within reason* was headed out the window. The full might and fury of the United States military wasn't going to be stopped by a town house on the Upper East Side. Thankfully, going by the fact that they hadn't been shot out of the air as they'd fled the USS *Elsie Downs*, and that the temporary White House—White House Manhattan was what everybody was calling it—wasn't just a smoking crater, Broussard wasn't ready to go that far.

Yet.

He looked out the window. He was on the top floor of the town house, in one of the bedrooms that had been converted to an office. Steph's office was next door, which had been a fight. The Secret Service wanted her belowground at all times, but Steph won that argument, throwing back their own claims that the whole residence was hardened. Right now, however, she was a floor down, in an actual bedroom, sleeping. That had been another argument—

one that he'd won. She needed to sleep. He'd handle everything else for now and catch a few winks in the wee hours of the night. Although it would help if Champ brought him his darn soda.

As if his thoughts could produce actions, Champ came through the door holding a glass full of the dark elixir that powered Manny through his days, followed by Cathy Silverberg.

They'd met a few times over the years. She had a relationship with the mayor that was analogous to his own with Steph. Well, probably without the affair part, he thought. But he knew both Silverberg and the mayor believed that if things had shaken out just a little bit differently, they, and not Steph and Manny, would have been the ones occupying the White House. Or, in this case, White House Manhattan.

He shook Silverberg's hand and then took a sip of his soda. The glass was cold enough in his hand that he already felt the relief before he even had any liquid in his mouth. But as he drank he knew something was desperately wrong.

"Champ!" he barked at his admin before the soldier had a chance to close the door. "What the hell is this?" He held up the glass.

"Diet Pepsi, sir."

Whatever warm feelings he'd had for his new assistant fled. Manny stared at Champ. "Diet Pepsi?"

"Yes, sir. There's no Diet Coke on the premises."

"You're telling me that the United States government can secretly own a terrorist-proof town house with an extra-double-secret three-level basement in the middle of Manhattan, a block from Central Park, and we can't stock the place with Diet Coke? You expect me to drink . . . this?" He held out the glass as if it were an infectious dying animal.

Champ took the glass. "Do you want me to send someone out into the city, sir?"

Silverberg laughed. She was somewhere close to Manny's age. She had her brown hair twisted up off her shoulders and was professionally dressed. She looked more put together than Manny did; he was still wearing the same suit, wrinkled and mussed, although somebody had acquired a new shirt so he could replace the bloodstained one.

Silverberg said, "There's a bodega a couple blocks away. I'll give you the address. There will be a pair of cops in front of it to prevent looting. Tell them you've got orders from the mayor's office. Tell them Cathy Silverberg authorized it."

"No," Manny said. "You know what, I'll go get it myself. Get some fresh air. You up for a walk and talk?" he asked Silverberg.

"Only if you don't call it a walk and talk."

They took the elevator down and walked out through the front door. Silverberg had four plainclothes police officers with her, and four soldiers in uniform accompanied Manny. As they walked down the front steps, Manny suddenly stopped.

"Crap." He patted his pockets. "I don't have a wallet."

Silverberg rolled her eyes. "I can spot you a few cans of Diet Coke."

They started walking again. "What do you need?"

He knew she wouldn't have come to see him if it wasn't important. Right now she was as busy as he was. They'd done a tremendous job of keeping the lid on things in New York City. A certain amount of that was, of course, help from the National Guard and federal troops, but the mayor had stepped up. Behind the mayor, of course, was Silverberg.

"You know what I love most about New York?" It was a rhetorical question, and Manny didn't bother answering. Even though it sounded like she was going to take the long way to get to her point, he didn't care. Getting outside had been a wonderful idea. Sure, maybe it wasn't exactly fresh air—not with the smells of the city always hanging about—but it was nice out. The streets were completely empty of civilians. There was a contingent of Secret Service agents outside as well as a mélange of military—God, he hoped these particular men and women were more loyal than Broussard—but it seemed almost normal. The buildings around them were a mixture of darkness and light, and he wondered if, were it darker, he'd be able to see the stars.

"What I love about New York," Silverberg continued, "is that nobody is alike. Millions of people, and each one of them has their own story, their own life, their own opinions. There are only two things New Yorkers can agree on. The first is that you don't block the sidewalk. Seriously, is there a bigger sin in all of New York than walking slowly or stopping in the middle of the sidewalk? That's why we hate out-of-towners as much as we love them. But the other thing New Yorkers agree on is that you never, ever mess with us. You mess with New York City, and we'll come at you."

They turned the corner. Silverberg's cops were on point, with Manny's protective detail behind them. There didn't seem to be a great need for security right at that moment, he thought, but he was used to it.

"I've been a New Yorker my whole life," she continued. "I'm old enough that I've lived through Times Square turning from a war zone into a tourist trap. I've lived through Koch and Dinkins and Giuliani, and I saw the towers fall. I've lived through Bloomberg, though he was a heck of a mayor, and Hurricane Sandy and Mayor de Blasio. Heck, I've lived through eating chicken I bought from a street cart parked next to the Gowanus Canal. I mean, come on, is this all you've got? Spiders? You'll have to try harder than that to scare New Yorkers."

She stopped walking. Manny saw the bodega across the street. Sure enough, there were two uniformed cops in riot gear standing outside. The store was open, however, and he could almost taste the Diet Coke.

"Manny," she said. She glanced ahead to make sure that her protective detail was far enough away that she could speak without being overheard. "There's a reason I came myself. We're hearing things."

"What kinds of things?" he asked, but he had a sinking feeling.

"Rank and file would be one thing, but we're getting pushback from the brass, too. There are a lot of people who think Broussard might be right."

Manny nodded. There was no point arguing and there was no point drilling down. He didn't know Silverberg that well, but he knew she was as tough as they came and she was thorough. She wouldn't have come to Manny with this if there wasn't a real problem. There might have been a political angle during normal times— there was always a political angle—but she was a straight shooter.

"How long?" he asked. "How long do you think you can keep the police in line?"

She looked down and opened her purse, rummaging around until she pulled out a wad of cash. "Here." She stuffed the money into his hand. "For your soda."

"You're not coming in?"

"No. I don't have much to add to what I just said. And to answer your question: I don't know. Two days? Three? Maybe less. You know how it is. What's the saying? A powder keg ready to explode? I'm telling you, we're already riding hard on this, and I think the longer you guys go without giving us something solid, the harder it gets to convince people that Broussard is wrong. And all bets are off if we get a third wave of those damn spiders."

"I thought you said it would take more than spiders to scare New Yorkers."

"I was lying," she said. She turned, walked over to the two cops at the door, introduced herself and Manny, then waved good-bye.

He went in, handed the cash—close to sixty bucks—to the guy at the register, and then cleared the cooler of all its cans and bottles of Diet Coke. Three paper bags full. He gave a bag each to two of the four soldiers on his security detail, and carried the third bag in one hand, leaving the other free to drink a soda. He didn't feel like waiting until he was back at the town house. The first sip hit his mouth with a jolt that felt like he'd stuck his finger directly into a light socket. He took a gulp, enough that he choked a little and then had to cough. It was invigorating, however. Between that and being outside, he was wide-awake again. There was something kind of pleasant in the idea of walking through the streets of New York as the clock approached midnight. When he'd visited the city as a young man, in his twenties, he stayed out until all hours of the night, and one of his favorite things had been—

He stopped walking so abruptly that the soldier behind him actually banged into him.

"Sorry, sir."

Manny turned and stared at the soldier. Like a lot of soldiers, this one seemed spectacularly young-looking up close, and he was taken aback by Manny's behavior. Manny couldn't help it, though: what Cannon had said to Steph as they were about to flee from the *Elsie Downs* had suddenly come back to him. They'd talked about Operation SAFEGUARD, and how that would buy them about seventy-two hours—he took a quick look at his watch, thinking it was less now—and then Cannon said something about—

"Soldier," Manny said. "Are you a Christian? What's Matthew 5:45?"

"Uh . . ."

"Don't worry about it"—Manny glanced at the kid's name tag—"Specialist Ward."

"Sir?"

He turned to look at one of the soldiers who had taken point. Her voice came as a surprise. He hadn't looked at any of them closely, and, geared up, Specialist Green's gender hadn't been obvious.

She held herself with confidence, despite looking no older than Specialist Ward. "My mother's a minister, sir," she said. "Lots of Bible camp growing up."

"Matthew 5:45?"

"It's from the Sermon on the Mount." She stared at Manny's face for signs of recognition. "Jesus?"

"Okay, even I know that much. But what is it? What's Matthew 5:45?"

"I used to have it memorized, but—"

"I'll settle for the approximate version, soldier."

Specialist Green scrunched up her eyes in concentration. "No. Give me a second. Uh, this is the English Standard Version. If you want King James or something, you'll need to find somebody else."

Manny tried to be patient, but it was all he could do not to shake Specialist Green, to yell at her to hurry. He could feel it, knew there was something important there. The way Steph had been surprised that Cannon knew about Matthew 5:45; that Cannon thought it might save them from Broussard; and the very fact that this was something Manny didn't know about.

"Okay, so this is the last couple, not just forty-five, but it goes something, something, 'Love your enemies and pray for those who persecute you,' something, something, then 'he makes his sun rise on the evil and on the good, and sends rain on the just and on the unjust. For if you love those who love you, what reward do you have? Do not even the tax collectors do the same? And if you greet only your brothers, what more are you doing than others? Do not even the Gentiles do the same? You therefore must be perfect, as your heavenly Father is perfect.'"

As she got more comfortable, her voice rose and fell, the cadence of a preacher's kid coming through; by the time she finished, Manny thought maybe she'd missed her calling by picking the military.

"That's it," she said. "It's the part about the rain. 'He makes his sun rise on the evil and on the good, and sends rain on the just and on the unjust.' Mom was big on that, the idea that you couldn't just pick and choose God's love. It fell everywhere."

Manny's heart was beating hard in his chest. It was too soon for the caffeine to have kicked in, he knew. "Jesus Christ."

"Exactly!" Specialist Green said brightly.

"No, I . . . Never mind," Manny said. He started walking briskly back toward the town house.

He didn't run, because he wasn't in the shape for that, but he didn't dither either. At the front door, he paused only long enough for the Secret Service agents to verify him, and then hustled up the steps. Inside, he tucked the paper bag full of soda under his arm so that he could hold the open Diet Coke and have one hand free to jab impatiently at the elevator button. He thought for a second about taking the stairs, but he didn't want to get to Steph's room and have to catch his breath before going in. When the elevator arrived with a charming *ding*, Manny stepped in and hit the button for Steph's floor. The ride couldn't have been more than ten seconds, but it felt like an eternity. The entire time he kept saying the words over and over to himself: "He makes his sun rise on the evil and on the good, and sends rain on the just and on the unjust."

As always, there were a pair of Secret Service agents standing sentry outside the president's door. He ignored them and knocked hard. Pretty much the same way he'd started the day, he thought. And once again it was George who opened the door. Manny's knocking had clearly woken the president's husband. He was wearing a pair of surprisingly nice pajamas, royal blue with thin red pinstripes. The pajamas threw Manny off for a moment. Had the pajamas been waiting inside this room the whole time, in case the president needed to use this top secret hideaway? Had whoever planned these New York City bunkers been that thorough? No. Eyes on the prize.

"I need to talk to her," he said. "Five minutes."

"She just fell asleep, Manny. Can it wait?"

Manny didn't say anything, and he didn't need to. George blinked as he realized that Manny wouldn't have knocked in the first place if it were something that could wait. He stepped back and let Manny in, hesitated, and then stepped out into the hall, closing the door behind him to give Manny and Steph privacy to talk.

Steph was already sitting up and leaning against the headboard by the time he got over to the bed. He saw her glance at the clock on her nightstand and then at him. He sat down on the edge, holding the paper bag on his lap.

"They're back?"

"This isn't about the spiders."

"What is it?" She didn't waste any time. Like George, she knew Manny wouldn't have woken her if it were for something small.

"Matthew 5:45. 'He makes his sun rise on the evil and on the good, and sends rain on the just and on the unjust,'" Manny said.

"As we were leaving the USS *Elsie Downs*, Billy said you could exercise Matthew 5:45."

"Manny . . ."

"This isn't the time, Steph. Look, I'm a big boy. I'm okay with the idea that there are things the president knows that I don't. I figure from your surprise when Cannon said it that not that many people know about whatever this is. The number of people who know about Operation SAFEGUARD is minuscule, but I know about *that*, so I figure that whatever this is, it must be an even bigger deal. But I asked a soldier about Matthew 5:45. The Bible verse. It rains on 'the just and on the unjust,' right? Cannon was talking about a way to disable our nuclear weapons, and I was thinking of Operation SAFEGUARD, but that's single authorizations. This is something that cuts across the whole nuclear program, isn't it? Like a master switch?"

Steph reached out and took a sip of water from the glass on her nightstand. "I don't know how Cannon found out about it. It was one of those pie-in-the-sky ideas, you know? The entire program was designed for a scenario like this one."

Manny was taken aback. "Spiders? Really?"

Steph gave him a long, slow blink. "No. Of course not spiders. No, the entire thing was designed around the worry that we would have a coup. Our military is as good as they get, but you always have fringe elements, and, well, our last president was both paranoid and unpopular, so it was a worry for him. Besides, great democracies don't stay great if they aren't vigilant, and our military is so large that bad actors do occasionally slip through the cracks. Anyway, after the Vail incident, my predecessor wanted to make sure we had a way to shut everything down as needed. He didn't get a second term, but the Matthew 5:45 project was almost complete by the time I took office. I decided that, in light of Vail, it wouldn't hurt to have a backup to Operation SAFEGUARD."

She didn't mean the ski town. The Vail incident had happened three years before she'd taken office, and it was so classified that he knew only the general outlines: a lone mentally unstable officer in the United Kingdom had, for an extremely brief period—less than three minutes—gotten control of the entire British nuclear arsenal and initiated a system-wide launch protocol. Thankfully, three minutes was not long enough for anything other than a good scare, and the British government did such a good job of keeping it quiet that not even a whisper had gotten out to the public. In fact, that was all Manny knew about what happened. He didn't even know why it was called the "Vail" incident. But he knew that in the very small circles of those in the United States government who knew the details—and they were small circles indeed if they didn't include Manny Walchuck—there was real concern that something similar could happen in the United States. What Steph had said was right. As good as the military was—and he fervently believed it was the best in the world—among the hundreds of thousands of men and women wearing the uniform, not all of them could be trusted.

As evidenced by Broussard and those who were following him.

"And?"

"And, Manny, quite obviously, yes, Matthew 5:45 is designed to shut down our entire nuclear system in the event that there is some sort of internal breach." She crossed her arms, frowning. He couldn't tell whether she was pissed because he'd woken her up or because of something else.

"There's more to it, I'm guessing," Manny said. "Otherwise you would have already initiated it, right? Because I'm sure Broussard and his folks are working really hard right now to circumvent things."

"We've got a couple of days until Operation SAFEGUARD goes down. You could have waited to ask me about this until the morning." She looked down at his lap. "Are you holding a grocery bag full of Diet Coke?"

"Steph. We don't have a lot of time." He leaned down and put the bag on the floor. "I just talked to Cathy Silverberg. Back-channel stuff. We're losing the NYPD. Broussard's message is echoing. She thinks, best case, we've got forty-eight hours. And right now the soldiers we've got surrounding us are loyal, but there's no guarantee they're going to stay that way. You're the president. For now."

Those last two words sounded bad, even to Manny, and he could see Steph flinch as he said them.

She ran her fingers through her hair and was about to speak when they both heard a noise behind them. Manny looked back to see George sticking his head through a crack where the door was open.

"Need a few more minutes?"

"Sorry," Manny said. "I know it's late."

"Well, I'm awake now. Maybe I'll go down and see if I can find some ice cream."

They waited for the door to close. Steph smiled a little ruefully. "Poor George. I don't think he ever really believed I'd win the presidency." She bit her lip. "Manny, am I doing the right thing here? Could Broussard be right? Maybe it's better to go down swinging."

"Do you really believe that?" Manny asked.

She considered. "No. Normally, I'd say yes, but if Broussard gets his way, there's no hope. We kill the spiders, but we kill ourselves, too." She chuckled and stared at her hands. "It's actually funny, believe it or not, because Matthew 5:45 works in this case. The reason the program is called Matthew 5:45 is because of the idea that rain falls on both the just and the unjust. You know, the idea that nuclear weapons don't discriminate. Supposedly we've got nukes as a way of keeping the peace. The whole idea is that they're such powerful weapons that we'll never need to use them. Mutually assured destruction. That's the thing, isn't it? During a nuclear war, it's going to rain on the just and the unjust alike.

"I don't think anybody ever thought we'd deliberately use nuclear weapons on our own citizens as a protective measure. But it fits here, doesn't it? Broussard thinks he's doing the right thing. But in blowing the hell out of the spiders, the just will suffer as well." She looked up from her hands at Manny. "After the Vail incident, the worry was that we'd have a single officer or a small number of officers who go rogue and are able to wrest control of the *entire* nuclear arsenal. Operation SAFEGUARD is terrific in terms of managing individual nukes, but that assumes the president is in control. So yes, there's Matthew 5:45. But the problem is that if I initiate Matthew 5:45, there's no rewind. It's a one-way street."

"So what? If it locks Broussard out from using nuclear weapons, it buys us—"

"No, Manny, you don't understand. It won't lock only Broussard out. It will lock everybody out. Permanently. There's no take-backs on this. It's some sort of computer virus. Once we set it in motion, we're crippling ourselves permanently. I can't order this and then decide a couple of days from now that I do, in fact, want to keep nuking those goddamned spiders. Look, when this first started, Broussard and all the brass were pushing hard for me to go nuclear, and I pushed back. I was adamant that we weren't going to use nuclear weapons. The thing that appealed to me about the Spanish Protocol was that it seemed like a way to protect America from herself. We could carve the country up with minimal casualties. Give those parts of the country that hadn't been infested the best chance to survive. Cripple some of America and hope that we'd last long enough to heal.

"We tried. I thought it was a good plan, and I think maybe, if we'd done it sooner, it might have made a difference. If we'd initiated the Spanish Protocol in the hours after that container ship spilled its spiders onto the streets of Los Angeles. Despite second-guessing, nobody really thought nuking LA at that point in time was the right thing, but I could have ordered something more aggressive than a quarantine and a full stop of domestic flights. But you know how that turned out. And you know how the Spanish Protocol turned out. We crippled our highways and infrastructure and it barely slowed those monsters.

"I don't regret ordering those nuclear strikes. I don't," she said, and she was quiet for a second, staring at Manny beseechingly.

"You did the right thing. You did what you needed to do," he said.

"I know, but that doesn't make it feel any better," she said. "And what if it comes down to that? What if we reach a point a few days from now when it's clear that we've lost? When it's clear that I should have followed Broussard's advice? If I initiate Matthew 5:45, I'm not giving myself any leeway."

Manny realized he was still holding his open can of soda, and he took a sip, but Steph was waiting for him to respond. He thought for a second and then remembered one of the first times he realized Steph was going places.

"Do you remember, in college, when you threw your medical-school applications in the trash? I asked you how you knew that you didn't want to be a doctor. Your parents were both doctors, and you had spent your entire life—your entire time in high school and up to the beginning of your senior year of college—planning to go to medical school. And there you were, dumping your applications in the trash so that you could instead apply to law school, because you'd decided that politics was your calling. I mean, I had no idea what I was going to do with my life at that point, but you were so sure of yourself. Do you remember what you said?"

Steph gave a little shake of her head. She was looking down at the covers of the bed, but he knew he was getting to her. She had a small, warm smile on her face. "No. I honestly don't remember this at all, but I'm guessing you're about to tell me."

"You said that, for every person, there are only a handful of moments when you have to consciously make a truly important decision that will alter the entire landscape of your life. The trick, you said, is that when you make one of those decisions, you have to throw yourself entirely behind it. The moment you commit yourself to a direction, you have to act like it was inevitable, as if your entire life was leading up to that moment and that decision, and never, ever look back with regret. You said that to look back was to be like Orpheus."

"Orpheus? Really?" She laughed a little. "God. I was a smarty-pants, wasn't I?"

"A little. Total honesty here? I had to look up what the myth of Orpheus was," he said, and that made him smile, too. Orpheus. The ancient Greek musician who charmed his way into the underworld to bring his wife back from the dead, and who lost her just at the moment of salvation because he looked back to make sure she was really following him.

"That's pretty good. Did I really say all of that?"

"More or less."

She flicked her hand at him. "Okay."

"Okay, as in you're going to initiate the lockout?"

"Okay, as in it's after midnight, I'm exhausted, and my husband is downstairs eating a bowl of ice cream. Get out of here, let me go back to sleep, and I'll decide in the morning. We've got that long, don't we?"

Manny took his bag of Diet Cokes and left the room. His security detail—the two soldiers still carrying the other bags—followed him to his office, where he gave Champ the Diet Cokes and strict orders to reserve them for Manny's personal use. There were ten people still waiting outside his office for an audience, and he moved through them as quickly as possible, finishing up about half past one in the morning. There was a bunk room downstairs in the basement that he could have gone to, but there was also a perfectly good couch in his office and he sent Champ to scare up a blanket and a pillow.

Once Champ had come and gone and closed the door behind him, Manny closed his eyes and thought of Orpheus. It was a beautiful story, really. To love someone so much you'd literally walk through hell to bring them back? But it bothered him, too, because he knew there was more to the story—that there was something else that happened *after* Orpheus looked back. He couldn't remember what it was, but he was sure it was another tragedy. Wasn't it always that way with the Greeks?

Operation SAFEGUARD, Undisclosed Location, Top Secret

The most important job in the world was wildly boring. Or it had been until very, very recently.

As far as the general public, his family, and his girlfriend were concerned, Lieutenant Colonel Lou Jenks had earned his silver bars through distinguished service in the air force. Which wasn't completely untrue. What was completely untrue was that he commanded a company that was essentially a roving force responsible for maintenance of helicopters and planes used in active-duty SpecOps missions. As cover, it worked well. All he had to say when asked was that he couldn't divulge any details about where he was or it might compromise the safety of the SpecOps forces. Sometimes, if he wanted to seem particularly mysterious, he would add that he couldn't even tell them whether he was working with SEALs or Rangers or Air Force Special Tactics or whomever this trip, because all of it was just so darn sensitive. Loose lips sink ships and all that.

His cover story even explained why he was gone for six weeks

out of every eight; he was, ostensibly, in the field. His girlfriend
didn't like that he was gone, but she did seem to get a kick out
of the whole international-man-of-mystery thing. She asked him
constantly where he'd been just so that he would have to say,
"No, sorry, I can't even give the smallest hint, no, not even to
you, sweetie, even though we've been dating for three years and
of course I trust you, but we're talking about a sacred trust that
the United States government and the fighting men of our armed
forces have given me to keep the faith. I'm sorry. I just can't tell
you."

Of course, even if he'd been allowed to tell his girlfriend or
his family or his friends where he'd been, he *couldn't* tell them. He
had to submit to a sedative and a hood that blocked out all visual
stimulation both coming and going. His job was simply to spend
six weeks out of every eight sitting in a bunker that was so secret,
he doubted there were more than a thousand people in the entire
military or government who even knew it existed; heck, it was so
secret that even though he worked and lived there, he didn't actually know where *there* was. All he knew for sure was that when he
went to the bunker, he had to fly from where his family lived in
Denver to Washington, DC, and from there he was draped with a
hood and sedated, and then he woke up in the bunker. When he
left the bunker, he always woke up to his hood being pulled off in
the same nondescript room in the Pentagon. He was pretty sure
the bunker was somewhere on the East Coast, maybe in North or
South Carolina, or Georgia, but even then he was guessing a bit.
So if his family and friends and girlfriend thought he was out in
the field supporting SpecOps, well, that was fine. Besides, when it
was all over with, he'd be able to at least tell them what his real rank
was. In public, he was Air Force captain Lou Jenks, but the truth
was that part of the deal for being assigned to Operation SAFE-

GUARD was that he'd been promoted well past captain, to the rank of lieutenant colonel. So what if he hadn't been near an actual aircraft in an official role in more than two years, and so what if he didn't have even a single man under his direct command?

Plus the bunker was way nicer than he'd expected. He'd spent some time on a nuclear submarine as part of a training program that allowed officers in one branch to do limited tours shadowing officers in another branch. Although he'd written a relatively positive after-action report, mostly all he'd gotten out of it was the deep understanding that he was truly grateful he hadn't joined the navy. He had a lot of respect for what they did, but he spent a lot of emotional energy trying not to panic at the idea of being in a metal tube that was traveling under the ocean. Which, when he thought about it, was kind of funny, because he had devoted his career to the branch of the military that specialized in being in metal tubes flying through the air. Regardless, when he'd learned of his new orders, he was, to put it mildly, less than thrilled.

The Strict Actual Failure and Error Guardians Under All Radioactive Decrees program's name had clearly been chosen only because it made a cool acronym: SAFEGUARD. The entire point of Operation SAFEGUARD was to serve as a control over the use of nuclear weapons, so it would have made sense to call it something like Nuclear Fail-safe and Oversight, but that would have made for a crappy acronym. Not that it actually mattered, since basically nobody knew it even existed, and Lou faced imprisonment for disclosing classified information if he told anybody outside Operation SAFEGUARD where he worked. Besides which, the thirty people who actively worked on Operation SAFEGUARD, split equally between operators like Lou and support staff, didn't even call it Operation SAFEGUARD. They just called it "the bunker." As in: "Yeah, another two weeks until I can leave the bunker for my R&R." Or: "Man, I can't tell you how good it is to be back in the bunker after the last two weeks. My parents were on my case the whole time about when I was going to finally ask Susan to marry me. I'd rather do back-to-back tours here than have to deal with another day of that."

They all complained about the bunker, but the truth was, aside from the restrictions placed upon them by the classified nature of the program, the bunker was actually a pretty sweet gig right up until this whole thing with the spiders. There were no women in the bunker—it was an all-male crew—because the isolation and small size of the crew would certainly have led to issues, but he had a serious girlfriend anyway. And, sure, Lou had to suffer through six months of incredibly intense training in cyberwarfare and security, but he had assurances that at the end of the two-year assignment his new top secret rank of lieutenant colonel would no longer be top secret. He figured that two years in the bunker was worth it if it meant he got promoted early to captain and then immediately from there to O5. There was no way during peacetime he would have made it from first lieutenant to captain to major to lieutenant colonel so quickly. Plus, honestly, the bunker really was pretty luxe. Not gold-plated-faucets-and-plush-hotel-robes luxe, but nicer than anything else he'd experienced in the military.

It had to be twenty thousand square feet. There was a full-size basketball court as well as workout facilities, including a close-quarters-combat room and a two-lane lap pool. The dining room was nicely appointed, and there were always at least two cooks in the bunker at any time. Having tasted a whole lot of military chow in his day, Lou wondered if maybe Operation SAFE-GUARD had poached some outside talent. Because while there were some damn fine cooks in the military, the cooks working in the bunker could have held their own in any white-tablecloth

civilian restaurant. He had to spend some serious time on the
treadmill and doing CrossFit workouts every day to make sure he
didn't put on weight during each six-week stint. He had his own
quarters and private bathroom, which felt like a luxury, and the
bunker was stocked with pretty much every movie ever made and
an unlimited library of e-books. For all that, however, the job was
boring. Boring, boring, boring. Boooooooring.

Part of his training had been hours upon countless hours em-
phasizing that he had *the most important job in the world!* That was
how he always heard it come out of the mouths of the man and the
woman—both civilians, both of them using names that were obviously fake, and both extremely annoying—who ran the six months
of training before he was physically assigned to the bunker. They
said it every time so that he could hear the italics and the exclama-
tion point: *the most important job in the world!* He and the other operators, all of whom had gone through the same training, constantly
joked about it. "Hey, Joe, pass the potatoes. Wouldn't want to be
hungry while I'm working *the most important job in the world!*"

Even though they joked about it, Lou figured all the operators
took it seriously. The thing was, at the end of the day, it might just
be the most important job in the world. No joke.

Sometime in the aughts—nobody working in the bunker
seemed to know exactly when or how, only that it had happened
under GWB's watch—every nuclear weapon in the US arsenal
had been outfitted with two-factor authentication. It worked,
more or less, like two-factor authentication did when you signed
on to Google. When the president dipped into the nuclear football to order a strike, there were a number of supposed fail-safe
checks to make sure that it was a legitimate order before things
went *kaploowee*. They were all along the same chain of command,
however. Before GWB, there were a terrifying number of near

misses in the history of the United States. Lou didn't even want
to think how much worse it had probably been in other countries.
But Operation SAFEGUARD had added that second step. Like
when you enabled two-factor authentication and you signed into
your e-mail on a new computer, you had to enter your password;
but then you would also get a verification number texted to your
phone, and you had to have that number to proceed. That was
what they did in the bunker.

In the event of an ordered nuclear strike, once it was determined that the president had, in fact, given the order, the bunker
authenticated it. It meant that a strike couldn't be authorized by
accident, and it also meant that in the event some crazy dude got
the opportunity to press the button, it wouldn't do anything more
than fizzle out.

The thing was, even though they took the job seriously, they
joked about it, because *the most important job in the world!* was both
boring and really easy. It was the sort of thing that would probably
have looked all high-tech and sexy in a Hollywood movie, but the
sad reality was that the command room in the bunker was basically
a pair of cubicles equipped with PCs that you could have bought
at your local Best Buy. There were always two men in the room,
and they worked eight-hour shifts. And what you did, essentially,
was . . . sit. You sat and waited for the order that never came. Supposedly, for the first few months of Operation SAFEGUARD, operators were not allowed to do anything that might distract them,
which included talking to the other operator, reading, listening to
music, etc. You had to just sit at your desk and stare at your screen.
As a result, pretty much every operator fell asleep at his desk. Repeatedly. In order to prevent that, they quickly changed orders so
that operators could bring in a book or watch a movie on a tablet
or do whatever they needed to do to kill the time while still staying

alert. Still, *the most important job in the world!* basically involved being stuck in a cubicle killing time while waiting out your shift, knowing that the thing you had trained to do would never be required.

Until, all of a sudden, it was required.

They had Internet and television and relatively unlimited access to outside media, so they'd been following the spider outbreak from the jump. They'd seen footage from Delhi and Los Angeles. They'd seen pretty much the whole thing unfold on their laptops and tablets and televisions, and even with the Chinese dropping nukes and the president authorizing the use of conventional weapons to destroy the highways, Lou never truly believed he would have to verify a nuclear strike order.

He'd been five minutes from the end of his shift when the president ordered the strikes and tripped all the alarms in the bunker. He was leaning back in his chair, finishing a crossword puzzle—the easier Monday puzzle, because the harder ones were way out of his league—when the big red light on the ceiling started flashing and a loud, piercing siren screamed at him. He was startled so badly that he tipped over and clattered to the floor. When he got back to his feet, rubbing his head, Hubbard was already going to the shelves to pull down the binder.

Operation SAFEGUARD was cutting-edge, one of the few places in the United States government where cybersecurity was properly considered even before the whole Russian election hacking fiasco, but it was weirdly antiquated at the same time. There were redundancies on top of redundancies, and even though the actual program could be run on a bare-bones PC, everything surrounding Operation SAFEGUARD was high-tech. Heck, the bunker was hardwired to the outside world just in case the other systems—cellular and satellite and radio—went down. Thousands of miles of cable, all to make sure that the two operators on duty could enter the needed codes in a timely manner. Yet they were required to go to a physical bookcase, pull down a physical binder, flip to the correct physical page, and look at codes printed on physical paper, and then type them in by hand. The reasoning was that if the codes existed only in this one place, and only in printed form, it made them virtually impossible to hack or steal. It seemed nuts to Lou, but then again, it was *the most important job in the world!*

Hubbard ran his finger along the shelf until he found the binder for that day's date and then walked back to his desk, flipping through to find the page that corresponded to the time and to the authorization code that had been used by the president.

Lou liked Richard Hubbard just fine. Even though pretty much all he wanted to talk about was Brazilian jujitsu, he was a nice guy. He spent all of his downtime either watching You-Tube videos about Brazilian jujitsu or working out in the gym and trying to persuade the other guys to spar with him in the close-quarters-combat room. Nobody would, because Hubbard wasn't a drive-by dojo practitioner. The one time Lou had agreed to spar, thinking he knew how to take care of himself, Hubbard had handed him his ass, bouncing him off the padded floor until he was black-and-blue. Since then Lou had made it a point to call jujitsu "karate" as a way of needling him. Of course, if it bothered Hubbard, he never showed it. He was one of the few operators who never joked about it being *the most important job in the world!* He was a rah-rah kind of guy who took his job seriously, and as Lou watched him work his way through the binder, he thought that maybe Hubbard had the right attitude after all.

Quickly they ran through their checklists, confirming every-thing, and then Hubbard called out the code: "Echo Romeo India

November Sierra Echo Papa Tango one zero one nine seven zero."
Dutifully, Lou typed in the letters and numbers.

The funny thing was that as they successfully executed the
confirmation procedure, Lou really did feel like it was the most
important job in the world—no joke. What they were doing was
going to help save the entire world.

It was only later, when he'd been relieved, when he was back in
his quarters, that he thought to check to see where the nukes had
been delivered. It was a long list, but one city stood out: Denver.

Denver was gone.

His parents. His brothers and his sister. His girlfriend.

He'd had to debrief with the bunker's commanding officer,
Brigadier General Yoats, the next day, and by then, he'd come to a
decision: he could stomach the loss if it meant he'd helped to save
the world. He was heartbroken and devastated, but he'd joined the
military because he believed in the higher good. Yoats had cleared
him to resume duty, and his next shift he'd gone in fully expecting
and prepared to confirm the use of more weapons.

And then there'd been the coup.

The brigadier general had done something unprecedented:
he'd called the entire bunker in for a meeting. Every single man in
the bunker was in the common room. There had been all-bunker
meetings before, but the two operators on duty had always been
patched in on the intercom. Not this time.

"If the sirens go off, well, that's why we're having this meeting,"
Yoats said. "We're getting two sets of conflicting orders. Much of
the armed forces seems to be reporting to the chairman of the Joint
Chiefs of Staff. I've spoken to him directly, and he is ordering us
to report to him. But there's still a large part of the military that is
under the command of President Pilgrim, and she still holds her
title. The president has ordered us to deny any and all requests for

verification through Operation SAFEGUARD. I'm not telling you anything you don't know."

That was true enough. They'd suffered some communications failures that were clearly a result of the outside world going to hell, but the bunker hadn't been designed to keep the operators out of the loop. Operation SAFEGUARD was there to make sure a rogue commander or a small group of men and women or even a mix-up in the chain of command couldn't cause the use of a nuclear weapon. When it was designed, the idea of a military coup hadn't even been considered.

Lou knew he *should* have been relieved at the president's orders. After all, he'd been on the desk and, with Hubbard, had confirmed the use of the nuke that wiped out Denver and pretty much everybody he loved. And yet. And yet he couldn't help but feel that it was foolish to stop. Wasn't the sacrifice in vain if they failed to keep going? If they didn't burn every one of those spiders into nothingness, then what was the point of those first launches? Had Denver been sacrificed for nothing? When you had your foot on your enemy's throat, you didn't let off. Why use nuclear weapons in the first place if you weren't going to finish the job? The president wanted to just, what, watch and wait? To risk having the death of his family, his friends, his girlfriend, be for nothing?

They talked for a little while, Yoats giving all of the men, even the ones who were support staff, a chance to vent or ask questions.

Lou kept his mouth shut.

After close to an hour, Yoats wrapped things up: "Men, we all know that with most of the military under his command, Broussard"—Lou couldn't help but notice the lack of a title and the disdain in Yoats's voice as he named the chairman of the Joint Chiefs of Staff—"is going to be able to circumvent Operation SAFE-GUARD in a matter of days. But until then, we are going to do what we have sworn to do, which is to obey the commander in chief."

Lou looked at the other operators. Some of them, like Hubbard, were sitting up smartly and looking at Yoats like good officers, but he noticed not everybody seemed to be hanging on every word the brigadier general said.

Those were the men he was interested in talking to.

USS *Elsie Downs*, Atlantic Ocean

"**W**ould a satellite phone work?"

The scientists turned to stare at Fred. He was sitting on a stool in the corner of the lab. One hand was reaching down to scratch Claymore's head. In the other hand he held up a phone. Melanie realized her mouth was hanging open. She closed it, hoping nobody had noticed.

"What?" Fred said. "I mean, I have an iPhone, too. I'm not a complete savage. But we don't exactly get good cell phone reception back in Desperation." He looked at Melanie, Julie, Mike, Laura, and Will. "Desperation? California? A couple of hours from LA?" They stared back blankly. "It doesn't matter," he said. "Middle of nowhere, really, and no cell phone towers, so Shotgun got us satellite phones."

Amy also held up a phone. "Gordo and I have them, too. I don't use it much, though. It's, like, a dollar a minute. And before all of this happened, I don't think Gordo ever actually used his. He only carries it because I make him."

Mike Haaf walked over. He eyed the dog warily, although, in

117

Melanie's experience, the worst you could expect from a choco-late Lab was that they'd jump on you or shed on you. Or eat your lunch if you were dumb enough to leave it near the edge of a table. Mike moved like he was afraid the dog was going to tear his throat out. Definitely a cat guy.

Finally, Mike motioned toward the phone and waited for Fred to give assent before taking it. "You're saying that you both have satellite phones?" Mike said. Amy and Fred nodded. "And why are you just telling us about them now?"

Fred gave Mike a look that could have cut glass. "Because, until now, you haven't needed to call anybody."

Mike looked up from the satellite phone. "Okay. Fair enough. Do they work?"

Fred reached out and took the phone back. "Well, duh. Of course they work. Not that I actually set them up or anything. Shotgun handles all the tech stuff. We have what I like to call a di-vision of responsibility in our marriage. He takes care of all the bor-ing things, like making money and making sure that when I press a button, stuff just works. I take care of cooking and entertainment and making sure that our life is generally fabulous. Which, I have to admit, has been a challenge of late. This whole spider thing has been an absolute drag."

"Fred!" Amy smacked him on the shoulder. "Ignore him. Please. I'm sorry, Mike." She looked around the room. "He's just trying to get a rise out of you. Fred is a menace when he gets bored. But, yes, we've got satellite phones, and near as I can tell, they're still working. Both of us sent texts to our husbands about the . . . Is this a coup? I guess this is a coup. But we haven't heard anything back." She held up her hand, closing her eyes for a moment, and Melanie was reminded that whatever threat they felt they were under here, on the USS *Elsie Downs*, Gordo and

Shotgun had been left behind when the overloaded helicopter took her to safety.

"Sorry," Amy said. "We haven't heard anything back, but it's only been a couple of hours, and we agreed ahead of time that if they weren't sure they could charge their phones they would only turn them on once a day. But both our phones show a signal and connection. The texts went through."

Even though Melanie knew the door to the lab was closed, with two sailors standing guard outside, she still looked at the door. She and the other scientists had been told of the "change in leadership," and they'd been given a chance to present their findings to Ben Broussard, the chairman of the Joint Chiefs of Staff. When Melanie said they weren't quite ready yet, she'd been swiftly and rudely shuttled back to the lab. After an hour or so, however, a young soldier bringing coffee slipped Melanie a note: *President safe. In NYC. Wants info. Help on the way.*

It was all a little much for Melanie. She'd never actually enjoyed the politics part of being married to Manny, and she sure as hell hadn't expected to be in the middle of a coup; but, as Manny always said, even in the midst of their divorce, you play the cards you're dealt. And the cards, in this case, were that they were trapped in a makeshift lab on an aircraft carrier in the middle of an attempted overthrow of the United States government during the spiderpocalypse. Which were some messed-up cards. Plus, ostensibly, there were people on board the USS *Elsie Downs* who were still on President Pilgrim's side, and Melanie and company were supposed to wait for some sort of rescue attempt. In the meantime she had information that she needed to get to Steph as soon as possible, and the two least useful people on the whole ship, Fred and Amy, evidently had satellite phones.

Melanie sighed. She had a headache, and she realized she'd

been grinding her teeth. "Okay. Obviously, that's great. Seriously, though, how did they let you keep your satellite phones? Nobody searched you? I got searched. We all got searched."

"Of course they searched us," Fred said. "Ask me where I hid mine!"

"Don't!" Amy sighed. "For the love of god, don't ask him where he hid his phone. He's just looking for an excuse to use that stupid 'Wrecked him? Almost killed him' joke."

"Party pooper," Fred huffed.

"It's not really the time, Fred," Amy said. She turned back to the scientists. "They gave us a cursory search, I guess for weapons or whatever, but neither of us seems too threatening. Plus everybody always gets distracted by the dog. Evidently, Claymore is more interesting than either me or Fred."

"Maybe you," Fred said drily.

Amy ignored him. "Anyway, I don't think the kid who searched us realized they were satellite phones. If you don't know any better, they look like crappy old-school dumb phones. He probably thought we were just old people with old-people phones. He looked at them and then handed them back. I think they were all a lot more focused on you guys. Fred and I don't matter much in the scheme of things."

"Hey!"

"Well, it's true, Fred. We're an afterthought. I bet the only reason they're letting us stay here in the lab instead of confining us to quarters or putting us with the rest of the civilians is that nobody's actually thought of us one way or another. It's easier, anyway; they still only need one set of guards on the door. I suspect they are going to leave us alone as long as we don't upset the apple cart."

She fiddled with her satellite phone and then held it out to

Melanie. "You might not get another chance with this. I'm sure if they figure out we've got satellite phones, they'll confiscate them."

Melanie had to think for a second to remember the number. She was so used to just hitting *Manny* whenever she wanted to call him that having to come up with the actual number took some effort. He'd kept the same number he had when they were married, and it was the number associated with their loyalty accounts at the bookstore, the coffee shop, even the grocery store, but it had been years since she'd had to rattle it off. Fortunately, it came back to her. She punched it in, waited, and then shook her head. "No dice."

"It's not working?" Amy was surprised.

"No," Melanie said. "I mean yes. I think it's working on your end but not on his end. I'm getting a message that the cell phone circuits are overloaded."

"What about sending an e-mail?"

"You can do that?"

"Sure," Amy said. "It's slow, so we can't send a video or anything, but a text file would be fine. And that might get through, right?"

"If he's checking his e-mail, yeah. He wouldn't get it on his phone, obviously, not without Wi-Fi, but I'm sure they're somewhere with Wi-Fi and laptops."

Laura Nieder raised her hand like an impatient schoolchild and then, when everybody looked at her, she spoke. Her voice was glum. "I hate to be a Negative Nancy, but the Internet is broken."

Will sighed. "The Internet is *not* broken. The problem is—"

"Holy crap, Will, seriously?" Laura said. "This isn't the time to be pedantic." Melanie thought if Laura rolled her eyes any harder they would have popped out the back of her head.

"You know," Fred said, "every few months there's some stupid meme and everybody's all, like, 'It broke the Internet!' And finally something actually broke the Internet! I guess what it really took was man-eating spiders."

Will couldn't help himself. "It's *not* broken. There are only so many relays . . ."

Melanie felt the words washing over her like white noise. She folded her arms and then rested her head on the desk in frustration. Fred she could live with. There was something charming about his willful childishness, but trying to keep the other scientists on the same page drove her kind of crazy. Will getting sidetracked into explaining the root cause of the Internet's failure was pretty standard, and all of them had their own peccadilloes. She rested for a few seconds, the hum of Will and Laura arguing its own sort of comfort.

"Okay," Melanie said, even though she knew that with her head resting on the desk her voice was muffled. "I can't get through on the phone, I can't send an e-mail, but I've got to get through to Manny and the president. How are we going to do that without getting off this ship? Send a frickin' telegram? A carrier pigeon?"

Nobody answered, and, in the quiet, Melanie thought she heard a thud followed by another. She wasn't sure what the first noise was, but the second thud was distinctive and sure sounded a lot like a body hitting the door.

And then, slowly, the door to the lab swung open. The man standing there was so big that Melanie couldn't see his face, but she didn't need to: Special Agent Tommy Riggs was easy to pick out of a crowd.

Riggs stepped to the side, and Melanie saw the body of a sailor on the ground. He looked as if he were sleeping peacefully, knocked out. In place of Riggs, Billy Cannon moved into the doorway.

"Quit staring and get hustling," Cannon said, grinning at them. None of them budged, and he shook his head. "Good god, you civilians. Oh, and great. You've got a dog."

"The dog is coming," Amy said in a tone of voice that brooked no dissent.

"Of course he is," Cannon said. "Why not? We're just trying to escape from the middle of a coup in the middle of the apocalypse. Sure, let's bring a dog!"

Melanie stared at him. He looked . . . he looked like he was having fun.

Cannon clapped his hands together. "Chop-chop. Come on, let's go. This here's a rescue mission. Broussard's got the bulk of the military behind him right now, but there are enough sailors on board throwing their lot in with the president and the rule of law that we can get you out of here. I think. But let's not be lackadaisical about it, okay?"

As the scientists scrambled, grabbing notes and laptops and tablets, Melanie could have sworn she heard Fred giddily say, "Now *that's* how you make an entrance."

Nazca, Peru

Dr. Botsford was paying for dinner, which was both rare and unimpressive. Rare, because although Dr. Botsford liked to cultivate the image of a freewheeling, devil-may-care bon vivant, those impulses did not extend to the inclusion of his graduate students in his acts of largesse. Unimpressive, because even though he *had* offered to pay tonight, the bill wasn't going to be more than the equivalent of twenty-five or thirty bucks no matter how much Pierre and the other students ate and drank. As a graduate student, however, Pierre thought, free food and beer was free food and beer.

Pierre actually liked Dr. Botsford, despite everything. He was a good professor in most ways. He was engaging and engaged, and if he could be condescending at times, he could also be inspiring. There was a reason Pierre had chosen to study with him, after all. Probably his biggest issue with Dr. Botsford was his penchant for trying to dress like Indiana Jones. According to Dr. Botsford, people frequently told him, unprompted, that he looked like Harrison Ford. *Raiders of the Lost Ark* is what Dr. Botsford said, though given Botsford's age, *The Kingdom of the Crystal Skull* was a more accurate comparison. Still, he wore an old bomber jacket and a fedora as often as he could. During the day, the heat of the Peruvian high plains was too much, but tonight, despite the temperature still being in the low seventies, he was wearing both.

The restaurant was on the second floor of a stubby building on the main drag. It was covered by a roof but was otherwise completely open, a waist-high barrier running the perimeter. The kitchen and bar were crowded into the back corner, and the rest of the space was overtaken with a mishmash of tables and chairs, no one matching another. It was raucous and fun, and it was the only restaurant that Pierre had been to in Nazca. That was partly because they went into town so infrequently—Dr. Botsford was the kind of professor who insisted that proper research meant living and working in the field—and partly because, when they did go to town, Dr. Botsford insisted they eat at this specific restaurant. He claimed that after all his years coming here to do research, it had the best food in all of Nazca. Cynthia Downs, who could be a bit of a snob, had remarked that "the best food in all of Nazca" wasn't setting the bar too high, but to Pierre the food seemed spectacular. Back home in the United States, it might even have been the sort of hipster restaurant that billed itself as serving "street food." Tonight he'd ordered *sanguche de chicharron*: a pork-cracklings sandwich with salsa, onions, and cilantro, served with a side of rice and beans. And since his professor was paying, he was washing everything down with as much beer as he could drink.

He caught the waitress's eye and made the universal motion for another beer. They kept bottles of Cusqueña behind the bar in a huge bin filled with ice. Beer that was weeping with cold felt like an unimaginable luxury in general, because, well, Peru, and specifically because Pierre had grown wearily accustomed to drinking all his beverages warm and tepid out in the field. He didn't even know if beer was normally served cold or kept on ice or how it was supposed to be done in Peru, but he didn't care. He wasn't even sure if he liked Cusqueña, but that wasn't going to stop him from trying to run up Dr. Botsford's bill.

In some ways it was surprising that Dr. Botsford didn't prefer a more formal restaurant, he thought, leaning back in his chair against the railing and looking out at the street below. A restaurant with walls, at least. Although maybe he shouldn't have been surprised. The general rowdiness played to Dr. Botsford's self-image, and the patrons were almost exclusively ex-pats and English-speaking tourists, which meant that for all the noise and loud music and the occasional fight between tank-top wearing, sunburned, college-aged macho brats, it was safer than seeking out something more authentic. The food, however, *was* authentic. Slow to come out because it was made fresh. And tonight the restaurant was going double time. Not just tonight. He'd talked to an Australian backpacker who'd been stranded in Nazca since the spiders emerged, and she said the restaurant was mobbed *every* night.

"We're all just looking for somewhere to be, you know?" She had long, dark blond hair that had been bleached in streaks from the sun, and she wore it braided down over her shoulder. She fidgeted with the braid while she talked to Pierre and occasionally glanced back at the two other women sitting at her table. "Nazca's just a stop. Just a day or two. You've got to do it if you're in Peru. Come on. But once you've done the flight, there's no point in staying. Of course, there's no point in leaving right now either."

She shrugged.

Pierre wondered if she'd have felt so sanguine about her exis-

tence in Nazca if she'd been there when he and Dr. Botsford and
the other graduate students had tossed the egg sac into the fire
by their campground. If she'd seen the way the sac split open as
spiders spilled out into the coals, turning to ash as quickly as they
could skitter out.

When he turned back to his own table, Beatrice was scowling
at him.

If he were a braver man, he would have confronted her. He
would have pointed out that they were *not* dating, that he was *not*
her boyfriend. He would have reminded her that they were sleeping together only because everybody else was paired off and they
were bored, and you could spend only so many nights alone in a
tent watching videos on your laptop. He would have said that there
was nothing wrong with his having a completely innocent conversation with another woman, and besides, if she really wanted to be
worried about another woman, it should be Julie Yoo, who he was
sure was the love of his life.

Pierre was not a braver man, however.

Instead, he took a sip of his beer and picked up his sandwich.
He offered it to Bea. "Want a bite?"

Bea shook her head and returned her attention to her stew.
Her refusal of the sandwich was a relief to Pierre. It was a peace
offering but, unlike most peace offerings, it was begrudging. He
had no real interest in sharing his sandwich. The bun was light and
fluffy, and the fried pork cracklings inside were crunchy and hot,
and salsa dripped down his hand and wrist when he took the first
bite. Good god, he thought, was this the greatest sandwich ever?
He could die a happy man having eaten this sandwich.

As he had the thought, he glanced over the railing to the street
below again and saw a young man—a boy, really—run past at a full
sprint.

Huh. He put the sandwich down and surreptitiously wiped his hand on his pants. Below, a few more people ran past. And then a moped sped by, the woman driving it with a look of terror on her face. She glanced behind her several times—quick looks, the moped wobbling a little each time.

Of course.

Of course, he thought. How stupid could he have been?

The whole reason he, Dr. Botsford, Natalie, Bea, Cynthia, and JD were here was to work on the Nazca Lines. It was an academic coup, unprecedented access, and sure to make Pierre's career. And when they carefully dug the calcified egg sac out from where they'd found it, buried near the spider line, Pierre shipped it to Julie for study, thinking it was going to be something cool to write a paper about. But then there'd been the horror. Spiders everywhere, people eaten alive, spiders hatching out of people's bodies. And the attempts to contain the spiders were worse. All that seemed far away, however. In Nazca, out by their campsite, with the sky so dark at night that the stars seemed like coins in a video game, Pierre figured he was safe. The spider line, so much older than the other Nazca Lines, was a warning, and he'd been warned. They'd found that other egg sac and burned it. That was it.

Naturally he'd worried about Julie's safety. She'd sent him a few e-mails before the Internet stopped working, but he figured she was on the East Coast of the United States. So far, that had seemed out of harm's way. He had other friends, school friends who he hoped were okay, and he despaired over the general destruction of the world; but his parents and grandparents had all passed away before he graduated from college, and he was an only child. If he was being completely transparent, he figured that as long as he and Julie weren't the people getting eaten, well, how bad was it really? When everything was done, he'd even have some extra credibility with Julie because he'd sent her that egg sac. Really, in some ways he was a hero!

Except that, right then and there, he didn't feel like a hero. He felt sick.

A small car, something that wouldn't have looked out of place in a circus, came barreling down the street and then veered left and into the building across from the restaurant. By that point, anybody who hadn't noticed the people running on the street was alerted that something was wrong.

Pierre stayed in his chair. He watched Dr. Botsford trying to push and shove his way to the exit, his hat knocked from his head and his panic and his thinning hair making him look decidedly unlike Indiana Jones. Not once did Dr. Botsford look back for Natalie, the graduate student with whom he'd been having an affair since the day they landed in Peru. On the side of the restaurant opposite the exit, Pierre saw a group of young backpackers climbing over the railing and jumping the ten feet to the ground. In the middle of the scrum of people mobbing the doorway that led to the stairs down to the street, he could see Cynthia tugging at her fiancé JD's arm. JD was frozen, swiveling between looking at the group jumping over the railing and the group that was bunched up at the door. But Bea was still sitting there next to him. She hadn't made any move to flee.

For whatever reason, looking at her made him feel calm and composed. He offered up a weak smile. "Doesn't seem to be much point in running, does there?" he said.

She rolled her eyes and stood up. "You've been an absolutely crap boyfriend. You know that, right?"

Without giving him a chance to respond and without another word, she turned and walked over to the mass of bodies trying to get out the door.

A part of him wanted to yell after her, to insist that he wasn't her boyfriend—that he'd never been her boyfriend—but instead he took another bite of his sandwich. He scraped the chair back against the floor so that he could easily see out over the railing and into the street. He could see the first people from the restaurant emerging onto the street and running away. One of them, the Australian he'd talked to earlier, stumbled, her braided hair bouncing, but she managed to stay on her feet. She was fast, Pierre thought as he watched her run.

He looked in the direction everybody was running from and saw them: black threads. Or, rather, dots that were packed so closely together that they looked like a solid mass. It reminded him of that painter, the one who made pictures using only dots. He could remember what the technique was called. Pointillism. He could clearly see the image of the famous painting that hung in the Art Institute of Chicago: French people spending the afternoon by the banks of a river. But he couldn't remember the painter's name.

He sighed. Was this going to be the way he went out? Sitting in a second-floor restaurant that didn't have walls, feeling defensive about being a bad boyfriend to a woman he was not actually dating? Eating a fried-pork-rind sandwich while trying to remember the name of some painter? It was certainly lacking in romance.

On the street, the fleeing people had become a mob. He saw a man go down, but the people behind just trampled him. Farther back, Pierre saw people overtaken by the scourge of spiders: men and women running in horror, turning into black pillars, then—slowly enough that it was more terrifying than if it had been quick—flattening out. Other people simply fell and lay still as if paralyzed, spiders swarming over them, coating them with hazy films of silk.

But here and there he saw people left untouched. An old woman who had fallen to her knees in prayer. A child frozen in fear. A man in a suit. The spiders simply flowed around them, splitting and rejoining like a river washing around a rock.

Soon enough, the first black tendrils reached the restaurant. The spiders were either pure black or black with red stripes. They moved quickly and together. He watched as the crowd became even more panicked. He thought he saw Dr. Botsford, but it was hard to tell as the spiders washed over the struggling figures. Inside the restaurant, the choked pack of people at the door trying to get out suddenly reversed course, like an ocean's waves pulling back into the water. He saw Bea knocked backward and over a table, her head banging painfully off a chair. Around her, people scrambled and panicked: they no longer wanted to leave the restaurant, and there were cries to close the door and lock it.

It was fruitless, of course, Pierre realized. Why bar the door when there weren't any walls?

He couldn't understand why he wasn't panicking, but as he heard the sick brush of the spiders pushing against the ground floor and starting to skitter up the outside of the building, he reached out to take a last sip of his beer.

Seurat! The painter's name was Seurat!

It felt like some sort of a victory to remember the name, and he closed his eyes, readying himself for the inevitable.

And yet, as he heard screaming and shrieking, prayers and pleas, the sound of furniture being overturned, bottles breaking—as he felt the overwhelming rush of spiders moving around him—he remained untouched and his eyes stayed closed.

He counted to thirty, forcing himself to go slowly, each number a separate word, a separate moment. It was hard to do, to summon the willpower to keep his eyes shut, but it was also somehow easier; the sounds of the world around him were too much to consider.

By the time he got to thirty, it had grown quieter. Not quiet, because there were still screams and cries and sobbing, car horns and the breaking of glass, but it had moved farther away, to the next building, and the next, and the next. But he scrunched his eyes tight for one second longer, listening as hard as he could. There, underneath the sounds of fear and panic, a soft brush that sounded like fabric rubbed together, like hundreds of leaves tumbling down from a tree in a gust of autumn wind.

When he opened his eyes, he took it all in at once: tables and chairs overturned, clothing that covered only bones, and perhaps half a dozen people slowly disappearing beneath layers of silk. A young woman, eighteen or nineteen, was staring at him, her eyes unblinking as spiders worked over her, coating her in webbing. Pierre could see a thin stream of tears coming out of her eyes, and although she couldn't move, that didn't stop Pierre from reading the terror in her eyes. To be paralyzed like that? To feel the spiders crawling over you, the silk wrapping around your body, to know that you were doomed?

He had to look away.

Which was almost weirder, because there were those left untouched: a diminutive but muscular man standing still in the middle of the restaurant, his hands over his ears, his eyes bugged out and his mouth moving silently; a black college-aged dude who was kneeling and rocking back and forth gently, his hands folded in a tent of prayer; a lumpy woman wearing a colorful patchwork dress, sitting at a table and crying with hysterical gulps of air.

And, near the middle of the room, Bea, slowly getting to her feet, rubbing at her head where she'd hit it. She looked bleary-eyed

and was probably concussed, but there was no panic in her de-
meanor. Even as a spider skittered up her leg and across her chest
and then off again, moving over a table and joining ten or more
other spiders diligently cocooning a body on the floor, Bea didn't
seem bothered.

She saw him and then worked her way across the room. He
couldn't decide which was worse, watching her or watching the
way the spiders—perhaps a hundred, two hundred of them—
that were still in the room spun silk in quick layers over the men
and women on the floor, the frozen, terrified faces disappearing
beneath translucent webs. No. That was actually an easy call: he
watched Bea.

The chair's wooden legs made a sharp sound against the floor
as Bea pulled it out from the table so she could sit down. "It figures, doesn't it?" she said. Her voice was glum.

He looked at her and then around the room again. The spiders
seemed to be completely uninterested in them. One of them ran
across the top of the table, scrambled over the remains of his sandwich, and then disappeared over the edge.

"Should we, I don't know, run or something?" he said.

"Doesn't seem much point. I think if they were going to eat us,
they would have done it already."

Pierre nodded. He couldn't tell if he was nodding because she
made sense or because he was just too freaked-out to do anything
else. Except, he thought, he didn't feel freaked-out. Did he? He
tried saying it aloud. "I don't feel as freaked-out as I should." And,
having said it aloud, he decided he believed it. "Right? Shouldn't
we be more freaked-out?"

Bea sighed. She looked sullen. "Aren't you even going to ask
me what I meant when I said, 'It figures'? I think, clearly, I was

fishing for you to ask me what I meant." She reached out, grabbed his beer, and took a sip. "Because what I meant is, it figures, doesn't it, that everybody else gets eaten, and it's just the two of us?"

"Technically, it's not just the two of us. There are a bunch . . . well, not a bunch, but *some* other people. Plus there's . . ." He trailed off and sort of waved one hand pathetically at the bodies being cocooned on the floor. It felt so unreal. Like he was watching this happen to somebody else. He put his hands flat on the table and stood up. He didn't want to sit here and watch those poor men and women get covered in silk anymore. He wanted to leave.

"You're going?" Bea said, clearly surprised.

"Yes," he said. "I think so."

"Where?"

"I don't know," he said, but then he did know. "To the spider line, I think. To see what's there. You should come with me."

It was odd picking their way through the restaurant and down the stairs. They were both very careful not to step on any of the bone-filled pieces of clothing or to accidentally hit one of the spiders still skittering about. Outside, on the street, there was more space to move. There were cocoons everywhere. Black spiders with red stripes across their backs scuttled about, spinning webs and completely ignoring the other survivors, people like Pierre and Bea, who were wandering around. He thought the other people looked dazed and forlorn, and, looking at Bea, he realized they must look that way, too.

They walked a hundred feet or so, moving slowly, walking together but separately. After a bit of hesitation, Pierre reached out and took Bea's hand. As he touched her fingers, the warmth of her skin was reassuring. After all that had happened, what else did they have if not a human connection? What point was there to survival if they couldn't survive together?

As he had the thought, he turned to look at her.

She was scowling and she stopped walking. She yanked her hand away from his with a fierceness that was matched by the venom in her voice. "Good Lord. You really think *that's* what I want?"

She strode off, leaving him scrambling to catch up.

God, he thought, he wished he were with Julie Yoo.

Càidh Island, Loch Ròg, Isle of Lewis, Outer Hebrides

Aonghas opened the wardrobe as quietly as possible. There were a number of wool blankets folded neatly on the top shelf. They had the faintly musty smell of all wool, and it made him smile. It reminded him of his childhood.

On the bed, Thuy was already under a small mountain of covers. Aonghas wasn't sure if he was imagining the draft or not, but the wind wicking the waves outside was real enough. The temperature had dropped enough over the last two days that even his stoic grandfather commented on it.

"Sweater weather."

That's all his grandfather had said, but from Padruig it amounted to shouting it from the rooftops. He wasn't emotionally reserved—or no more so than one would expect from a man of his generation—but he was not prone to complaining about the weather or physical ailments.

Carefully, Aonghas opened a blanket and added it to the ones covering Thuy. He'd heard from his friends who'd gotten a head start on him with marriage and children that the first trimester could leave a woman wiped out, but he thought they'd been exaggerating. However, for the last couple of days, Thuy had been taking early-afternoon naps and going to bed almost immediately after dinner. Not that there was much else to do. They were stuck on the island.

He stood up, feeling dizzy at the thought. They were stuck on Càidh Island. The world had gone to hell, and he and Thuy and his grandfather were on one of the few places on earth that seemed entirely secure. His grandfather kept BBC Radio nan Gàidheal on constantly, to the point where Aonghas felt anxious without the quiet, clipped voices in the background. Not that radio made him feel less anxious: the list of places that had been overrun by spiders or destroyed by men was overwhelming. They'd stopped trying to keep track of what pockets of the world were still safe—though, at least for now, it seemed like Thuy's family was doing okay. Other than that, the only thing Aonghas was sure of was that the world apart from Càidh Island was terrifying, all the more so because he was now an expectant father. Here, at least, they were surrounded by the ocean, and the chance of any boat—let alone one carrying that scourge of eight-legged monsters—happening upon them seemed remote at best.

For how long, though? How long were they going to be stuck on this rock? He loved it here: loved the way the castle sat brooding and sharp above the ocean, loved the smell of the library, loved the deep maze of the cellars filled with wine and port, loved the winding staircases, loved the grand sweep of windows that he could look through while he was cooking. But that was always a love based on knowing that he could leave this solitude whenever he wanted. And, good god, Thuy! What if she got sick? What if they were still here in . . . how many months until she had the baby? She tracked her period, so they'd been able to figure out her due date was New Year's Day, but what if they were still stuck here? What if the baby came early? Or late? What if he had to deliver the baby on his own?

He leaned over, putting one hand against the top of the head-board for balance, and kissed her hair. It was all he could do not to start crying. She wasn't a delicate sort, but wasn't it his responsibility now to take care of her? A terribly sexist thing to think, he knew, but he couldn't help it. Wasn't that what the ring he'd given her meant?

He straightened and then moved to the rocking chair by the window. For a while he simply watched the light and the white of the waves frothing against the rocks. And then, for another while, he watched Thuy softly breathing.

It could be worse, he thought. To be stuck here with Thuy and his grandfather? That wasn't so bad. There were so many worse places in the world to be right now.

They could ride out the storm.

The Interstate 80 High Times Truck Stop and Family Fun Zone Restaurant and Gas Station Taco Bell Pizza Hut Starbucks KFC Burrito Barn 42 Flavors Ice Cream Extravaganza Coast-to-Coast Emporium, Nebraska

H e'd seen news footage of refugee camps before. That was the closest equivalent that the Prophet Bobby Higgs could come up with. He was up on a rise that overlooked the truck stop, and from his vantage point the sea of people reminded him of nothing less than a refugee camp. Which was almost certainly a fair comparison, he thought, because what was a refugee camp but a place for people who were fleeing from danger?

His best guess was that there were two or three thousand people down there. Enough to create a sense of chaos but not so many that he was worried. His flock was easily double that. And, judging by the lack of armed sentries, the people below weren't expecting any sort of an attack. At least not from people. He was sure that they were worried about spiders, although perhaps the relative iso-lation of the truck stop was enough to give a false sense of security.

He was surprised that Macer didn't have sentries out. It was unlike the man. Macer wasn't just opportunistic. He was a forward thinker. How else could he have turned somebody like Bobby Higgs into the kind of religious leader who could gather the num-ber of people needed to break through a military quarantine zone? Why else would Macer, that son-of-a-bitch, leave Bobby on the side of the road and then end up here, in the middle of nowhere, running his own fiefdom? That wasn't the sort of thing that hap-pened through luck and happenstance. You needed to be a planner for outcomes like that. A thinker.

And yet, inexplicably, there wasn't any sort of security perim-eter. There were a few armed men apparently guarding a tractor-trailer, and Bobby wondered what could be in the truck that was of enough value for Macer to post men there but not around the grounds.

One of his disciples started to say something, but Bobby shushed him. He wanted to think.

For the next five minutes he looked through the high-powered binoculars, trying to find what he was missing. Was it a trap? Did Macer know he was coming?

He saw movement. Nothing sudden or suspicious, just the swirling movement of humanity that indicated something was happening. Sure enough, a group of people parted and Bobby saw Macer with Lita beside him, followed by a small cadre of men who were clearly serving as bodyguards. They all had the looming pres-ence that Macer preferred in his flunkies, although they didn't have the professional swagger that Bobby recognized in some of his own men who were former military. He counted four, no, five men, plus Lita. She almost floated, moving so gracefully that from this distance he would have been willing to believe that she wasn't touching the ground. She was the dangerous one. Even more so than Macer, because she existed solely as his weapon. Without her, he thought, Macer was a toothless dog.

He watched for a few more minutes as Macer moved around the facilities, stopping to chat here and there, occasionally smiling, at one point directing one of his goons to help a woman get something down from the roof rack of a car. Macer called out to the men by the tractor-trailer, and one of them gave him the thumbs-up. But that was it. There was no sign of any security beyond men watching the truck and Macer's small group of bodyguards. It was as if Macer felt invulnerable.

Bobby lowered the binoculars and crawled backward until he was behind the rise of the hill. And then he did something he would have laughed at even a few weeks ago: he prayed.

He knelt on the soft dirt of what had been Nebraska farmland before this all began. Around him, his disciples followed his lead, kneeling and praying. It moved outward from him in a wave, those closest to him stopping whatever they were doing—which was mostly waiting for him to make a decision—and mimicking him, dropping to their knees to pray, and then, as those people knelt, those farther out saw and copied. It was an odd sensation, hearing and feeling the way hundreds of people and then thousands came to stillness in prayer. What *they* prayed for, he didn't know, but he prayed for guidance. He prayed to know how, exactly, God wanted him to exact his vengeance. Because if there was one thing the Prophet Bobby Higgs was sure of, it was that Macer needed to suffer.

When he finally got to his feet, he knew.

If Macer felt invulnerable, Bobby could fix that.

He went and talked to a select group of three men—all former military, all extremely good with a rifle—and made sure they were ready. The trio had taken to calling themselves the Angels of Death, and although he thought it was a bit silly, he'd run them through their paces during the march, and the name was not unsuited.

Then, silently, without motioning or explaining to anybody else, he walked over the hill and down to the truck stop. He didn't look back. He didn't need to. The sheer number of men and women and children following him was such that he simply knew they were there. And, likewise, he didn't need to check that the men and women who had experience with weapons—he shouldn't have been surprised to find so many veterans out here in the heartland—were close to him. He had ordered that they stay with him at all times, and thus it was so.

As they got closer to the ragged rings of people around the truck stop, he could see the refugees stop what they were doing and take stock. Some of them just stared, unsure what to make of the Prophet Bobby Higgs leading his flock down from the mountain, but others seemed to sense that the winds were changing.

He walked past tents and parked cars and shelters made of little more than cardboard and garbage. He walked past gas pumps and a truck wash. As he passed, the men and women who were not part of his flock came to join them. As he moved by the tractor-trailer, the three guards—each carrying a shotgun—watched him warily, but none of them made any move to try to stop him. At the building, a crazy conglomeration of bright plastic colors and logos, he closed his eyes, waiting to be shown the path. When he opened them, Macer was in front of him. Lita was by Macer's side, her right hand stuffed deep in the pocket of her jacket, a shiny black number that looked like something a triathlete would wear. He knew that her fingers were wrapped around the butt of a gun. The burly men whom he'd identified as bodyguards were standing in a semicircle behind Macer. They looked even bigger up close, and they were all armed.

"I fear not," the Prophet Bobby Higgs said. He kept his voice deep and made sure he projected it so that not just Macer and Lita but everybody around could hear him. "I fear not, for the Lord is my armor, and the Lord keeps the just and the true safe from harm. I have come from the land of lost angels, and I have come through the desert, and I have walked here with my disciples and my flock." He turned slowly, his hands raised to take in the people around him. He cast a quick glance at the top of the hill. It was three hundred, perhaps four hundred yards away. He couldn't see the Angels of Death, but he knew they were there. "I fear not." He kept both hands raised.

Macer tilted his head back and let out a loud, cackling laugh. "Ah, for the love of it. Don't tell me that you're swallowing your own crap, Bobby?"

Lita, Bobby noticed, was not laughing. She was scanning the crowd of men and women who were beside Bobby. Her eyes were narrowed, and she turned her head a bit and said something indistinct to the guards standing behind Macer. One of the men moved a little bit to have a clearer look.

"The Lord is just, and the Lord provides, and the Lord demands that those who have sinned against him pay." His arms were still up, the soft breeze kissing his hands.

Macer had stopped laughing. He was angry now. "Get the hell out of here, Bobby. I did you a favor when I left you on the side of the road. Figured it wasn't worth wasting a bullet on you. I was wrong. Not too late to fix that mistake, though. Lita?"

One of the men who'd walked down the hill with Bobby—a man named Glen Twaits, a car salesman from Cozad who'd done two tours in Afghanistan—slid partly in front of Bobby, shielding him with his body.

It was a nice gesture, and Bobby appreciated it, but it wasn't necessary. He was perfectly safe. All he had to do was drop his arms.

As he did, Lita crumpled. Macer's other bodyguards were on their way down before Lita hit the ground. The echo of the gunshots was still washing over them when Macer realized what was happening.

Bobby looked back at his snipers on the hill and nodded his approval. He could hear people screaming, but his focus was now fully on Macer. He reached out and patted Glen on the shoulder, and the man moved out of the way so that there was nobody standing between Bobby and Macer.

Macer had turned pale. It might have been the first time Bobby had seen the man look surprised, and he couldn't stop himself from giggling. "Didn't see that one coming, did you? I have to admit I was surprised you didn't have any sort of patrol or guards out watching for something like this."

Macer recovered quickly. "I kind of figured, given where we were, it was a waste of effort." He looked down at Lita's body and sighed. "It hadn't occurred to me that you'd track me down." There was something in the studied nonchalance with which Macer then shrugged that enraged Bobby.

"You thought you were safe here? You're not safe from the wrath of the Lord anywhere, Macer."

He meant it to be frightening, threatening, to let Macer know exactly what he was in for. He still burned with the bright shame of having been used and then dumped unceremoniously on the side of the road. He didn't just want to kill Macer—he wanted to punish Macer.

Except Macer didn't react the way Bobby had expected. The man actually had the temerity to smile.

"You're kidding, right?" Macer looked around him, making eye contact with as many people as he could. "Is he kidding?" He stared at Bobby again. "Of course I didn't think I was safe here, Bobby. Nobody's safe here. Nobody's safe anywhere. I just wasn't worried about being ambushed by a two-bit hustler from Hollywood."

Bobby seethed, and he was about to order his men to restrain Macer, but then Macer said, "The spiders are already here, Bobby."

The response from the men and women around him came like a flood. Harsh whispers turned into moans and then into the kind of fear that was palpable. It took Bobby several seconds of raising his hands and shouting to the crowd to get them quiet again.

"Peace! Peace!" he yelled. To Macer, he spoke with a deadly seriousness. "Here?"

Macer pointed. "That truck. Why do you think I've got men guarding it? What, you think it's full of televisions or cell phones or something? Civilization is on its way out, man. There aren't any *things* that are worth protecting. That truck could be full of cash and it would be completely worthless. Sure, I suppose food and weapons and things for survival are going to have some currency, but none of that matters if the spiders come romping through."

Bobby glanced at Glen. The man was the sort of salt-of-the-earth midwesterner who could be counted on to come through. Bobby doubted that, under normal circumstances, Glen would have had anything to do with him. Macer hadn't been too far off the mark calling Bobby a two-bit hustler. But that had been before, and Bobby took some strength from Glen's unyielding solidness. The crowd around them positively radiated with anxiousness, but Glen trusted him. Glen was counting on him. Bobby bowed his head for a moment, closed his eyes, took a deep breath and then another. It calmed him and, in ways he couldn't understand, it seemed to calm the crowd around him. It was, all of a sudden, as quiet as several thousand people could be.

"Okay, Macer. So why, then, if there is nothing of value—if there aren't televisions or cash or whatever in that truck—why are you guarding it? Who exactly are you trying to keep out of that truck?"

Macer shook his head sadly. "Not out, Bobby. In. We've got four of them in there."

"Spiders?"

For the second time in as many minutes, Macer seemed taken aback. "No. Not spiders. Carriers. Are you telling me you haven't checked your people? The signs are—"

But Bobby wasn't listening anymore. He didn't need to. He knew exactly what Macer was saying. There were *people* locked in the back of that tractor-trailer, and each of them bore the telltale mark of a person who'd been bitten by a spider, who'd had a spider slip through the thin membrane of their skin, take up residence, and lay eggs.

"Grab him," he said to Glen. The man moved without hesitation, and several other members of his flock helped, holding Macer by his arms and frog-marching him after Bobby.

As Bobby walked, he felt a sense of serenity that he could attribute only to the knowledge that he walked in God's path. He stopped in front of the men guarding the tractor-trailer. They looked nervous, and the two white men glanced at the black guy, who was smaller but also older, so that was whom Bobby addressed.

"What's your name?"

"Deke."

"Deke, you have people in here who have been bitten, yes? Who you think have spider eggs inside them?"

Deke nodded.

"Why haven't they been disposed of?"

"Working on it, man." Deke glanced over Bobby's shoulder at Macer but barely hesitated before continuing. "Macer has a crew putting together a, uh, well, I guess an incinerator of sorts. Until then, this is the best thing we can do for a quarantine."

"And you're sure the spiders can't get out?"

"Worked it over pretty good. It's not exactly airtight, but it's close enough," Deke said. "Nothing's getting out."

Bobby smiled. "It must be pretty uncomfortable in there."

Deke shrugged, unsure of what to say. It was clear that the idea bothered him, but the situation had made pragmatists out of many people. He heard Macer say something foul behind him, and then the thump of a fist on flesh and a grunt. By the time he turned around, Macer was on his knees spitting out blood and fragments of teeth. The sight made Bobby happy, but then he had a better idea. He turned to Deke again.

"Can you be completely sure that there are no spiders that have hatched in there right now?"

"Actually, yeah. We rigged it up with a camera and a couple of LED lights on the ceiling so there's enough light to see." He reached over to the bumper and handed Bobby a baby monitor. The picture was grainy, but it showed two people sitting, one lying down, and a fourth person pacing back and forth.

"Open it up," he said.

"Pardon me?"

"You heard me," Bobby said. "Open up the truck."

Deke blinked hard and then took the measure of the crowd around him. "Forgive me for saying this, man, but are you out of your frickin' mind? No way we're letting those people out. They've got spiders cooking up inside them. Sooner or later those spiders are going to hatch, and I'm sure as anything I've ever been sure about in my whole life that I'd rather have them locked up inside that truck than out here with us." He licked his lips nervously. "You've clearly got yourself some sort of . . ." He spun his hand in the air, taking in the armed men and women who were escorting Bobby. "I don't know what's going on, but I know that we do *not* want to let these people out."

"Out?" Bobby showed his teeth. "Who said anything about letting them out? Nobody's getting out of that truck." He stepped forward, clapped Deke on the back, and then pointed at Macer.

"He's going *in*."

Soot Lake, Minnesota

"You know what I really wish?" Mike popped the clip out of his pistol. He checked it for what had to have been the tenth time that morning. He'd already cleaned his Glock and reassembled it twice.

Leshaun, who was relaxing on the top bunk, grunted. "That spiders hadn't come out to eat everybody?"

"Well, yeah, but what I really wish—"

"That the president didn't decide to bomb the ever-loving heck out of our country?"

"Okay, sure—"

"Or, no, wait for it . . . You wish that the president didn't decide to use nuclear weapons, so we could have stayed here in this lovely cottage on this picturesque lake and simply gone fishing and hung out while we waited for the whole spider thing to be sorted out, instead of being so worried about fallout that we've decided it's actually safer to try to get your daughter and your ex-wife's unborn child out of the radioactive Midwest and all the way to the East Coast with no real plan besides trying to sort of drive even though all the highways have been bombed into oblivion? Is that it? Is that what you really wish?"

Mike put the clip back into his pistol and secured it in his holster before turning to the dresser. The Mossberg 500 and his other pistol, a Glock 27, rested on a blanket that had been neatly folded to cover the top of the dresser. The Glock 27 was a subcompact. It fit well in Fanny's hand, and she was a better-than-average shot with it. She was also, Mike thought, the kind of person who would pull the trigger if necessary. He was less sure what to do with the shotgun. Fanny's husband, Rich Dawson, had already come close to accidentally shooting Mike once. On the bed, which he'd made out of habit, he also had four rifles. The Remington 700 was his. Neither he nor Leshaun was really a gun guy, but the Remington was a great rifle. It was what both of them had trained on when they'd done SWAT work and, with the scope, either one of them was comfortable to three or four hundred yards. The other three rifles they'd taken off the yahoos who had tried to do them dirty, sneaking through the night with plans to do God knew what to Mike and his family. Not for a second did he feel guilty about or second-guess the decision to take those men down. Their rifles, though, were the kinds of crappy bargain buys that felt flimsy in your hand. And when he and Leshaun had broken them down and cleaned them, it seemed clear that it was the first time anybody had done such a thing. They hadn't fired them either, figuring that, with the limited ammunition for the rifles, they didn't want to waste a shot. That made Mike nervous. Which was an answer in and of itself, he thought. He picked up the Remington and put it on the dresser with the shotgun and the spare Glock. They'd leave the three crappy rifles behind.

"Are you done?" Mike asked. He was trying to suppress a grin, but he couldn't. "Yes, sure. Those are all good things to wish for.

When you say it like that, I feel kind of stupid; and even though I thought my thing was pretty good, now I don't want to say it."

Leshaun chuckled. They'd been partners long enough that half the fun was that almost everything was an inside joke, and they had a long history of interrupting each other when one of them was trying to get a punch line off. Leshaun sat up and swung his legs over the edge of the bed.

"Come on, man. Just say it."

"Nope. You ruined it. I'm not saying it until you apologize."

"Okay, fine. I'm sorry. What, Mr. Mike Rich agent man, do you really wish?"

"If I'm being totally honest here—and obviously I'm excluding wishes that have to do with making it so none of this ever happened, because, well, those would be good wishes . . . so if I could, what I would have changed is that I really, truly wish I hadn't bothered paying my taxes this year." Mike checked the shotgun now. He wasn't sure whether it was worse to hand it over to his ex's husband loaded or unloaded.

Leshaun pushed off, landing lightly on the floor. He really didn't look too bad, given the bullet he'd taken in his arm a few weeks earlier and the broken ribs. Mike looked him up and down. Maybe Leshaun had been milking it a bit when he'd made Mike fix the gutter. He went back to checking the shotgun and continued: "I'd forgotten that I was going to have to write a check come tax time. I kept looking at my savings account and getting excited. I was planning on taking Annie to the Caribbean over the summer. Go to one of those all-inclusive resorts, one that has activities for grown-ups and kids. Snorkeling, paddle boarding, windsurfing, beach volleyball, fishing. Some of the ones I was looking at even had circus stuff."

"Circus stuff? You mean like clowns?"

"More like trapeze classes. How cool would that have been? Don't you think Annie would have loved that?" Mike said. He made sure the safety was on the shotgun before putting it down. Loaded, he thought. He'd just make sure Dawson kept the safety on. He picked up the Glock he was going to give to Fanny and released the clip. "And it would have been perfect, because they have a sort of camp thing for kids. She could have gone in and out of it however she wanted. If she wanted to do something with kids her age, she could do the camp thing, and if she wanted to hang out with me . . . I had the whole thing priced out and was on the verge of booking it. I even got a new credit card, one that doesn't have any foreign-transaction fees and came with a big bonus of points when you spent a couple grand in the first three months. I figured it would be like a two-for-one. I'd use the credit card to pay for the trip with Annie; then, when I paid my credit-card bill, I'd get a bunch of airline miles and I could use those for another trip with Annie the next year. It would have been amazing. And then I did my taxes and realized that all the money I thought was going to go into a trip to the Caribbean was going to have to go back to the same dang government that gives me my paycheck."

"How long have you and Fanny been divorced now?" Leshaun motioned to the bed. "We leaving those junk guns here?" Mike nodded and Leshaun didn't argue. "Never mind. Doesn't matter how long you and Fanny have been divorced, because one thing I know is that every year since you've been divorced, you've been surprised come tax time. Every year it's the same thing. 'Ah, man, Leshaun,'" he said, doing a surprisingly good impression of Mike's voice, "'I forgot I was going to owe on my taxes.' And every year I get on your case to put in a new W-4 so that your withholding is done properly. Look at me, man. Come April? No surprises. I zip through TurboTax, get a refund for a couple hundred bucks, and have a great weekend."

There was a knock, and Mike opened the door. Annie stood there wearing the hoodie he'd given her. "Mom says we're ready." She looked past him to Leshaun. "Do I get a gun?"

"Uh, not yet," Mike said. The truth was, he'd thought about it. Part of being his kid meant that she was familiar with firearms. He knew Fanny and Dawson weren't pleased with it. Neither of them thought Annie was old enough. It wasn't an argument, however. He was a federal agent and he had guns. It was as simple as that. As long as he had guns in his apartment, it was better to make sure Annie knew gun safety than to pretend there were no guns around. He had a gun safe in the back of his closet where he kept the shotgun and rifle and his spare Glock and all his ammunition, but he wasn't naïve. Kids were curious creatures, and sooner or later Annie would figure out how to get into the safe. Or, more likely, his bad bachelor habits would catch up with him. Most nights when he came in, he dumped his keys and wallet and holster on the kitchen counter. What if he did that one of the nights he had Annie? So, despite his ex-wife and Dawson's concerns, he'd gone through gun-safety training with her and even taken her on a couple of trips to the range. The Glock 27, Mike's backup—a gun he thought of as almost dainty but that was well sized for his ex-wife—looked like a cannon with Annie firing it two-handed. The lock-screen photo on his cell phone was of Annie wearing the earmuff-style hearing protectors and safety glasses while she was shooting. He thought it was adorable. Fanny, however, was not amused.

The funny thing, which he'd tried to tell Fanny and Dawson, was that Annie was a natural. By the end of the first trip to the firing range, Annie could consistently hit a body-mass shot from ten meters. After their third trip she was a better shot than some of the federal agents he knew who skimped on range time. She wasn't exactly ready to enter shooting competitions or anything, but it did make him feel less nervous about the accoutrements of his profession. He was confident that she understood guns well enough that if he did screw up and leave his gun out, she wouldn't accidentally kill herself. Or, for that matter, him. Still, that didn't mean he was ready for her to carry a gun of her own. Not right now. "I think we'll leave the guns to the grown-ups."

"How long is it going to take to get there?" she asked, already moving on.

Leshaun laughed. "You know how your dad is," he said. "Even if he gave you a time, he'd be late."

Annie snickered and then ran off down the hallway. Mike turned to look at his partner. "Seriously?"

"What?"

"Just throw me under the bus like that," he said, and Leshaun laughed again.

In the living room, all the adults spent a few more minutes fussing with gear and food, stalling. None of them wanted to go. They'd spent several hours arguing about it already, and although they were in agreement that the risks of trying to get east were fewer than the risks of staying where they were, it didn't mean anybody was excited to leave Dawson's cottage. Finally, however, travel couldn't be put off, and they headed down to the boat. It was another gray day, and Mike wondered if it was simply the weather or if it was fallout. He wasn't familiar enough with nuclear weapons to know, but that was part of why they were getting out of there. If he knew, maybe they'd be able to stay.

He'd made everybody bundle up so that their hair and as much skin as possible was covered. Thankfully, with the weather finally turning appropriately seasonal, it wasn't uncomfortably hot, and they weren't complaining. All five of them were also wearing face masks they'd made out of T-shirts. Mike couldn't decide if they looked menacing or fashionable.

The lake was calm. There was enough of a breeze to send ripples across the surface of the water. The tops of the trees ticked back and forth like metronomes. If he weren't so afraid of nuclear fallout, it would have been a pleasant day.

Dawson drove the boat. He kept it cruising at a relatively low speed, no more than twenty miles per hour. As much as Mike wanted to put miles between them and Minneapolis, he'd decided that it was best to be overly cautious, particularly while they were still in the boat. The truth was that none of them knew what the hell they were doing. They were leaving because it seemed dumb to just try to hunker down so close to where there'd been a nuclear explosion, but it wasn't like any of them actually knew what it meant to be so close to one. Was it in the water? The dirt? The air? The only thing Mike knew for sure was that the longer the exposure to radiation, the more at risk they were. Maybe if instead of a fancy house on a lake Dawson had had himself a good old bomb shelter, they could have stayed in place, but he didn't have a lot of faith in the efficacy of duct taping garbage bags over the windows.

"Hey, hold up!" he yelled to Dawson. He stood, holding on to the back of Dawson's captain's chair, looking around. "Cut the motor."

In the sudden silence he could hear it clearly. The throaty buzz of a motor. It wasn't a boat. It was—

"There!" He pointed up and behind them.

The airplane was gaining altitude off the lake. It had floats on the bottom. A seaplane. It had come from farther down the lake and was clearly just taking off. It looked like a small plane, maybe only a two-seater, but Mike couldn't tell if that was just a trick of distance. The plane banked lightly, a gentle turn that put the pilot in prime position to see them on their boat. Mike raised his hand and then, frantically, pulled the shirt off his face and started waving. Leshaun did the same.

The plane kept turning, a half circle, but then it kept going, disappearing over the treetops and past them. It was low enough that after a few seconds, it was hidden by the trees.

"Crap," Mike said. "I was really hoping . . ."

He fell quiet. They all did, and they heard the change in the sound of the motor. The plane was turning again.

They watched it come toward them, so low that the perspective made Mike momentarily afraid it was actually brushing the heavy pines. Once it cleared the woods and was over the water, the pilot came down smoothly. There was none of the wobble that Mike sometimes saw with amateur pilots. It touched down much closer than Mike would have expected, so that the plane passed by them. By the time it did so, however, it was moving slowly enough that he could ID the pilot: the older-looking black dude who'd done them a solid the previous week.

The plane was bigger than Mike had originally thought—still small, but big enough to give Mike a little hope—and Dawson waited for the plane to turn a slow circle and come back near them before firing up his motor and bringing his boat alongside.

"Keep it about twenty feet out," Mike said. "Don't want to make him nervous."

Dawson did as he was told and then cut the engine again so that they were drifting quietly. The plane quieted, too, and then the door opened.

The pilot leaned out. His beard was still gray and unruly, but he was wearing a big smile on his face. "Glad to see all is well with you, my friends. I take it those miscreants I warned you about weren't a problem. You said you were feds, so I figured you'd have it in hand."

Mike could see a figure that was no more than a shadow standing behind the man. He remembered the man saying that his wife was a good shot, and he figured she was back there keeping him covered, but Mike decided to play it cool. "Nothing Leshaun and I couldn't take care of," he said. "Which isn't to say no, they weren't a problem." He thought of the way the three men had come hiking through the woods, their ill intentions as clear as their flashlight beams in the dark night. He and Leshaun had treated them like rabid dogs.

He felt Annie pull his sleeve. "Are you talking about those men you shot?"

Her voice was high and clear, a bell rung in a quiet space. With the stillness of the lake and all the motors cut, he knew it carried across to the plane.

"Uh . . ." He looked to Fanny for guidance, but her eyes were panicked; and when he turned to Leshaun, his partner gave him a "Don't look at *me*" grimace. "Sorry," he said to the pilot. "Just give me, uh—just a second." He lifted Annie up with a grunt. She'd grown so solid the last few months. She was still his little girl, but he wasn't sure how much longer he'd be able to just pick her up like this.

"You know about that? How do you know about that?"

She was straddling his front, and he had his arms hooked under her butt to keep her up. Her arms were wrapped around his shoulders, but she leaned back a little so she could look at him. She blew a puff of air from between her lips. "I'm not stupid, Daddy."

"No, of course not. I'm not saying . . ." He trailed off. He was lost here, and he could have used some help from Fanny. Heck, he would have happily welcomed help from Dawson. The funny thing was that he usually didn't mind having serious talks with Annie. He was okay with the birds-and-the-bees kind of stuff, and his daughter didn't hesitate to ask for his advice if she was having problems with friends at school. But, no, he was not exactly equipped to explain to her why he had killed three men. He'd done it coldly and quickly, and he knew as much as he'd ever known anything that it was the right decision. The three men had ridden by in a boat, shirtless but gunned up, scouting the property at least twice, and then they'd come in the night, doing a poor job of sneaking along a trail that ran through the woods. They came with malice in their hearts and were sent to hell by cold copper-jacketed bullets. It was complicated, though. Too complicated to explain to a—

"They were bad guys," Annie said, interrupting his thoughts. "And you were keeping us safe."

Or maybe it wasn't so complicated. "You got that right, sweetie." She wriggled a bit to get down again, and he turned his attention back to the pilot. "Sorry about that."

"No worries, son. I served in Vietnam, and like I said when we first talked, I was a sheriff up until a few years ago. I know from bad men." He called to Annie. "Your daddy did the right thing, honey."

Mike nodded. "And I'm trying to do the right thing now, too."

"I take it you mean that the five of you aren't just out for a pleasure cruise."

"Well, between my daughter and"—he almost called her his wife but stopped himself in time—"Fanny, who's pregnant, we thought it might make sense to try to get away from any fallout."

The man nodded. "I can see why you might think that. That's what I was thinking myself. In fact, if we weren't so dang slow in packing up, we— *Ow!*" He turned, rubbing the back of his head, and said something to the shadow standing behind him. Mike didn't hear a response, but the man looked back at Mike with a rueful smile. "I am not apportioning blame in terms of how long it took us to get going. Let me be clear about that." He paused, said something over his shoulder again, and then let out a barking laugh before continuing. "Anyway, point is that if we'd left any sooner, we wouldn't have seen you out and about. I'm planning to hopscotch north and then east about as far as we can get. Of course, I've got myself a plane," he said, flashing his teeth. "You, my friend, have no such thing. I have to wonder if it's a good idea for you to be out on the roads and all. My understanding is that things are torn up pretty good."

"That's my understanding, too," Mike said, "and I can't help but notice that nifty little plane of yours is not actually as little as I might of thought. In fact, I wonder if it might be big enough to fit all of us . . ."

"Cessna 185. She's called the Skywagon, kind of like a station wagon. I'm counting five of you. I've got me plus one, and technically she's only a six-seater."

"Seems like a nice little puddle jumper."

"She's amphibious." He waved at the floats. "Land or water, it's all the same. Costs me some range with the extra weight. Costs a bit of extra cash, too, but we don't have kids, so what's the point in saving it?" He gave Mike a winning smile. "We live in Fargo. Well, lived. I guess a lot of things are in the past now. But it meant we needed the wheels for home and the floats for here."

"You said it costs you some range having both?"

"Yep. Fifty miles, give or take. Can still get about three and a half hours of flight time. About five hundred miles." He stopped talking for a second and then turned and said something inaudible to the shadowy person behind him. Mike could see that there was some sort of back-and-forth before the man turned back to him. "Of course, if I really want to push things, I can go a bit faster and a bit farther." He reached out and patted the side of the plane. "But between my age and the age of my plane, I'm not really interested in pushing things."

Leshaun, standing next to Mike, called out, "You know, I've got to ask. How old?"

"The bird or me?" The man laughed. It was a deep chest laugh, warm and full of life. The kind of laugh that would have been well suited to a man dressed up as Santa Claus. "The plane's a '67. But she's been babied. I've got a good mechanic and I probably take care of her better than I take care of myself. As for me, let's just say I'm old enough."

Mike felt Annie leaning into him. Without looking down, he put his arm around her. "I'm thinking that you probably have it right about the roads being torn up. You've got the right idea in terms of just hopscotching over everything. I like the sound of that. Might you be amenable to a few passengers?"

Behind the man, the shadow took shape out of the darkness. A woman holding a rifle. He'd been right about that. They might be friendly and they were clearly good people, but they weren't suckers. Not in this new world. Not when the kind of men Mike and Leshaun had put down were roaming about. The woman let the barrel of the gun drop and leaned to whisper into the man's ear. Without looking away from Mike, the man tilted his head a little and said something back. Then he nodded and stepped out of the way. The woman took his place. She was white, which Mike knew shouldn't have surprised him, but did anyway. She was about the same age as the man, with long gray hair loose around her shoulders. "Rex is being a stupid mule. What is it with you military men?"

"We're not military, ma'am," Leshaun said. "We're—"

"Same difference," she said, motioning with her hand as if to brush off his words. "Military. Cops. Federal agents. 'Gee, what kind of a plane is that? Might you be amenable to a few passengers?' Men." She huffed the last word. "Talking around things like you're in some silly Western." Mike could hear the gruff laugh that came from behind the woman, and she turned and said rather sharply, "I'm including you in that, you darn fool." She shook her head and spoke to Mike again. "Rex said he visited you and you seemed like good people. And we both know that's not the case with everybody around. The long and the short of it is that we're two old people and you've got yourself a young one and another on the way. So the answer is yes."

Mike felt Annie wrapping her arms around his waist. He glanced down at her and then back at the woman. "Yes?"

"Yes," she said. "We'll fly you out."

Her name was Carla, and she and Rex had been married for ten years. It was a second marriage for both of them. They interacted with the ease of people who'd fallen in love well into their lives, when both of them were clearly comfortable in their own skins. They had to spend some time moving things around to fit them in, as Carla and Rex had packed the plane as though they weren't going to carry any passengers. The Cessna was a six-seater, and they were one person over that—although, given Annie's size and age, she was just going to be shuttled from lap to lap.

Rex had a heavy-duty camping water filter, and while it was useless against radiation, it would do anywhere they could find water. With a floatplane, they figured that would be easy enough, so they dumped the water first. Mike had made his group pack lightly as it was, but they had some basic camping gear—as did Carla and Rex—and they all decided it made sense to keep as much of that as possible. Clothing was deemed expendable, as was a lot of the packed food, particularly anything canned. They kept enough so they'd be good for a couple of days. Last to go were two large tote bags full of personal mementos that Carla had brought with them from their home in Fargo. She held the bags out for Dawson to pass down into the boat.

"Are you sure?" Dawson asked.

Mike was busy stuffing the gear they were keeping under seats and in nooks and crannies, but he snuck a peek at Carla's face. It was clear she was trying not to cry, but she held the bags out until Dawson took them.

"I've got a flash drive with photos on them, and I took photos of everything in these bags, too, so that'll have to be good enough."

Rex turned around from where he was sitting in the pilot's seat and reached out to touch his wife's arm. "Carla, we can—"

"They're just things, Rex."

"But—"

"Rex Millington, I said they're just things. We've got seven people in a six-seater plane, and even if one of those people is a munchkin like Annie, space is tight and weight is at a premium. If getting rid of a few tchotchkes might buy us a few extra miles of range, and those few extra miles of range might make the difference, then, well, I'm willing to get rid of them."

Everybody was quiet for a moment, and then Fanny stepped from the boat to the pontoon, climbed up into the already crowded plane, and gave Carla a hug.

Chincoteague Island, Virginia

Shotgun sat with his back against the tire of the pickup truck. His ankles and feet were in the light, but the rest of him was sheltered from the sun and the breeze by the shadow of the truck. It wasn't comfortable, exactly, but it was comfortable enough. More important, it made him and Gordo look like they were relaxing instead of plotting an escape. Nearby, Teddie fussed with her camera and other equipment, but that, too, was just an act.

"It'll be dark in a few hours," Shotgun said.

"That's going to be worse, don't you think?" Gordo said. He sat cross-legged with his satellite phone in his lap. He kept running his fingers over the rubber buttons as a way of keeping his hands busy, but he tried to keep the phone low and mostly out of sight. Given the text messages he and Shotgun had gotten from their spouses, it didn't seem like a wise idea to advertise. As it was, Shotgun had to talk him out of phoning Amy directly. "Let's not call attention to ourselves. Rodriguez will definitely have guards out. They'll be jumpy. Best bet is to just try to slip away before it gets dark."

Teddie started packing her gear into her new backpack. There was an outdoor-gear store a few blocks away that the Marines had taken them to. The store was surprisingly well stocked, given the size of the town; it had enough camping and hiking gear that all three civilians were able to get fresh clothes and backpacks and even a pair of hiking boots for Teddie, and most of the Marines were able to supplement their own gear. Across the street from where Rodriguez had the Marines parked, there was an off-brand motel that catered to summer tourists. Even with the rush to flee from the cities, it still had a few empty rooms, and the manager, a former army infantryman, had provided them with a stack of clean towels and temporary access to showers so the platoon could clean up.

Gordo had been surprised at how refreshing five minutes in a shower and clean clothes could be. The new underwear was made from some sort of space-age material that wicked away sweat and supposedly didn't get smelly. Between the new underwear and the new cargo pants designed for hiking, a smart-looking T-shirt with a stylized wave design, a Windstopper jacket, and a pair of thin wool socks, he both looked good and felt good. He'd topped everything off with a trucker's cap and a pair of sunglasses, and then grabbed an Osprey hydration pack. The pack had a three-liter water bladder and enough space for another pair of clean underwear, socks, and a T-shirt, as well as a dozen Clif Bars. Since he'd lost his multitool somewhere between Desperation, California, and Chincoteague Island, Virginia, he'd also snagged a Leatherman Skeletool RX. He'd already been wearing a good pair of boots, so he kept those.

Shotgun had similarly decked himself out, although he'd managed to keep hold of his multitool the entire way. To Gordo's surprise, he'd also brought along two of the metal nozzles they'd fashioned back in Shotgun's workshop. Those nozzles and a few pieces of gear readily attainable at almost any hardware store could make a pretty kick-ass flamethrower.

As for Teddie, she'd been wearing an assortment of borrowed clothes and military gear with a pair of shoes that might have made sense for her back at CNN but weren't of much use out here. She'd found sensible travel clothes, and Shotgun had convinced her that a pair of lightweight hiking boots that wouldn't take any real break-in time were the way to go. She'd also opted for a hydration pack, and—thanks to the miracle of modern technology, which meant that her video stuff was all pretty compact—she was able to fit her camera and all her attendant gear in the bag as well as a change of clothes, some nutrition bars, and something called a Mooncup. She'd started to explain to Shotgun how the Mooncup worked, but as soon as she said the word *menstruation*, he threw his hands up in the air.

"I'm gay," he said, "but I'm still a guy." He walked to the back of the store and started looking closely at the dehydrated camping food while Teddie and Gordo laughed.

While they'd been in the store, there wasn't any explicit talk about cutting and running, but there was a tacit understanding between Gordo and Shotgun. Even before they turned on their satellite phones and got texts from Fred and Amy, Gordo had known what their decision was going to be. Rodriguez had signaled his alliance with the breakaway faction of the military, but with what the ST11 was telling them?

Without the satellite phones, Gordo wasn't sure what they would have done. But they *did* have the satellite phones, and Amy had given a clear and concise account of the coup and the choices facing them. While Gordo understood the drive behind the military men who had tried to seize control—when you see a spider, isn't the impulse to smash it?—he and Shotgun were being given an opportunity to *perhaps, maybe* do something that could potentially save lives. Gordo and Shotgun had been friends for long enough that he knew it wasn't a question of *if* they were going to try to split off from the Marines and get to Amy and Fred and Dr. Guyer; it was a matter of whether they were going to risk taking Teddie with them. He still wasn't sure what they would have decided had it been up to the two of them, because Teddie had asked them point-blank if they were splitting, and when Shotgun hesitantly said yes, she told them she was coming with them.

"So let me just make sure I've got this one hundred percent," she said. She kept her voice low. Not whispering, nothing to call attention to herself, but quiet enough that it wouldn't carry. They were sitting by the pickup truck they'd driven from the NIH, but Kim Bock had left it parked at the far side of the lot, and the closest Marine was still thirty or forty feet away. It hadn't occurred to Rodriguez—not yet—that his three civilians were a flight risk.

Teddie kept stuffing her gear into her bag. "Your little doohickey can tell us where the spiders are, and we can use that to tell the president where to attack instead of just willy-nilly bombing stuff."

Shotgun glanced at the ST11. It was relatively small. Among other modifications, they'd also rigged up a battery pack, so it didn't need an inverter or standard electricity anymore. It wasn't an ideal setup, but they'd stuffed it into another backpack from the outdoor store and run a cable out so that they could keep the ST11 in the bag and plug it into the laptop. Not pretty, but functional.

"Not all the spiders, no," Shotgun said. "Again, think about how you've said they move like they're fake. Like they're all following orders. That there's not enough randomness for a bunch of spiders. Well, you put that together with the way the ST11—as we originally intended it—made the spiders sort of pacifists. I'm sure that Dr. Guyer—Melanie—will want to study it, and there's more to it than this, but basically we think that you're right: the spiders are essentially following orders. The basic idea of the ST11 was that we were going to use extremely low frequencies as a weapon, but instead it seems like we ended up blocking the spiders' transmissions. The orders, so to speak. And what we did when we reworked this beast," he said, elbowing the bag with the ST11, "was to figure out how to receive the transmissions instead of blocking them. Then we combined that with some proprietary software I developed for the government that taps into the GPS satellites. With the GPS system on board, and using what we know about longwave and shortwave and sky wave propagation—"

"Got to be honest," Teddie said, "you sound a bit like a Bond villain right now."

"—*and* sky wave propagation," Shotgun continued, as if he hadn't been interrupted, "I think I can pinpoint where the orders are coming from. So, yes, we can figure out where to attack. In theory."

"In theory?"

Gordo put the satellite phone into his jacket pocket. "I mean, it seems to check out, but we thought we had something that would work to kill the spiders with the first version of the ST11, and it just sort of made them sleepy. So, you know, we think we're right, but . . ."

"But?"

"But," he said, "it wouldn't be the worst thing in the world to give it a real-world test."

"Okay," Teddie said. "How do we do that?"

"Go to Atlantic City." Gordo pulled his backpack closer. "We confirm that we're not actually crazy, and then we bring this to Dr. Guyer, who has the ear of the president, and then the president figures out how to pinpoint the attacks and kills all the spiders."

He paused, considered, and then continued. "And then, honestly, once the day has been saved, we're big old heroes. They'll have a ceremony where we stand in front of a bunch of people and get medals like at the end of the first *Star Wars* movie."

"You mean the first *Star Wars* movie, like, the old one, or episode one?"

Gordo couldn't stop himself from glaring at Teddie. "The *first Star Wars* movie. The first *Star Wars* movie is always episode four, *A New Hope*."

Teddie closed the flap of her backpack. "Whatever, nerd. Are you Chewbacca in this scenario here?"

"I'm literally just going to say the word 'sigh,' Teddie, and move on. The point is, we're getting a ping out of Atlantic City. So we go there; the closer we get, the more we can narrow down the signal; and hopefully . . ."

"Hopefully, what?" Teddie said. "Hopefully we don't get eaten? Because that sounds like a crappy plan."

"Actually, pretty sure we've got that one figured out." Shotgun brought his hand up to shade his eyes. Gordo turned to look where Shotgun was looking. Across the parking lot, a small cluster of Marines was huddled around the hood of an SUV staring at what Gordo thought was one of the military radios. "Once we're in Atlantic City, I'm ninety percent sure I can keep us safe. We'll have to make a stop along the way, but, yeah, we need to go to Atlantic City."

From above them, out of the open window of the pickup truck, Gordo heard Kim's voice.

"Atlantic City? You really need to actually go there? You're telling me we can't just bomb Atlantic City and be done with it?" Her head popped out of the window. She wiped at one of her eyes. "God, can't take a nap around here without accidentally overhearing you all scheming away."

"Kim—"

"Lance Corporal Bock." She waited a beat, and then she laughed. "Just kidding. But you should have seen your face." She propped both her arms on the windowsill and peered at him and then at Shotgun and Teddie before looking across the parking lot to where the other Marines were gathered.

Shotgun scooted away from the tire so he could see her. "How much did you hear?"

Kim considered him. "Enough."

"And?"

She disappeared for a second and then opened the door and climbed out. "Do you guys know what the oath of enlistment is?" They all shook their heads. "You've heard it, and I'm going to get some of it wrong, but it's something like this: 'I solemnly swear I will support and defend the Constitution of the United States against all enemies, foreign and domestic.'" She paused and shook her head. "I guess that probably includes insane alien spiders. So, yeah, I will support and defend the Constitution of the United States against all enemies, foreign and domestic and spiders, and there's something else I forget, but then it goes: 'I will obey the orders of the President of the United States and the orders of the officers appointed over me, according to regulations and the Uniform Code of Military Justice. So help me God.'" Gordo and Shotgun and Teddie stayed quiet, watching her.

Finally she shrugged. "Maybe I didn't get all the words right, but that's the gist of it. I don't really know who's wrong or who's right, but when I swore that oath, I never really thought about the possibility that I'd have to choose between the president and my commanding officer. I've seen these suckers up close. We're lucky as hell that we managed to get away from them. It was chaos. I mean, this was back when we still thought a quarantine zone would work." She shrugged. "That sounds funny, doesn't it? 'Back when we still thought a quarantine zone would work.' Like it was years ago. Ancient history. But we're talking a couple of weeks, right? Anyway, this was on the fringes of Los Angeles . . . Well, more than that: way out of the city, on the highway. Or interstate. I'm not actually sure what the difference between a highway and an interstate is, and I guess it doesn't matter. The thing that matters is that we had the road blocked and traffic was backed up for miles and miles and then, when the spiders started swarming, the military went to town to try to contain them. I'm talking jets screaming overhead and firing missiles, helicopters firing chain guns, us Marines up in our JLTVs with our .50-cals spitting out bullets to the tune of hundreds of rounds a minute. And the civilians? Even with all that, people were more scared of the spiders. They ran *toward* us while we were firing on them.

"I'll tell you this: Those spiders? They're a black swarm of living death, and if I happened to be magically in charge of the universe, I'd never come within a thousand miles of those suckers again. But I can tell you this, too: when we were at the NIH, we were just a few miles from my parents' house. And we left because you made a very good point. We left the NIH and drove here because you convinced us that the Washington, DC, metro area was going to be next on the ticket for tactical strikes. We all know what that means. Tactical strikes. I doubt the fact that they were tactical strikes is much solace for the people living in Denver or Seattle or any of those other cities that are just piles of rubble leaking radioactive smoke. Living. Who lived.

"Let's be honest. Our whole platoon got a gift when we got tasked with bringing you folks east. If not for that, we'd probably still be somewhere near Los Angeles or somewhere else that ate a nuke. As my grandmother liked to say, I didn't fall off a turnip truck. I'm not dumb enough to think that the men and women in the armed forces out west were somehow left miraculously unscathed by those tactical strikes."

She looked up at the sky for a moment, then back down at Gordo and Shotgun and Teddie. "And right now, near as I can tell, there are two choices: the president of the United States of America, who authorized those original nukes but who is now saying enough is enough, or a group of brass who've seized control of a big chunk of the military and want to keep slinging atom bombs. Do I know what the right decision is? Of course not. I'm a lance corporal and I'm only eighteen. I've got less than a year in the Corps. What I do know, however, is that if there's a chance to save Washington, DC, from getting lit up—if there's a path that might keep my parents alive, might save more lives—well, I have to take it."

She bit her lip and then motioned generally across the parking lot. "I think the same could be said for a bunch of us. Not all of us. But there are a few I trust, and I think you'll have better luck getting where you're going with a little help. What do you say?"

Teddie looked at both Gordo and Shotgun wide-eyed, but Shotgun gave a nod. It was his call. Shotgun was better at engineering and math and, hell, almost everything, but Gordo was better at reading people. He thought about it. It worried him, the idea that she'd tell the other Marines. The more people who knew, the more likely it was to cause a problem. He wasn't sure what Rodriguez would do if he got wind of their plan to go AWOL. Except, Gordo thought, it was only Kim and her platoon mates who were going AWOL. He and Shotgun and Teddie were civilians. Again, though, that was the problem: he didn't think Rodriguez would see it that way. In Rodriguez's eyes, they and the ST11 were "high-value assets," and that meant, when it came down to it, if they tried to leave and Rodriguez didn't want them to . . .

So was it worth the risk? He stared at Kim. He trusted her. She was a smart kid, and they'd been together for a while now. The stress and pressure had made days feel like months, and he believed her, that she would help them. And if he trusted Kim, he figured she knew her men well enough to know whom *she* could trust. Because, ultimately, Kim was right: with the chaos on the roadways and with all the potential for problems, they were better off if they had a few Marines accompanying them than if they were on their own.

"Okay," he said.

She nodded. "You three get in the truck. And try to seem inconspicuous."

"Now?"

"Now," she said, already turning to walk across the parking lot. But then she stopped and looked back at Gordo. "I'm a Marine. Civilians like to talk about things," she said, flashing him a white-toothed smile. "Marines like to get stuff done. Let's saddle up, head to Atlantic City, and let's figure out how to be heroes. And, oh," she added, "if there is a medal ceremony like from *Star Wars*, I get to be Princess Leia."

Central Park,
New York, New York

Melanie watched Amy lift the dog down from the helicopter. Even though she knew it wasn't necessary, Melanie was hunched over. It was a reflexive action. The Osprey was powering down, but the spinning blades made her nervous. The whole thing had made her nervous: donning a borrowed US Navy uniform, climbing onto two different helicopters with close to fifty other people, half of whom were just dressed in military uniforms, half of whom were actually in the military, as if they were *supposed* to be leaving the USS *Elsie Downs* in the middle of a coup that was occurring in the middle of an apocalypse. The worst part, actually, was the five or ten seconds when the Osprey rotated its wings to turn from a helicopter into a plane. She didn't like that at all.

But they'd made it to Central Park. Billy Cannon, the secretary of defense, had told her during the flight that the White House—"I don't know: White House in exile?"—was being cagey about the president's location in New York City, so they had to land in Central Park and wait for a convoy of vehicles to bring them to Steph.

She was impressed by how calm Amy seemed about all of it.

Fred nervously made jokes the whole time, but Amy took it all in stride. Even now, as Melanie watched, Amy led Claymore off to one side and unclipped his leash so that the dog could do his business in the bushes. The dog seemed to take his cue from his owner; as he bounced off into the undergrowth, he seemed completely at ease with what had just happened.

As Melanie watched Amy and the dog, she felt a hand on her shoulder. She turned to see Fred, who was preening for her.

"My god, do I look good in a uniform or what?" he said.

She had to laugh. There had been a few times when she'd wanted to tell him to bring it down a notch, but mostly he'd been exactly what she needed: a release valve. It was funny how different Fred seemed from his husband. While Shotgun was cerebral and circumspect, Fred was all glitz and charm. Shotgun, Melanie knew from the limited amount of time she had spent working with him, liked to engage directly on an intellectual level, but Fred needed an audience, and at the moment Melanie was happy to oblige. She watched him spin around in his uniform and then touch a finger to his backside and pretend it sizzled.

Special Agent Riggs came up beside her and motioned to Amy and the dog. "You might want to keep them close. We've got a convoy on the way. Things are a bit hectic, and if I'm being honest, your friends," he said, indicating Fred now, who had drifted off and was primping for Julie, "aren't top priority. If they don't stay close to you, they're liable to get left behind."

Melanie nodded and Riggs walked away, toward the potpourri of people milling around the two helicopters. She looked again at Amy, who had her satellite phone out and appeared to be talking to somebody: finally gotten in touch with her husband, Melanie figured. She'd sent a string of texts to Gordo, who'd responded, but they hadn't actually talked. As soon as Melanie had a chance, though, she was going to borrow Amy's sat phone and try to talk to Gordo and Shotgun herself. Amy had shown her a text the guys had sent that said they had figured out a "tracker," but she wasn't entirely sure what to make of it. However, it made her think to walk over and tell Amy to stay close. Before she could move, she got distracted by the sound of sirens. It took her a second to pinpoint the source: a line of vehicles approaching with their lights flashing. When she looked back, Amy was waving frantically at her. She had the satellite phone pressed up against her ear, her eyes wide.

"You okay?"

Amy held out the phone. "You better listen to this," she said.

And as Melanie watched Amy clip Claymore back on to his leash and then followed her over to the convoy of vehicles, she listened to Gordo explain how the new and improved ST11 had changed the game.

USS *Elsie Downs*, Atlantic Ocean

Ben Broussard took another sip of his coffee. He was exhausted. But now was not the time to weaken. You didn't rise to become the chairman of the Joint Chiefs of Staff without being able to power through. He'd sleep later. He indicated that General Roberts should keep talking. Roberts was an icy prick, but he was as relentless as Broussard was.

"It's a lot easier because the strikes we already carried out were authorized by the president. The door is already open. We're well positioned in key places, but there are some holdouts." Roberts lowered his voice and leaned close to Broussard. "Things are fragile, sir. I think if we get into firefights with our own men, this will all fall apart. Even though we both know it's the only option, using more nuclear weapons on our own soil is a hard sell. I'm not sure we'll be able to keep things together if we engage in broad action."

"I don't want to spill the blood of any of our men and women," Broussard said. He flashed to Alexandra Harris's body hitting the ground. That had been a shame.

Roberts nodded. "Yes, sir. But that brings me to Operation SAFEGUARD."

"How much longer will it take for us to have control?"

"Forty-eight hours until we've compromised it. We're making progress. There's a chance we can speed that up, though."

"How?"

"We've managed to establish contact with the men working inside, and it's not a straight ticket for Pilgrim. The commanding officer, Brigadier General Yoats, is a die-hard loyalist. There's definitely dissent, however, and I think we could leverage that. But . . ."

"What?"

"Sir, if you want to minimize action against our own troops, we'll have to allow things to play out. Forty-eight hours and Operation SAFEGUARD should be off-line and we can proceed as you wish."

Broussard rubbed at his eyes. They'd already gone this far, he thought. It was too late to stop. He had never been the kind of man to look back. Once he considered all the variables and determined a course of action, Broussard kept going until he achieved his goals. It was how he'd risen through the ranks. Sheer, brutal stubbornness and determination. First it had been physical. He'd never been the fastest or the strongest man, but he learned a trick early on: he could swallow an endless amount of pain. There was always a point when other men would succumb to that voice inside their head that said, *Enough, I can't keep going,* but Broussard drowned that voice out. When he was qualifying for his Special Forces training, he had to complete a wilderness course in less than one hundred hours in order to move on. Broussard finished in seventy-one, setting the course record by forgoing sleep and walking without stopping. When he peeled off his boots afterward, enough flesh pulled away that he was confined to a hospital bed for a week.

But this was the hardest thing he'd ever done.

He'd never liked Pilgrim. Never trusted her. He probably had to admit that there was some truth to the accusation that it was because she was a woman. He was old-school and old enough that women in leadership and combat roles rankled him a bit. He accepted that the world was changing, but taking orders from a female president . . . No, that wasn't the part that was really the problem. It was that she was a civilian through and through. He understood that there were plenty of times where diplomacy was called for over military strength, but soft power was not always the way to go. Sometimes the only thing people understood was a good old-fashioned ass kicking, and that was something that the American military was good at.

For all that, Pilgrim had been his commander in chief. His job had been to give her the best advice he could. To speak honestly and clearly and make sure that when she made decisions that required his input, he had given her the best information he could. No matter how angry she had made him, how often he disagreed with her orders, he'd never questioned that they were her orders to give.

This was different, though. This wasn't some spat over oil or the Russians getting frisky. This was the end of the world. If she'd listened to him and the military right away . . . if she'd only acted . . . And then, when he finally *could* get her to act, to implement the Spanish Protocol, even then she'd held back at first. When she finally authorized the use of nuclear weapons—those were the United States' trump card, and if there was ever a time to play the trump, wasn't it now?—he'd almost yelled out, "Praise Jesus!"

And even then she'd held back. Instead of trying to make up for her mistakes—to make damn sure there was no way those little monsters kept coming, kept tearing the country apart—she did as little as she could. Best case, he figured, she'd bought them a little time.

Time.

Roberts was telling him that it was going to be another forty-eight hours until Operation SAFEGUARD was off-line, which meant it was going to be forty-eight hours until Broussard could finish the job that Pilgrim had been too cowardly to complete.

Did he have forty-eight hours?

"No," he said.

"Sir?"

Broussard placed his hands firmly on his desk. He was a man of action, and he wasn't going to wait. Better a little blood be spilled than for those spiders to come back and capitalize on the president's weakness. "If we've got men inside, give the orders. Whatever the cost. I want Operation SAFEGUARD taken down."

Oxford, Mississippi

Santiago had expected to be hot and uncomfortable wearing his homemade hazmat suit, but he hadn't really expected it to be this bad. The worst, honestly, was his hands. He was wearing rubber dishwashing gloves, and the heat was just trapped inside, aggravating his poor, burned, blistered hands. They ached miserably, and he wondered if he somehow managed to survive all of this he would bear permanent scars. The good thing, however, was that the soreness of his hands occasionally distracted him from how much he was sweating. He could feel rivulets of sweat running down from his head and down his back. He was sure that he must have soaked through the clothing he was wearing, and every step gave him an unpleasant squishy feeling in his boots.

For all that, he'd take the discomfort over being eaten by spiders, because, at least so far, the getup appeared to be working. For the first few blocks after he left his house to go after Mrs. Fine, he hadn't seen any spiders. It actually made him panic. Was he dreaming? He was already hot and sweaty, and there was a part of him that wondered if this had all been part of some fever dream, delirium, a nightmare brought on by some illness. But when he turned onto North Lamar Boulevard, he was quickly assured that he was not, in fact, dreaming.

All the spiders he'd seen up close so far had been burned and charred, empty husks and damaged shells that were no match for the fiery moat he'd built around his property. The spider in front of him was very much undamaged, though. It was alive and skittering across the sidewalk and directly in his path.

He couldn't stop himself from freezing, one foot forward, his body stopping in an awkward impersonation of a man on a walk.

The spider went past him without stopping. It was as if he weren't even there.

He crossed himself, an action he hadn't performed in many years. The news, such as it was, had been so sketchy and so full of obvious falsehoods that he hadn't dared to be honest with his wife about how hopeless this quest seemed to be. But here he was, a knight in armor made of rubber boots, a raincoat and rain pants, a pair of dishwashing gloves, a full-face respirator, and almost an entire roll of duct tape. He was pretty sure he didn't look like a knight, however. Not with the raincoat's hood completely covering his head and the full-face respirator. If anything, he probably looked more like Marty McFly in *Back to the Future* when he snuck into his dad's bedroom and used his Walkman to . . . Santiago paused. Why was it exactly that McFly had snuck into the bedroom and put the headphones over his father's ears? He could remember the scene clearly, the visual of Michael J. Fox looming over the bed, appearing alien and menacing, playing loud rock and roll as a scare tactic . . . but what the heck had that been about?

He shook his head. Not the time or the place. He was on a quest. Mrs. Fine. The problem, he realized, was that even if his homemade hazmat suit did work as he hoped, he didn't actually know where Mrs. Fine had gone. He had to get to her before—

Oh. Crap. He knew where she'd gone. Of course.

He was about to start walking again when he felt something on his leg. He looked down and let out a scream that turned into a wild laugh. The spider was one of the ones with red stripes across its back. It skittered up his leg, across his crotch—that was a sensation he hoped to never feel again—and back down his other leg and over his boot before continuing on its merry way. The eight-legged demon had felt so heavy on his body, and yet the only thing he could think to compare it to in terms of size was one of the rubber duckies that his son, Oscar, had so loved when he was a little boy. The spider was larger, of course, if you counted its creepy, knuckled, and hairy legs, but its body was the same size as a duckie's. Of course, one of these terrible spiders bobbing in a bathtub would have been unlikely to bring Oscar as much joy as the yellow duck he'd had that was decorated as an Ole Miss football player.

He realized he was still standing in his tracks and wondered if it was because he knew. Here, still blocks away from the university, he was starting to see spiders, and if he kept going, how long until he saw Mrs. Fine's body? Or something worse?

But he couldn't stop. He'd proven to himself that this hodge-podge getup would keep him safe. Now he owed it to the woman who had treated him like a son and who acted like a grandmother to *both* his children. Because that meant something. They had plenty of friends. His wife, in particular, was social. And, of course, Oscar was never a problem. But Juliet? He loved his little girl so, and he understood why some people looked at her without seeing what was wonderful about her. Understanding and forgiving were two separate things, however, because if Mrs. Fine treated his kids as though they were her own grandchildren, his mother-in-law had not. He would never, ever forgive his wife's mother for saying that she wished they had decided on an abortion when they'd found out Juliet was going to be developmentally disabled. It didn't matter that there had been times, in the deepest, darkest corners of the night, when he himself admitted that their lives would have been easier if Juliet had never been born. It didn't matter, because he understood that while it would have been an easier life, it would have been a life lived less fully. Although they'd never talked about it, not in so many words, it seemed as if Mrs. Fine had always understood that, too.

From the very beginning, Mrs. Fine had been there for them. Before Juliet was born, she'd babysat only occasionally for Oscar. But in those first few months after Juliet came, when Santiago and his wife were constantly at the hospital, Mrs. Fine was an extension of their family. She brought them food at the hospital, took Oscar to the park, even worked at the gas station when Santiago couldn't find coverage for certain shifts, sitting at the register and knitting a blanket for Juliet, just as she'd made a blanket for . . .

Oh, goodness. He was crying now. Mrs. Fine. She had been a glorious, giving woman. She deserved better than this, and he realized that in all the years he'd known her, with all the things she'd done for them, he'd never once told her that he loved her.

It was too late for that.

He set himself walking forward, however, because it was not too late to do right by her. He would find her body and he would bring her home and bury her and if he and his family lived through this, they would keep her memory alive with every breath they took.

He turned right on Jackson, left on Ninth, and right on University. As he walked, the mass of spiders grew thicker, from a few here and there to scattered groups to dozens and dozens. By the time he was on campus proper, they were everywhere. No matter where he looked, he saw them skittering about. And yet there was no sign of Mrs. Fine's body. He passed a hundred, maybe two hundred bodies, all of them wrapped in cobwebs, but he checked each and every one of them. Most of the time, there was enough exposed that he could rule out the body as Mrs. Fine's, but on twenty or thirty occasions—enough for him to lose count—he swallowed his disgust and used his rubber-gloved hands to part the spider silk to get a look.

He wondered if he was wrong—if perhaps Mrs. Fine had gone in a different direction—but by that point he was close enough to the stadium that it seemed silly not to at least look.

He was surprised to see the gates standing wide-open. He'd never been much of a sports fan, but he assumed the football field was off-limits. When he got close enough to see the field, he stopped dead. The field was littered with bodies. Piles of them. There had to be at least a hundred, perhaps a hundred fifty silk-swathed bodies on the field, and another fifty or so that had managed to get some distance before being overtaken. There was even a golf cart with the Ole Miss logo on it that was overturned in the end zone, a body splayed on the ground beside it, half-covered in white spiderwebs.

"It's a shame, isn't it?"

He shrieked and jumped at the same time, catching himself just before he fell.

"Mrs. Fine?"

She was in the stands, barely twenty feet away. She looked . . . normal.

But all around her he saw black skittering shadows moving across the seats, crawling up and down every vertical surface. Where she was standing, there were a lot of spiders; but in the far corner, up and away from Mrs. Fine, there was an uncountable number. A black, glistening mass that pulsed and swirled. It was hypnotic and horrifying. It reminded him of the time he'd found a dead raccoon in the alley between his house and the store and he'd nudged it over with his foot. The raccoon's belly had been a snarled, teeming mess of maggots that made him retch.

"How are . . ."

He trailed off and just stood there, waiting, as she slowly made her way toward him. It was not until she was standing right in front of him and wrapping her arms around him in one of her warm hugs that he allowed himself to believe it was true.

"I don't know," she said, releasing him. "The entire time, I kept waiting and waiting. There was a moment, right when I came in here, when I started walking up there." She didn't have to point or motion for Santiago to know she meant the swarming sea of black at the top of the stadium. "I could see a wave of them rolling toward me, but then I stopped, backed up, and it was like I ceased to exist. As long as I stayed over here, they left me alone. Oh, here and there a few of them crawled across me, and I can tell you," she said, shaking her head and giving a short, clipped laugh, "I didn't like that. But I might as well have just been a part of the stadium for any interest they showed in me."

She reached up and gave a gentle knock on the faceplate of the respirator. "That doesn't look too comfortable in there. You're all sweaty."

"It's hot," he allowed.

"Well, the news did say that some people have been left untouched. I suppose I'm just lucky." She gulped and then she started to cry. "I'm so, so sorry. Some luck, huh? I thought I was doing something noble, and instead you put yourself at risk to look for me. I was trying to make sure I wasn't a burden on you, and I couldn't even get that right."

He reached out and swept her into his arms as though she were one of his children. He just held her while she cried.

When she'd composed herself, she took a few steps back, pulled a tissue out of her purse, and blew her nose with a great honking noise that belied her size. "I can't believe you came for me," she said.

"Of course. It's what you do for family. We love you. *I* love you. We don't call you *abuela* for nothing."

A line of spiders—twenty, thirty, perhaps forty—came bristling past them, but although they passed close, they seemed to take no notice of the two people, one old, one not as old, standing and looking out over the football field.

"Well, then, we should head home," Mrs. Fine said. "But Lord, oh, Lord. What a shame about them boys." She waved her hand to indicate the lumpy, cobwebbed remains of the Ole Miss football team. "How about that? The world's falling apart all around us, but Coach had the boys out here practicing. He always favored getting spring practice started later than I liked, and I guess nothing was going to stop him from putting them through their paces, not hell nor high water nor spiders. What a waste."

She pointed to somewhere near the twenty-yard line. To Santiago, it just looked like a mess of bodies and cobwebs, with a steady stream of spiders going back and forth, but to Mrs. Fine, it was the glorious future of Ole Miss football lying in ruins.

"We were returning eighteen starters. Eighteen! And this was a stud recruiting class, I'll tell you that. Giles was supposed to sit on the bench his freshman year, but I saw his first couple practices he graduated high school early and enrolled in the spring just so he could get on the field for spring practices and get the reps—and he was *electric*. He threw a pretty ball, just a spiral for the ages, but even from up in the stands you could see the velocity. If I didn't know better, I could have sworn I heard the zip on the ball as it left his fingers. With a quarterback like that? If my husband had been alive to see Giles throw that ball, he would have had another heart attack."

Santiago nodded, but the truth was, he was a rarity in Oxford. He didn't care one whit about football. He looked at the writhing mass in the stands. "What do you think is up there?" he asked. "Why are they clustered up there?"

"Oh, who knows? And who knows why my old bones weren't tasty enough for them? Let's head home and you can get out of your crazy getup and I can sit with Juliet for a spell and maybe read her a story."

That seemed like a good plan to Santiago, and so they turned and began walking.

Oslo, Norway

She had yet to venture outside the high school auditorium. She'd felt the burning destruction of the egg sacs that had been in the barn only a few miles away, and so she had kept to the darkness and the deep safety of the auditorium. Her little ones could seek the light. They could bring her what it was that she required.

Soon. Soon enough she would be ready to emerge. She could feel the tight shell beginning to crack. It wouldn't be long before she would slide out of that shell and take her final form.

Operation SAFEGUARD, Undisclosed Location, Top Secret

Lieutenant Colonel Lou Jenks checked his watch. He'd always wanted to do something where he got to synchronize watches, but it seemed significantly less exciting now that he was actually doing it. The truth was that he felt conflicted.

About whose side he was on, there was no question. He'd done everything that the United States Air Force had asked of him. He'd gone from being a somewhat tubby towheaded teenager to a chiseled man who could give and follow orders. Even though he'd never seen actual combat, before his posting to the bunker, he had actually done the job that was his cover story: providing maintenance to aircraft used during SpecOps activities in hot zones, and he'd been close enough to action that he'd been able to hear it. When he'd been ordered to Operation SAFEGUARD, he obliged without a single complaint, even though it meant being sealed up underground six weeks out of every eight, bored out of his skull. And when the president ordered the use of nuclear weapons, he did what he'd been trained to do, running through his checklists, entering the codes Hubbard read to him.

His whole life he'd wanted to be a pilot. He wanted to be a badass, flying a fighter jet and taking down the bad guys in cinematographic dogfights. By the time he was ten, however, he needed glasses, so he settled on the next best thing: join the air force and work on those fighter jets. His dad wanted him to go into the army, like he had, but his pops never made it sound all that glamorous. Lou wasn't particularly interested in crawling through mud and taking long marches with heavy packs on his back. Sure, there'd been some of that early on, but mostly it had worked out. Better than worked out, because once he was in, he realized that all he wanted to do was stay in the air force. He was a lifer through and through, and he studied and jumped through all the hoops to make officer. And from there it was a hop, skip, and a bunch more hoop jumps until Operation SAFEGUARD greased the skids for a few more promotions. His whole life was air force, air force, air force. He gave them everything, and in return they'd given everything back.

That's why it hurt so much when the president betrayed him.

He knew it wasn't personal, that Stephanie Pilgrim wasn't sitting in the White House scheming about how to stab Lou in the back, but it felt that way. Denver was gone. His parents were gone. His friends, his girlfriend. The city of his birth was a dead zone. And all because he'd done his job the way he'd been trained, because he'd followed orders and allowed the president to use nuclear weapons on domestic soil.

He kept telling himself that if it meant they'd won, if it meant the end of those spiders, then, yes, he would have done it again. He would have sacrificed his own life. But they hadn't won. The spiders were still out there, and the entire coup had been over that basic fact: the president had started a job but wouldn't finish it. She'd sacrificed Denver for no reason.

A few of the other operators had tried arguing with Yoats, but the brigadier general wasn't having any of it. He'd given his orders. They were under the command of President Pilgrim. It didn't matter to Yoats that at this point most of the armed forces had swung around to Lou's way of thinking. One of the operators, Gomez, couldn't let it go, and Yoats had ordered him confined to the brig, which, since they didn't have a brig, was actually a storage room with a lock.

Still, Lou was conflicted, because even though he knew which side he was on, Yoats wasn't the only person who was dead set against Broussard's coup. Hubbard, who had been on the desk with Lou when the strike orders came in, was also adamantly pro-president. They were friends, of a sort, and Hubbard had confided that he was worried.

"Look man, we both know that Yoats is right about sticking by the president," Hubbard said, and Lou worked very hard to make sure he didn't give anything away. They were in the back corner of the dining hall, lingering over the remains of their breakfast. Hubbard was a tea drinker, but Lou had made himself a soy latte in the fancy machine by the beverage station.

"You join up, the first thing you do is swear an oath," Hubbard continued. "We take our orders from our commanding officers, they take their orders from theirs, and it goes all the way up. I know that not everybody loves having a chick as the commander in chief, but she's got the job. Chain of command, you know? You've got to respect that or what do you have?" Hubbard snagged the last nub of the powdered donut on his plate and threw it in his mouth. He chewed aggressively, swallowed, and then leaned toward Lou, clearly worried about being overheard even though there was no-body else left in the dining hall.

"The thing is, even if you and I know what's what, I don't think everybody sees it the way Yoats does. I mean, obviously Gomez, but he's got an excuse."

Lou took a sip of his latte, thinking of poor Gomez. He was the youngest operator and originally from Los Angeles. He had it worse than anybody. First spiders and then nukes. Crap.

"It's not just him, though. There are the guys who are obvious about disagreeing. Chappie and McNair are walking around like dogs looking for a fight. But that's not who I'm worried about. I think something's going on, Lou. You would have asked me a couple of weeks ago, I would have said never in a million years would any of the men in the bunker disobey a direct order from Yoats; but if you would have asked me a couple of weeks ago, I also would have said that never in a million years would there be a coup in the United States."

"What are you saying?" Lou was surprised at how calm his voice sounded.

"I'm just saying keep your eyes and ears open. Okay? And stick with me. If things go to hell," Hubbard said, not able to stop him-self from smiling, "you've got a black belt at your service."

It left Lou feeling crappy. He didn't care about Yoats. The guy had been a good commander, but it was the cost of doing business. Hubbard, though . . .

He looked at his watch again.

It was time.

He knocked on Hubbard's door.

"Sec!"

After more like thirty seconds, Hubbard opened up. "Sorry, man," he said. "Just got out of the shower."

"Oh, ah, yeah. Bad timing, I guess. I was going to ask if you'd maybe come to the gym with me. I was thinking about what you said earlier." Lou lowered his voice. "You know, about maybe some guys thinking about something, and I thought you could maybe show me a few moves, just in case. Work up a little of that jujitsu."

It was like waving bacon in front of a dog. Lou had barely finished speaking before Hubbard was bouncing down the hallway toward the gym.

The walk took maybe forty seconds, and the whole time Lou was looking at his watch. He'd been afraid that he was going to be too late getting Hubbard in the gym, but the guy was so eager to help that they were thirty seconds early.

Hubbard entered the close-quarters-combat room ahead of him.

The room was maybe twenty by twenty and covered in wrestling mats. It had the odd, funky sweat-sock odor that came from men trying to pulverize other men, and suddenly Lou had a visceral remembrance of the way Hubbard had embarrassed him the one time they'd sparred. It made what came next a little easier. He glanced one more time at his watch. Ten seconds.

"Hey, Richard?"

"Yeah?"

"What's this scar from?" He pointed toward Hubbard's head with his left hand while reaching behind his back and under his shirt with his right.

"What scar?"

"This one," he said. He whipped the pistol up, planning to put one right in Hubbard's eye. He didn't know whether he'd tried to be too cute or he was a second later than his brothers-in-arms and Hubbard heard a gun going off somewhere else in the bunker, but Hubbard skipped backward.

The bastard was fast. Lou had to give him that. But he wasn't faster than a bullet. It was enough to mess up his aim, though, and the shot tore through Hubbard's throat, right next to his Adam's apple. Crazily, Hubbard stayed on his feet. He was gushing blood even as he had a hand clamped over the wound, but he looked for all the world like he was—

Crap!

Suddenly, Lou was on the ground, Hubbard on top of him, spitting blood and just whaling on him with one hand and pinning down the wrist holding the gun with the other. And then, even as the blood came running out of Hubbard's throat like a fountain, Hubbard forced Lou's hand around so the gun was pointing at Lou's face, wrapped his fingers around Lou's fingers, and pulled the—

M anny kept looking at the dog. Why on earth was there a dog in here? And who were the woman and the man who came with the dog? They weren't scientists, but they seemed to be affiliated with Melanie and her small group of men and women who *were* scientists. Whatever, he thought. Not really where his focus should be, particularly when Melanie was promising a "game changer."

They were in the room they were calling the Oval Office despite being neither oval nor in the White House. Everybody was doing their best to inject some sense of normalcy into a situation that was nothing short of surreal. When everything was turned upside down, you had to look somewhere to keep your balance.

Not surprisingly, since it was the president's office, even if hopefully a temporary one, it was the largest office in the building. The desk was an ancient rosewood beast that would have worked as a banquet table in a pinch, and there was a sitting area with two heavy blue chesterfields plus a settee and a pair of chairs upholstered in a floral fabric that Manny thought was absurdly ugly, particularly given how tastefully the rest of the office had been decorated. While it wasn't the real Oval Office, it had the same sort of feel. Regal, serious, and authoritative, yet still a place where business could be done. Though right now it was crowded. The room was big enough that it could comfortably fit perhaps fifteen people, but they had at least double that number in the room.

Aside from Melanie and the other scientists and the mysterious woman and man with the dog, Billy Cannon was there with several other uniforms, plus a mix of aides, high-level members of the government, including the director of the National Cyber Security Division, the unfortunately named Bertha Biggins, and the president's science advisor, Dr. Hickson Churley, who was, in Manny's opinion, a buffoon. As he looked around the room, he was stabbed with a sudden sense of sadness as he realized who was missing: Alexandra Harris. He'd grown to appreciate Alex's presence. As his father would have put it, Alex could be a crusty old broad at times, but she was at the top of her game, and he often thought that she'd been born a generation too soon to be truly appreciated. Goddamned Ben Broussard. When all of this was over . . .

Manny was sitting next to Steph on one of the chesterfields, and he leaned over to whisper in her ear. "I still think you should go ahead and give the order. Activate the Matthew 5:45 protocol now. We've got a ticking clock here with Broussard, and—"

"Dammit, Manny," she hissed. "I know. And *you* know that once I go down that road there's no going back. Our nuclear weapons won't be of any more use to us than a bag full of rocks. I want to reserve the right to change my mind and use them for as long as possible. That's my decision, Manny."

Melanie came to stand in front of the room, the desk behind her, waiting to catch Steph's eye. Manny gave her a quick shake of his head and held up a finger to indicate he needed a second. "If you wait too long, it *won't* be your decision. It will be Broussard's."

Steph glared at him in anger. It was nothing he hadn't faced before. He didn't like it, but he knew that one of the things she most valued in him when it came to politics was that he had never been a yes-man. She let out a loud huff, then pursed her lips. "Fine. Let's listen to what Melanie has to say, and after we're done, we can revisit this. We'll take stock of where we are on Broussard's progress breaking down the firewalls."

Manny figured that was as good as he was going to get, so he signaled to Melanie that she could start. The room stilled as she began to speak.

"You should all have access to the slide deck on your tablets. Please go to slide one. You'll see a picture of a first-wave Hell Spider next to one of the second-wave Hell Spiders. First wave is all black, while the second wave has red stripes."

They both had tablets, but Steph shifted on the chesterfield, leaned over, and whispered "Hell Spiders?" out of the corner of her mouth. It was quiet, but Melanie heard.

"Sorry. Yeah, we're calling them Hell Spiders." Manny saw Melanie glance over at Julie and then back to the president. "Seemed like a fitting name, and we needed to call them something." She continued: "If you swipe to slide two, you'll see those two spiders as well as the third kind, which we are calling queens. So you've got first-wave, second-wave, and queen Hell Spiders. Please note that slide two is to scale."

Manny heard several people gasping. He'd seen the pictures already and was still wildly unsettled, so he knew how startling it was to see how big the queens were for the first time.

"Obviously, yes, this is way outside the sphere of what we are used to. The largest known spider before these events is about the size of a dinner plate. That's going by the legs, not the tagmata, which is— Sorry. I'll try not to slip into scientist-speak. The body is smaller—say, the size of, uh, a pear or something. When we look at the first-wave and second-wave Hell Spiders, they're quite large, but nothing that is beyond the scope of what we would expect in the natural world. The queens, however, are a different matter."

Across the room from Manny, Dr. Churley was shaking his head in obvious dissent. Before the man had even spoken, Manny found himself annoyed. The president's science advisor was new to the post. He'd come on board only the week before the spiders had emerged, a replacement for Dr. Pihu Agnihotri, who had resigned after she'd been diagnosed with stage IV breast cancer. Dr. Agnihotri had been a slam-dunk pick. She was brilliant and personable, plus she was a huge political win on both sides of the aisle. Manny could think of maybe only four or five times in his entire career when a decision had made everybody happy in the way that appointing Dr. Agnihotri had. Unfortunately, Dr. Churley was a win only in the politics department. He had a CV that looked impressive but was one of those compromise picks that Manny was willing to allow because it gave him and the president leverage on another front. It had been such a recent appointment that his interactions with Churley had been limited, but from the little he'd seen of the man so far, Manny would have been happy to watch the smug doctor get dropped out of a helicopter from a great height. Frankly, that was one of the reasons Churley hadn't been called on to consult since this began. Manny didn't actually know how the doctor had even gotten himself into this room.

"Are you really sure you've got the scale correct on this?" Churley said. "It's inconceivable that a spider of this size—"

"Yes. I'm sure."

Although Manny wanted Melanie to just cut to the chase,

there was a part of him that thrilled at watching her cut Churley off instead.

"Well, I don't know about that," Churley continued, as if he somehow had inside information. "There's simply a physical limit to how big spiders can get. Proportionally, they just keep adding weight, so at some point they'd be immobile. It's really inconceivable that—"

"Churley!"

Manny actually jumped. He hadn't expected the president to shout at the man, and—given the proximity of Steph's mouth to his ear—it startled him.

"I'm just saying that, with all due respect to Dr. Guyer, it's inconceivable that a spider of that size could—"

The president cut him off again. "Stop talking. I would like to hear what Melanie has to say."

"But—"

"Shut up." She said it firmly and coldly, and Churley's mouth snapped shut. She turned to Melanie expectantly.

Melanie considered for a second. "There are a lot of things we just don't know or understand, but we've got good data here."

Churley couldn't help himself. "It's just inconceivable—"

"Enough!"

This time Manny was ready for Steph's outburst, but he was still surprised that she leapt to her feet and pointed at the man. "You. Get the hell out of this room. In fact, get the hell out of my life. If I see you again, I'll have you shot."

Churley stood frozen for a second, then carefully smoothed down the front of his shirt and his tie, turned on his heel, and walked out of the room. The door shut with a heavy click, and the room was dead quiet for a second.

Melanie's eyes were so wide that she looked to Manny like a

deer caught in the headlights. She cleared her throat but didn't say anything. Steph sat back down on the couch next to Manny, and he shifted and said sotto voce, "You aren't really going to have him shot, are you?"

That was enough to get a polite snicker from Steph and break the tension in the room. Melanie continued speaking.

"Okay, so we're on slide two still. And I was saying, this is to scale. Apropos of . . . Honestly, I have no idea who that guy was, but apropos of Captain Inconceivable, we have never seen spiders the size of the Hell Spider queens, but it's not without precedent. At different times in the earth's history, there have been outsized creatures. There are the obvious examples like during the Cretaceous period, when we had T. rexes and the *Saltasaurus* and other jumbo dinosaurs. And at the end of the last ice age there were animals all over the world that were huge. There's a book called *The Sixth Extinction* by Elizabeth Kolbert, and she called it the 'too big to quail' strategy. There was supposedly a beaver in North America that was the size of a grizzly bear. And then, about thirteen thousand years ago, they all seemed to die out."

Steph leaned forward. "The spiders?"

Melanie wobbled the hand that wasn't holding the tablet. "Don't know. I don't think so. Most scientists seem to think the megafauna extinction was caused by the spread of humans. But the point is, we think the Hell Spiders are on some sort of extreme cycle of hatching and hibernation. I was fortunate enough to be able to examine an egg sac immediately prior to the emergence of the first wave. It was dug up during archaeological work on the Nazca Lines in Peru, and it was buried with items that were dated to about ten thousand years ago. So right now our best guess is that the cycle for hatching is spread out in the same way that certain kinds of cicadas go underground for thirteen or seventeen years. It

makes sense. It explains why there's no written record of the Hell
Spiders, why the hatching came as a complete surprise."

"It explains the hatching patterns, too." That came from Billy
Cannon, who was on the chesterfield opposite Manny and Steph.
"Right? One of the reasons this has been such a disaster is modern
transportation. On their own, they seem like they could only
spread a few miles. But with planes and trains and cars . . ."

"Yes! Exactly!" Melanie jabbed her finger at Billy, excited.

Manny ducked his head, trying to hide the small smile that had
come across his face unbidden. Things would never go back to the
way they had once been between him and his ex-wife, but seeing
how excited she could get when she was in her element reminded
him of why he'd fallen in love with her in the first place. Of course,
it was that same passion for her work that had ultimately undone
them, but that was another story.

"Ten thousand years ago, the spiders wouldn't have been able
to travel like this. We've done some analysis and, best as we can
tell, there are a number of locations in China and in India that
were primary sites for the emergence of the Hell Spiders, and then
those spiders found carriers who spread eggs to other, secondary
sites. Los Angeles was a secondary site. A hundred or two hundred
years ago, North America would probably have been spared all of
this. And, at least as of right now, New Zealand and Australia are
both completely untouched. Ironic, of course, given how many
poisonous things live in Australia."

"Peru." Manny said it quietly, and then he said it again, louder.
"Peru. The Brits . . . Before we left the White House. The Brits
said they thought this all may have started in Peru. Ground zero."

Melanie nodded. "It's possible. But that's not the important
thing right this second. What's important is that we've got these
three kinds of Hell Spiders, right? First wave seem like they're

there to spread as far as they can and to remove any possible threats. The second wave does something similar, but they also serve as feeders. They keep food cocooned up for safekeeping and seem to bring it to the queens while the queens are still developing in their egg sacs. Swipe over for slide three, four, and then five."

Manny felt the wave of revulsion sweep through the room as people swiped. The first photo was recognizably a human body underneath a shroud of silk. The spiderweb was thickest around the upper body and head, thankfully, so he didn't have to see the person's face, but it was gossamer-thin around the person's bare ankles and feet. The second photo was from a greater distance and a bit grainy, as if it had been lifted from surveillance footage, and it showed five different lumpy, cocooned bodies. The final slide was clearly satellite footage, and it showed a football stadium. He used his fingers to zoom in. He could see the Ole Miss logo partially and terrifyingly obscured by white-cloaked bodies at midfield. When he zoomed out so that he could see the whole stadium, there were a hundred bodies, maybe two hundred, and the stands were speckled with black dots that became more and more concentrated toward one end, until the southeast corner of the stands looked like a giant unified black mass.

Something caught his eye at the northeast corner of the stadium. He flicked his thumb and forefinger to zoom in. The picture was extremely high resolution, and as he kept zooming in, it didn't seem to lose any detail.

"Melanie," he asked, "how old is this photo? The one from slide five."

One of the aides standing behind his couch responded before Melanie could. "Less than an hour, sir."

Melanie cocked her head. "Why?"

"Well," he said, "either I'm losing my mind, or it looks like there are two people in the stands." He held up the tablet and pointed. "One of them is wearing what looks like a hazmat suit, and the other one is, well, an old lady. Near as I can tell."

There was a scramble and buzz as people in the room started zooming in on their own tablets, and it was ten or twenty seconds before Melanie responded.

"Maybe Dr. Dichtel should take over for a minute. This is out of order, but, well, Will?"

Will, who had been leaning against the wall, pushed off with his foot and came to stand next to Melanie.

"Okay, so spiders don't actually have teeth." He held up his hand to forestall the inevitable questions. "Or certainly not in the way in which you're thinking. The short version is that spiders use their fangs to secrete a venom that basically dissolves their prey. They might grind it up a bit with their pedipalps, but essentially they turn what they eat into a liquid slurry and slurp it up. What's astounding about the Hell Spiders is how quickly they can do this. I'm sure you've all seen footage of them stripping a person to the bone in seconds. Now, spider venom comes in all kinds of varieties and is incredibly complicated. Dr. Guyer is just one of many researchers who have looked at the efficacy of spider venom in medical treatments, which is of particular interest because latrotoxins, which have a high molecular weight, trigger neuromediators—"

"Will."

He glanced at Melanie. "Sorry. English. Okay, the point is that there are two types of venoms. The first kind is necrotic, or cytotoxic, which damages and kills the cells it comes into contact with. This is what the Hell Spiders are using to dissolve human flesh so quickly. Amazingly, the first-wave spiders seem to be able to alter their cytotoxic venom when they use a person or, I suppose, an animal, which would have been more likely in terms of evolution, as a host to lay eggs inside. That venom both dissolves flesh and heals it, allowing the spider to slip inside a body and essentially close up the wound behind it. We think this was probably a strategy developed in order to spread their reach. Allow the carriers to expend their own energy covering ground.

"The second kind of venom is neurotoxic, which acts directly on the nervous system. Here we're talking exclusively about the second-wave spiders, the ones with the red stripes on their backs. The neurotoxic venom that they inject into their victims acts almost immediately as a paralyzing agent. I haven't had the time to do extensive testing on its properties, but we've got video and enough accounts from witnesses to confirm that if one of them bites you, you go down like you've been shot, completely paralyzed. They seem to also have the ability to produce necrotic venom functionally identical to that of the first-wave spiders, which is not as surprising as you think; it's not uncommon for spiders to be able to exhibit both necrotic and neurotoxic venom. Given how old the Hell Spiders seem to be, they didn't develop these attributes specifically to kill people. And this gives us an advantage."

Manny caught himself actually letting out a guffaw. Will stared at him, as did pretty much everybody in the room. "Sorry," he said. "I guess I just didn't think of us as having an advantage here. I think it was . . ." He searched until he saw Dr. Nieder and then pointed at her. "You told me at an earlier briefing that you thought the spiders had stopped evolving because they didn't need to anymore. You compared them to sharks as the perfect killing machines."

As he spoke, Manny saw Melanie tap Will on the arm and whisper something in his ear. He whispered something back and then returned to his place against the wall, clearly annoyed at Manny's interruption. Admittedly, Manny felt a little bad, but come on, what was it with these geniuses?

"The reason I called on Dr. Dichtel out of order," Melanie said, "is that to go back to what you saw in the stadium, the man in what appears to be a hazmat suit, the lack of evolution *is* an advantage here. Yes, of course we should be terrified of these things, and the fact that they haven't needed to keep evolving means that they were perfect. Were. Past tense. Because even though their necrotic venom opens flesh like a hot knife through butter, there are some things it can't go through, namely, plastics, rubber, and glass. Dr. Dichtel has tested the venom on all those materials, and it seems to have no effect whatsoever. There might be other materials as well, but for right now, plastics, rubber, and glass are all fine, because those are the materials we use to make—"

"Hazmat suits." Manny was excited. He blinked and motioned with his hands, apologetic for interrupting again.

"Exactly. We know that at least one group of scientists in Japan was able to go into an infested area wearing hazmat suits and return unharmed. The suits also seem to function as some sort of disguise. The spiders don't seem to—and I'm using this word in quotes here—'see' people wearing hazmat suits. So it's quite possible that this guy in the stadium is . . ." She stopped, frowning. "Though that doesn't explain the woman," she said, touching her lips with one finger, "except that we also know the Hell Spiders leave a certain percentage of people untouched. We assume to ensure a food supply for the following waves, but we aren't sure."

"Snacks." That was Steph staring brightly at Melanie. "Get to the good part."

"Right. Snacks. Realistically, to the Hell Spiders, a human is just like a burrito, a soft wrapper with a tasty filling. The thing is, how is it that they know not to attack somebody? If a Hell Spider leaves a person untouched, how do the other Hell Spiders know to do likewise? And, more important, we now have many, many confirmed reports of people who have been left untouched more than once. In other words, it's not just a single Hell Spider or a group of Hell Spiders that decides a person is off-limits, but that understanding seems to get passed on to all of them."

Manny got it now. It meant the spiders were communicating. Melanie had alluded to that when he greeted her upon her arrival, but in the chaos and hubbub of trying to get the briefing going as quickly as possible—it had made sense to have her give the briefing just once, to a larger group, in order not to waste time—he hadn't really gotten it. So the spiders had a way of talking to one another, of passing on information, and suddenly Manny felt . . . optimistic? Because if the spiders could communicate with one another, perhaps there was a way to disrupt that.

Melanie continued, describing what the scientists had worked through in terms of the way the spiders seemed coordinated. She discussed Teddie's theory, that they looked almost fake in the way they moved, using the example of special effects made with early computer-generated images to illustrate her point. She covered some of the differences between types of spiders and how the Hell Spiders were both like and unlike all other spiders, moving through the briefing at a fast pace, occasionally stopping to answer questions and, as needed, having the other scientists, Dichtel, Nieder, Haaf, and Yoo, pitch in. It was a well-thought-out presentation, and she covered a lot of ground, backing away from the question of how the spiders communicated to explain as many things as possible before coming to the main point, to what Manny sure as heck hoped really was a game changer.

After nearly twenty minutes of talking, Melanie stopped, took a sip of water, and then looked around the room. She was clearly excited. Something approaching a smile was playing on her lips, and it reminded Manny of his thirty-fifth birthday. She'd never been good at keeping secrets, and the whole day she tried to play it cool, but at dinner, she pulled a small, elegantly wrapped box out of her purse. He was so surprised that he swore aloud in the quiet restaurant: a vintage TAG Heuer Monaco. The exact model Steve McQueen wore in *Le Mans*, with the iconic square case. It was the first watch ever to feature an automatic chronograph, and he'd mentioned to her that it was the kind of watch he aspired to. It must have run her five grand, and it was pristine. Absolutely cherry. And it was—right now, he realized—on a watch winder in the safe in his condo in DC. There was a good chance he would never see that watch again. He glanced at his wrist, not to check the time, but just to look at the tasteful Shinola Runwell Chrono he was wearing instead of the Monaco. He liked Shinola watches. They were made in Detroit, which sent a good message, and they were much more reasonably priced. This one had been about seven hundred new. He suddenly realized he couldn't remember if Detroit had been on the list of cities included in the thirty-one that were obliterated by tactical nuclear strikes; perhaps, going forward, all Shinola watches would be vintage.

He felt the sharp dig of Steph's elbow in his side. "Manny," she hissed. He straightened up. A bad time to be daydreaming.

"Which brings us to now. There's good news and there's bad news. The bad news first. When we, um, left our lab, one of the things we were watching for was signs of ecdysis. That's when a spider molts. They shed their exoskeleton—the hard, crunchy part on the outside—so that they can increase in size."

Manny felt a shudder go through the room.

"Our concern here is that we aren't sure if this molting is simply so they can grow or for something else. Given what we've seen

going from the first- to second-wave Hell Spiders and the difference between those two versions and the queens, we're nervous
that they might be preparing for something else—that there's a
new model, so to speak, on the way."

Manny heard somebody groan. For all he knew, it could have
been him. He asked, "Like what? One that spits fire or something?"

"Hardy-har, Manny," Melanie said. And yet, the way she said
it still reminded him of the night of his birthday, the way she had
clearly been pleased with herself.

"Here's the good news. There are a lot of reasons why the
Hell Spiders have been so scary: they can reproduce so fast, they
lay eggs inside hosts, they can swarm over somebody and strip
the flesh from their body. But the thing that's been the hardest
for us to deal with, in my opinion, is that they work together.
That threw us off for a while, because we were working under
the model of other kinds of creatures that have a sort of queen
structure, like ants, or bees. With them, however, there's a sense
that the queen is in control of the colony, but it's different." She
looked directly at Steph. "No offense to you, Madam President,
but when we think of insects that are controlled by queens, it's a
little bit like the way you work. The queens give orders, sort of,
and then those orders are passed on and on so that eventually you
get a bunch of people working together to accomplish something.
Basically, you give orders, and the federal government does what
you tell it—"

"You do realize a large portion of the US military is in the middle of attempting a coup, right?" Steph said drily.

Melanie continued unfazed: "—the federal government does
what you tell it to do, but it's not a monolithic entity. You've got
hundreds of thousands of people, all more or less trying to accomplish what you've ordered but also sort of doing their own thing.

With the Hell Spiders, it's different. They aren't individuals. They're extensions of one another. I think, from the very beginning, we've had this all wrong. We've been acting like there are millions and millions of these spiders, tens of millions of them. But that's wrong. It isn't millions of spiders. It's a few spiders in millions of parts."

She spent a few minutes explaining what had happened in the lab at the NIH when Shotgun and Gordo demonstrated their spider-killing machine, the ST11. "And of course, while it didn't seem to harm them, we realized that what it did do, essentially, was to disrupt their communication. The Hell Spiders seem to need constant input. Think of it like Wi-Fi. You want to watch a television show and you've got a great signal, no problem. Even with a cruddy signal, it will still download and you've got your show. But no Wi-Fi? You've got nothing. Just a dumb blank box on the wall with a spinning wheel instead of your favorite comedy. With the ST11 going, it's like the spiders don't have any Wi-Fi. They're essentially harmless."

The president leaned forward and slid her tablet onto the coffee table. She tapped her finger on the tablet's glass. "So can we just, I don't know, amp up this machine and block the signal? Can we do that?"

Melanie shook her head. "Even if we could, that's really just a temporary solution. As soon as the ST11 is turned off, it's like flicking a light switch. They go from being harmless spiders to being the Hell Spiders again."

"I want to talk to this Shotgun fellow, because, to be honest, Melanie, I'll take a temporary solution right now." Steph's face was deadly serious, her voice grim. "Our best efforts have left at least a hundred million Americans dead and vast swaths of the country in ruins. If there's a stopgap solution . . ."

"No, no," Melanie said, her voice wildly excited. "That's the thing. We think we've got something better. Shotgun's not here. He's on his way to Atlantic City."

"Excuse me?"

"Sorry," Melanie said. "It's a little complicated. But that's why Amy and Fred are here." She gestured over to the woman and the man with the dog.

The dog had been almost completely motionless the entire time, curled up at the feet of the woman, but as if he knew that he was suddenly the center of attention, he started thumping his tail against the carpet.

Fred raised his hand. "Shotgun's my husband."

Manny looked at Melanie and then back to Fred and Amy. "Okay, I'll bite: Why the hell is your husband in Atlantic City?"

"Because he's figured out how to find the signal."

"Fred," Melanie said, "I've got this." She turned to Manny and Steph. "They retrofit the ST11 so that instead of blocking the communications signals, it can track them."

Manny blurted, "Wait. You're telling me that the Hell Spiders all get these commands that turn them into flesh-eating dynamos, and, using this machine, you can block the commands so that they're essentially harmless?"

"Yes."

"And now the fellows who invented this machine have figured out how to determine precisely where the commands are coming from?"

"Yes. We think so. I mean, that's why Gordo and Shotgun and a few Marines are going to Atlantic City. To make sure that this actually works. They were . . . I don't know. Somewhere in Virginia? Anyway, the closest signal was in Atlantic City." She glanced down at her watch, a sporty number with a yellow band. "They should be there within the hour."

"Okay," Manny said. "So, assuming they don't get eaten, they know about the hazmat suit thing?"

Melanie nodded.

"Okay. So, again assuming they don't get eaten, once they get to Atlantic City, what then?"

It had been a bit like watching an odd tennis match, Manny thought, the way the attention in the room bounced from Melanie to Steph to Melanie to Fred to Manny to Fred to Melanie and then back, and then a nice little rally back and forth between him and Melanie. Except, with this last question, Melanie clearly hadn't been expecting the ball to be hit back, because she looked flummoxed.

"That," Melanie said, "is a great question."

There was a buzz in the room as people started talking, and Melanie looked over at the other scientists and her two civilians.

Manny felt a slight pressure on his shoulder and realized that while he'd been asking Melanie questions, an aide had come into the room and was leaning over the back of the chesterfield and whispering into Steph's ear.

And, judging by the way her face went pale, it was not good.

Steph turned to him and whispered, "Operation SAFEGUARD is compromised."

"What? How? It should have taken Broussard at least another two days to work around—"

"There was a mutiny in the bunker."

Manny slumped over, resting his head on his hand. He took a deep breath and then sprang to his feet. "Okay. Shut it!"

It was like a balloon popping. The room had been full of noise and people talking, and suddenly it was deathly quiet. He pointed at Melanie. "How good is this?"

"How good?"

"How confident are you in what you've told us? How confident are you that we can disrupt the Hell Spiders by tracking down the signals, and how confident are you that we can track down the signals?"

Melanie glanced nervously at the other scientists. "Maybe eighty percent."

"That's not good enough," Steph said. "I know what you're thinking, Manny. But I need better than eighty percent."

Julie motioned upward with her thumb and Melanie upped her estimate. "Maybe eighty-five percent?"

"It's one hundred percent." The voice was loud and self-assured. The man who came with the dog. Frank? No, Fred. He had his arms crossed and looked fierce as he continued to talk: "My husband said it works, and if he says it works, it's one hundred percent."

Everybody turned to look back at Steph. She took a deep breath. "One hundred percent? You're telling me that I can trust your husband—"

"Ma'am," Fred said, cutting her off. That was not something one did to the president, and Manny heard somebody in the room gasp. "Don't take this the wrong way, because I voted for you and we gave a lot of money to your campaign, but you don't question Shotgun. If you ever tell him I said this, I'll deny it, but that man is brilliant. If he said it's going to work, it's going to work. He's . . ." Fred trailed off, seeming to suddenly realize that the way he was speaking to the president might not be completely appropriate.

Steph turned to Billy Cannon. "Billy, Operation SAFEGUARD is compromised."

Billy went white, which, given his reputation and the medals he'd won for bravery under fire, was more than terrifying.

"Ma'am, are you talking about Matthew 5:45? You've got to do it."

She turned to Manny. "Manny?"

"Do it."

Stephanie took a deep breath, held it in, and then closed her eyes while she exhaled. "God help us all if I'm wrong," she said. "Bring me the football."

The room exploded in noise, and Manny once again had to shout to bring order. "Not a peep out of any of you, or I'll have the room cleared."

The president's emergency satchel was always carried by a military aide with Yankee White security clearance. The aide on duty, a stout woman who was a Marine, was in front of Steph in less than ten seconds. Normally the aide would have taken Steph aside, but Steph pointed to the coffee table.

"Let's get this over with."

"Excuse me!" The voice was loud, insistent. Manny had a sinking feeling in his stomach, and even before he looked he knew it was Fred.

Manny stood up. "I warned you I'd have—"

"I am *not* talking to *you*." For one of the few times in his life, Manny found himself speechless. Fred was seemingly incapable of observing the decorum attendant to the president's station. He either completely missed the seriousness of the situation or simply didn't care. As he continued talking, Manny realized it was the latter. "Are you planning to launch more nukes? Because we have people out there that we love, and I am not going to let you sacrifice them. I'm telling you that if my husband—"

Steph held up her hand, and to Manny's surprise, Fred actually stopped talking. "I believe you."

"What?" Fred looked taken aback.

"I believe you. And because of that, no, I'm not ordering a launch. This is so ridiculously classified that there are fewer than twenty people in the United States government who know about it, but, heck, *he* found out about it somehow," she said, nodding toward Billy Cannon. "No. I'm about to shut it all down, and after I do this, we aren't going to be able to launch any nukes. So I hope your husband is as great as you say he is. Is that okay with you?"

"Yes. Thank you."

Steph tilted her head, curious. "You really didn't get that I was asking a rhetorical question? Good gracious. Never mind." She turned back to the task at hand.

Manny had grown used to the sight of the black leather bag that went everywhere the president did, but he never expected to see Steph have to actually use it. Apparently, neither had Steph.

"Second time in a week I've had to open this," she said, sliding the metal briefcase out of the leather jacket. Manny nodded, but he hadn't been in the room when she authorized the thirty-one strikes. That time, although they'd been scrambling, she did it properly, keeping the sanctity of the football intact. This time, he realized, it wasn't going to ever matter again.

Manny was a little surprised at how unimpressive the contents of the briefcase were. A bound black book that was maybe one hundred pages thick, a bound green book that was significantly thinner, a manila folder with maybe a dozen stapled pages inside, and a single large index card dense with type. And . . .

"Is that a BlackBerry? Do they even make those still?" Manny asked.

Billy Cannon had come across the room to stand beside Manny. "Modified. It's got an extended battery so that it can be on standby for sixty days without a charge. Honestly, the BlackBerry part is more of a shell than anything. The insides are all proprietary, but Matthew 5:45 didn't need to reinvent the wheel. It just needed to figure out how to smash it so it never rolled again."

Steph had picked up the BlackBerry and was now staring at them, annoyed. "First of all, Cannon, when all of this is done, you're going to tell me how the hell you found out about Matthew 5:45. Second of all, for the love of God, would you please be quiet?"

She didn't wait for an answer. She typed in an extended phrase, her thumbs moving quickly enough that even though Manny tried to figure out what she was spelling, he lost track. She stopped, her thumb hovering over the green send button.

The room was dead quiet, the loudest noise a panting from that ridiculous dog. Claymore was sitting, but like everybody else in the room he was also staring intently at Steph as if he, too, knew something serious was on the line. The thing that caught Manny's attention was that while everybody else seemed to be holding their breath, the dog was panting. It caught Steph's attention, too. For the first time she seemed to notice the chocolate Lab.

"Why is there a dog in here?"

Fred arched a single eyebrow. "He has a name, you know. It's Claymore. And, what, we were just supposed to leave him behind?"

The president stared at Fred for a beat, nodded as if that made perfect sense, and then pressed the button.

The Interstate 80 High Times Truck Stop and Family Fun Zone Restaurant and Gas Station Taco Bell Pizza Hut Starbucks KFC Burrito Barn 42 Flavors Ice Cream Extravaganza Coast-to-Coast Emporium, Nebraska

They knelt underneath the midwestern sun, bodies casting short shadows. The Prophet Bobby Higgs registered fidgeting from some of the pilgrims around him. His own flock, he knew, was without question, but he'd absorbed many men and women and children from the group that Macer had gathered. They had come to this oasis seeking not the glory of God but simple shelter from the wrath of those eight-legged devils that had come crawling up from the depths of hell.

Bobby recognized that maybe he had lost his mind somewhere along the way. It wasn't that long ago that he really was just a grifter. He'd been good at it, but he had never resorted to violence. It was unlike him to do what he had done to Macer, condemning

him to a terrifying death trapped in a barely lit, poorly ventilated
tractor-trailer with four people who were surely infested with
spiders.

And yet it was so clear to him that what he was doing was
right. The voice of God was truly speaking to him. He didn't
know exactly when, but there had come a point between Los
Angeles and here when he stopped *playing* the Prophet Bobby
Higgs and had *become* the Prophet Bobby Higgs. He was the
Lord's agent. And as he knelt there, the Nebraska sky enfolding
him, he thought that perhaps these questions were the Lord's
way of telling him that he should let Macer out of the back of
the truck and allow him to enjoy a quick and merciful death.
No man deserved to be devoured by these spiders, not even
Macer.

He got to his feet. Making sure to project, he called out in a
booming voice, "Rise!"

The sound of thousands of people standing up was awe-
inspiring. Not a word was spoken, but the hush and brush of
clothing and feet scuffling against grass and asphalt sounded
like lush curtains opening. Bobby raised his arms in the air and
turned to address all of his followers. "The Lord has spoken, and
he has decided I must show mercy."

He walked over to the tractor-trailer. The men standing guard
were his men now. "Open it," he said.

The guards hesitated.

"Open it," Bobby insisted.

One of the guards finally moved, hopping up onto the rear
gate and then lifting the bar that kept the doors sealed shut. As he
was doing so, Bobby realized he could hear someone pounding
on the doors from the inside, accompanied by a man's muffled
yelling.

It was too late for him to say anything, too late to realize that perhaps the Lord had not, in fact, been speaking to him.

As the door swung open, Macer stumbled out screaming, his face a mask of horror. A thick, swarming carpet of black spiders covered his legs and chest, and Bobby saw one dart into Macer's open mouth. Even as Macer was falling, Bobby saw past him into the deep interior of the truck. The four other people who'd been in there, the poor men and women bearing the mark of carriers, were all lying on the ground, writhing and bursting open like sausages left too long on the grill. Streams of spiders were pouring out of the gaping holes, an infernal tornado of skittering legs and bodies scrambling to their first meal outside their hosts' bodies.

The Prophet Bobby Higgs had just enough time to register that some of the spiders had red stripes across their backs before he felt something hideously burning on his neck and then pain lance through his body so sharply that he couldn't stop himself from screaming. Except he couldn't scream. He couldn't open his mouth. He couldn't do anything other than slowly topple backward. The last thing he saw before cobwebs clouded his vision was the blue beauty of a Nebraska sky.

Berlin, Germany

The air felt blistering over her newly naked body. The husk she'd just shed lay discarded in a side tunnel. She wasn't ready to travel yet, and she wanted to keep her little ones close. It would be a while before her body hardened. There had been heat and fire aboveground, a neat circle of death surrounding this city, but the sewers had not been blocked off. Not to her, not to the little ones.

She'd been disturbed by how many of her sisters had emerged into the light and then stopped talking. And yet each pulsing pinprick of light that came to her told her that for every sister who was gone, there were still two more who had finished molting, as she had. All she had to do now was rest, to let her new skeleton harden so that she and all of her sisters could emerge and take what was theirs.

Airspace above Buffalo, New York

There had been no question whom to side with. He'd flown the Chicago mission, and by the time he'd released the missile, the videos and pictures the military had been able to gather of the city as it was overrun by spiders were chilling. He knew the seriousness of what he was doing. He knew what it meant to those who were still alive—knew that nothing would survive in the molten heat that came with what he was about to unleash—but he also knew that it was unquestionably the right decision.

Just as he knew now that the orders he'd been given were essential. They had to finish the job.

The missile detached cleanly, and he made distance, pushing the plane to its limits.

But as the time came and went, there was no sign that anything had happened.

USS *Elsie Downs*, Atlantic Ocean

"It's like we're dropping rocks. I don't understand it." General Roberts slammed his hand on the table. "Operation SAFEGUARD is online and in our pocket, but the nukes won't go. They're useless."

Broussard stared up at the ceiling. What the hell had the president done?

Central Park, New York, New York

"**L**et's go! Go, go, go!"

Melanie picked up her pace, Julie right beside her, but she had to admit that having Billy Cannon yell at her wasn't actually as motivating as one would have thought. She was already nervous enough that it was all she could do not to barf as she ran from the police car to the helicopter.

The crazy thing was that Cannon had actually volunteered to go. He seemed excited about it. Melanie and Julie *had* to go. They needed to have the scientists on-site to confirm everything. Melanie was going to Atlantic City because Steph wanted Melanie to see with her own eyes, and Julie was enlisted because it made sense to have scientific backup, but Cannon *wanted* to go.

They were keeping the party lean and mean, with a dozen men to accompany Melanie and Julie. Well, a dozen plus Cannon. She thought they were Army Rangers or maybe Navy SEALs, but, honestly, it had happened so quickly that she wasn't actually sure which branch of the armed forces her personal guard was from. All she knew was that half of them were carrying wicked-looking machine guns and the other half were carrying homemade flamethrowers. They'd gotten moving so fast that there was only time for Fred to proudly point out that the flamethrowers the men were carrying were based on a design that Shotgun and Gordo had come up with.

God. Fred. That man. She swore that if she didn't die, she was going to either kill him or make sure he got a medal.

One of the uniforms hauled Julie up into the helicopter and then reached down to help Melanie. She'd barely gotten into her seat when the bird leapt into the sky. It was already moving forward before it was even ten feet off the ground, and she bet the pilot was pushing the limits of what was safe in terms of how quickly he rotated the engines so the Osprey would be flying like a plane instead of a helicopter.

Cannon handed her a headset, and when she put it on, she heard his voice. "She can do a bit more than three hundred miles an hour at top speed, so we've got twenty minutes to gear up. If this guy of yours is right about there being Hell Spiders in Atlantic City, I sure hope *you're* right about the efficacy of the hazmat suits. If I'm going to die, I really don't want it to be in one of these ridiculous outfits." He handed her one of the hazmat duffels.

"You make sure your men don't act unless I tell them to, okay?"

"You don't have to yell, Melanie." Cannon tapped his microphone. "I can hear you."

"Sorry. Just make sure they don't go shooting at the spiders or firing up those flamethrowers on their own."

Cannon grabbed a duffel bag for himself. "Don't worry. Trust me when I tell you these guys are some of the most well-trained men in the world. If I ordered them to stop breathing, they would. They're here to watch our backs."

She nodded and started getting the hazmat suit on. Nobody else, including Julie, seemed bothered by the movement of the

Osprey, and one of the men helped Melanie with the finishing touches. As Melanie sealed up her helmet, the outskirts of Atlantic City were in sight. She pulled the satellite phone that Amy had given her out of the pocket of her jacket and awkwardly, because of her gloved hands, checked for a new text.

Here. Entrance to Pleasure Paradise Casino.

She relayed the location to the pilot, and after checking to make sure that everybody was suited up, Cannon ordered the pilot to take them down. He came in hard and fast over a couple of buildings before dropping down in an empty section of a parking lot. The Osprey gave a light bounce, enough for Melanie to have to grab onto her chair, and then settled. Six of the men went out first—three with guns, three with flamethrowers—and then Cannon helped Melanie and Julie out. The rest of the men followed. As soon as they were clear, the Osprey sprang back into the sky. No sense risking a stray spider getting onto the helicopter.

It was eerie how devoid of life the landscape around her seemed. The streets were completely empty, and though the parking lot was maybe a quarter full, with all the cars clustered near the entrance to the casino, there wasn't a sign of anybody other than Melanie and her entourage.

"They're waiting inside," she said. Her voice sounded muffled to her, but Cannon's response, a crisp "Roger," sounded good through the earpiece she was wearing.

They were maybe twenty feet from the entrance when the man on point held up his hand in a fist. With his orange hazmat suit, it looked almost comical. Almost. Because Melanie immediately saw why he'd stopped. There were twenty or thirty Hell Spiders skittering up and around the canopy that covered the entrance.

Melanie took a deep breath. "I'll go." Julie started to come with her, but Melanie held up her hand. It was okay. She'd go by herself. Only one of them needed to test the efficacy of the hazmat suits.

She stepped forward. This must be what it felt like to walk on the moon, she thought. The boots were too big for her, but the jumpsuit part fit fine. If she'd been a smaller woman, she probably would have been swimming in it. She was already warm and sweating, and when she stepped into the shade cast by the canopy, it was a bit of relief. Or it would have been if she hadn't been so conscious of the Hell Spiders moving along the metal framework above her.

She felt the hot thud of something substantial hit her shoulder, and she froze. She was too scared to move her head, but out of the corner of her eye she could see the staccato movement of the spider's legs. The weight shifted slowly from her shoulder toward her neck, spider legs pressing the material of the hazmat suit against her flesh. And then the ping of a leg tapping the glass of her face mask. The spider scuttled fully onto her face mask now; it was so big that she could see the world around her only in fragments.

"Steady now." Cannon's voice was calm. "Steady. There's just the one. The rest of them are ignoring you."

Melanie closed her eyes. She counted to ten, trying to control her breathing, and not for the first time wished she practiced yoga and meditation and all that hippie kind of stuff.

By the time she'd counted to seven, the weight of the spider had moved from her mask down to her chest. She opened her eyes to it flitting down her leg, over her boot, and across the ground toward the bushes that flanked the entrance.

"Okay," she said, but her voice cracked, and she had to say it again. "Okay. I think we're good with the suits."

"You'd engender more confidence if you didn't use the phrase 'I think,' Melanie," Julie said.

"Ha ha."

The rest of the group came toward her. She was impressed with how smoothly the men seemed to move even with the hazmat suits on. Once everybody was by the entrance, one of the men opened the door, and they went inside the building.

Pleasure Paradise Casino, Atlantic City, New Jersey

They'd been waiting for only five minutes, but it felt longer to Kim. First of all, the hazmat suits were uncomfortable. Second, trying to talk was exhausting. Everything came out muffled, and if you weren't right next to somebody, it was pretty much impossible to understand what the person was saying. And third, and really the only thing that mattered: the lobby of the Pleasure Paradise Casino was positively dripping with goddamned spiders.

She was sure that, without the spiders and the dozens and dozens of bodies that were wrapped in cobwebs, the entranceway would have been a lot of people's idea of classy. There were, like, an acre of marble, fluted columns, mirrors on the walls, and a round fountain with a stream of water flowing out of the tip of a cupid's arrow, and it seemed like anything that could possibly have been gold plated had been gold plated. To her taste, however, it seemed kind of chintzy and vulgar. Although, to be fair, her parents had always been of the "If you've got money, you don't need to prove it" school of thought.

Teddie seemed perfectly at ease, however. She was walking around with her stupid camera, filming everything. She'd even fitted everyone with microphones before they'd donned their hazmat suits. Unfortunately, the mics were connected only to the camera, so it didn't help them communicate. Kim watched Teddie bring the lens of the camera ridiculously close to a spider that was chilling out on one of the pillars. It was one of the ones with red stripes across their backs. Kim didn't know what the difference was between the ones with the red stripe and the ones that were completely black, but she figured if they didn't all die, Teddie would have a heck of a documentary.

Shotgun and Gordo were huddled over the ST11, looking at the laptop screen and occasionally touching their helmets together to talk. She could hear the dull murmurs of their voices but couldn't make out any words. Next to her, sitting on a plush red leather chair, Honky Joe tapped out a beat on the butt of his rifle. Elroy, Private Duran Edwards, and Mitts were standing a little closer in, near the edge of the casino floor. They'd already shown her that, in the first row of slot machines, there were at least two cocooned bodies. Two people who, even with this alien invasion, couldn't tear themselves away from the machines.

That was the whole crew. She'd thought about recruiting Sue and her fire team, but in the end she couldn't risk it. She loved Sue but she knew, deep in her heart, that Sue wasn't the kind of girl who would disobey Rodriguez's orders. Kim also knew that the bigger the group—the more people she tried to bring in—the greater the risk would be: not only was there a greater chance of somebody running to Rodriguez but it would also be harder to casually slip away. She finally decided to just stick with her fire team, but Honky Joe had sussed things out and invited himself along. Of course, Honky Joe, being Honky Joe, had more than pulled his own weight; he was the one who'd known that the Salem Nuclear Power Plant was more or less along the way and that it would be a logical place to score hazmat suits.

She walked over to where Gordo was working with Shotgun and was about to ask if he'd gotten any new texts, when a whole passel of people came breezing through the entrance. They looked as alien as Kim and her crew did, decked out head to toe in rubber and glass, carrying either M4s or . . .

"Hey! They made them!" Even muffled by his face shield, Gordo's voice sounded bright and excited. He whacked Shotgun on the arm. "They made the flamethrowers!"

The hazmat suits blurred the details of the people entering so that aside from the weapons they carried, they all looked alike. The giveaway was that two of them were unarmed. Those two had to be Dr. Guyer and Dr. Yoo. Kim started to talk, but one of the new guys stepped in and presented a rucksack. He pulled out headsets. They were bulky, like what you'd see a coach wearing on the sidelines at an NFL game, with a heavy padded earphone on one side and a boom mic. Both Gordo and Shotgun slipped on a pair, and then Kim made sure that Mitts, Duran, Elroy, and Honky Joe were similarly equipped before she took a headset for herself. The hood of the hazmat suit was a heavy rubberized material, but as soon as she had the earpiece in place, she could hear fine.

"—like playing hot and cold. We're in the right place, but we're going to have to basically go room to room. Even without the ST11, it's probably going to be obvious, though. The closer we get, the more concentrated the spiders seem to be." Shotgun picked up the ST11 and handed Gordo the connected laptop to carry.

One of the unarmed figures grabbed Shotgun's elbow. "You have no idea how much is riding on this."

"I think I've got a pretty good idea," Shotgun said. He pointed at Kim. "Okay. Just like we talked about. You guys are going to be our eyes and ears while Gordo and I deal with the ST11."

"We're good," Kim said. "Whenever you're ready."

One of the men who'd just come in held up his hand. "Hold up. I'm running this show."

Typical, Kim thought. Guy walks in and thinks that because he's got a pair of balls he's in charge. She walked toward him, careful to keep her rifle pointed at the ground. "Who the hell do you think you are to just come waltzing in and—" She stopped. She'd gotten close enough to see his face. "Holy crap. You're Billy Cannon."

Shotgun had walked over with her. He shrugged and looked at Kim. "Whatever. I trust *you*."

"Uh, Shotgun, I appreciate that, but Billy Cannon is the secretary of defense."

Shotgun stuck out his hand reflexively and Cannon shook it. Shotgun held on. "Pleased to meet you," he said. "Now *I'm* in charge, and Kim and her crew are going to take point."

There was an awkward static silence over her headset that was polluted by the sound of the games in the casino beeping and whirling. Kim glanced up and watched a line of seven or eight spiders with red stripes on their backs traveling across the ceiling. After a second Cannon nodded. "Fine," he said. He looked at Kim. "What's the drill?"

"Right. Okay. My fire team will take point, we'll keep . . . Sorry. Who are the rest of you guys?"

They spent a moment on introductions. She'd been right that the two unarmed figures were the scientists Dr. Guyer and Dr. Yoo—Melanie and Julie—and she decided to corral all five civilians in the middle, between her fire team and the group of Rangers led by Cannon. The plan was to let Gordo and Shotgun focus on the ST11 while Kim worried about moving them safely through the casino and hotel. It meant that Melanie and Julie could concentrate on . . . well, Kim thought, science kind of stuff. She figured Teddie would have her camera going the whole time. That was fine. As long as the civilians stayed between her team and the Rangers, they'd be out of the line of fire.

They started moving, heading out onto the casino floor. It was a carnival of nightmares. Neon lights and flashing LED displays washing color across the glass of Kim's faceplate. There were dozens and dozens of bodies wrapped in webs. Here and there, gossamer strands of silk floated and rippled in the air currents from the HVAC system. The gaming tables still had chips out, and there was a pile of bills on one of them, at least a thousand dollars in twenties spilled across the green felt. And through all of it there were spiders. Black spiders and the ones with the red stripes, skittering and dancing, moving in patterns that made sense only to them. They seemed uninterested in Kim and her party, but she stayed alert.

"Crap!"

Kim froze. She didn't recognize the voice.

"Sorry. It's Jones. I stepped on one. Squished it."

"Okay." It was a woman's voice. Melanie. "Hold up a second. Let's see if they react. Everybody just stay still. Hey, Julie, you seeing that over there? Have they started ecdysis already?"

Kim stood her ground, looking around the room. She wasn't sure whether she imagined it or it was real, but it seemed like, for the first thirty seconds after Jones stepped on the spider, the others in the casino grew frantic, moving more quickly, crawling across the casino games and the carpet and the ceilings and the walls in whirling circles. Like they were searching for something, she thought. After maybe sixty seconds, Melanie gave them the go-ahead.

"Try to shuffle step," Kim said. "I know they're everywhere, but let's do our best not to rile them up."

Gordo gave directions as they walked. They passed through the casino into the hotel lobby, and Gordo asked for a few seconds so that he and Shotgun could fine-tune the ST11. "The closer we get, the more data we have," he said. "Should be able to . . . Okay. Upstairs. Somewhere in the hotel."

Kim reflexively went to the elevators and then realized that might be a bad idea. Being stuck on an elevator in a hazmat suit with spiders crawling around? Because, what, she wanted her nightmares to be even worse?

In the stairwell the sound of nearly twenty people slapping their boots on concrete was a hollow echo inside her suit. They climbed four flights and she waited until Shotgun indicated they should keep climbing. She paused again on the seventh floor and the tenth, and each time Shotgun motioned upward. Finally, at the twelfth floor, they reached the top. She opened the door and had to bite down on a scream. There'd been quite a few spiders in the stairwell, but on the twelfth floor it was something else. The walls and ceiling and floor were a moving quilt of spiders. There were enough of them that the lighting was obscured in fits and starts, giving an almost strobe-like quality to the scene. She stepped out into the hallway. "Watch your step," she said, and then motioned to Honky Joe and Mitts to secure the right side. She went left herself with Elroy and Duran.

Gordo let out a whistle. "Holy crap. I think we're in the right spot."

"The ST11 is telling us . . ." Shotgun touched the screen with his gloved finger. "Left. Twenty meters. Must be near the end of the hall. Julie, Melanie? What do you want to do?"

"If you know this is where the signal's coming from— Sorry, this is Cannon speaking. If you know this is where the signal's

coming from, let's just get out, wire up the building with explosives, and take care of it that way."

Kim had her rifle up, in firing position. She knew it was ridiculous. She couldn't blast her way through these spiders. There had
to be a thousand of them in the hallway. Still, she thumbed her
rifle to full automatic fire.

Dr. Guyer's voice came through her headset. "We need to see.
We need to make sure."

Cannon's voice sounded absurdly like he was enjoying himself.
"I figured you'd say that, but thought it was worth a try."

"Okay," Gordo said. "Down the hall. Kim? You ready?"

Of course, Kim thought. Of course down the hall. She moved
forward in a shuffle step, trying to brush the spiders on the carpet out of the way instead of stomping on them, afraid of what
she might unleash if she just started squishing their bodies under
her boots. Through the hazmat suit she could feel spiders moving over her legs and arms and crawling across her back. One of
them moved quickly across her face mask and she almost startled
enough to squeeze the trigger.

As she approached the end of the hallway, the already thick and
frantic concentration of spiders seemed to get denser and denser,
until she couldn't see any carpet through their writhing mass. She
heard somebody swearing over the radio, a voice she didn't recognize.

She was shoulder to shoulder with Duran. A trickle of sweat
tickled down the back of her neck and she couldn't stop herself
from swatting at it. It was too easy to believe that maybe there was
an open seam in her suit and that spiders were silently working
their way inside.

"Through the door," Gordo said over the headsets. "Straight
ahead."

Straight ahead was the Presidential Suite. The door was ajar, but it was so densely covered with spiders that it was a swirling vortex. The light in the hallway was dim and wavering, and she wished to god that she had a flashlight on the barrel of her rifle. She tried to get a better look at the spiders concentrated in the doorway without actually moving nearer. "Dr. Guyer," she called out. "Melanie? Can you and Julie take a look at this, please?"

She listened to the sound of her own breathing as she waited for the two scientists. Once Julie and Melanie were beside her, Kim watched them lean in close.

"They're in the process of molting," Julie said. "Trying to shed their exoskeletons. That's why they look—"

"There!" Kim pointed. "That one. Did you see that? It's got a silver slash across its back instead of a red stripe."

There was only one of them, or maybe there were two, it was hard to tell. The mass of spiders, hundreds of them, maybe thousands, swirling and pulsing around the doorway, was moving constantly. Kim saw a flash of silvery gray that disappeared and then reappeared a moment later elsewhere in the pile. Both Melanie and Julie saw it, too.

"Those are new," Melanie said.

"Great. Because I'm sure they're friendly, unlike the other spiders." Kim shut up when she saw the look Dr. Guyer gave her through the glass of her faceplate.

"They're not going to be a threat," Melanie said. "Not with the hazmat suits on. We need to keep going. We need to see."

"Okay. Fine," Kim said. "Into the room?"

Gordo's voice was warm and steady. "Straight ahead, Kim. The signal's coming from in there."

Kim realized she was holding her breath as she reached out with the barrel of her rifle to push the door open wider. The room

had to have more light, because there was a halo in the opening, and she stepped through, hopeful that whatever those new
silver-slashed spiders were, they hadn't evolved to recognize a
meal through a hazmat suit.

It was better inside the room. Still gloomy, but compared to the
narrow hallway, the spaciousness of the Presidential Suite lessened
the feeling of claustrophobia. The main room was large and square,
thirty feet by thirty feet, and two of the walls were almost completely
glass. Spiders crawled over the windows in a moving horror show
that the afternoon sun turned into a speckled and demented series
of shadows. There were thousands of both the black and the red-
striped spiders in the room, maybe tens of thousands, and here and
there Kim thought she caught glimpses of the spiders with the silver slashes across their backs, maybe one out of every hundred. She
scanned the room quickly, looking for what, she didn't—

"Holy mother of . . ." Kim snapped her mouth shut. In the
back corner, near an open door that must have led to the bedrooms, she saw the great glistening body of the giant spider twitch
and shiver. There were twenty or thirty of the spiders with silver
slashes crawling over the beast's body, and it made her think of
piglets trying to feed. She heard the sound of someone vomiting,
and despite how scared she was, she was able to feel a moment of
pity for the poor soul who'd been sick inside his hazmat suit. She
slid sideways, careful not to trip as she moved all the way into the
room. She stopped when she was right next to the window. Not
once did she take her eyes or the barrel of her rifle off the giant
spider in the corner. It was huge. A beast. Each leg was twice the
size of one of hers, and the body . . . She would have bet the thing
weighed two hundred pounds, dwarfing the silver-slashed spiders
dancing across its body. It's back was turned to the room, and all
Kim could think of was that she didn't want it to turn around,

didn't want its many eyes staring at her. As if being subjected to the spider's gaze would mean a sure and instant death.

She felt a heavy bump against her side, but it was only Gordo. "Sorry," he said. He looked back at the screen of the laptop and then angled it so Melanie and Julie could see it.

"Holy crap." Dr. Guyer looked at the screen and then at the monster. "The signal's coming from right there? It's really coming from one of the queens? She's controlling all these spiders!"

Kim wanted to look away from the spider, but she was afraid to. A queen. That's what Dr. Guyer had called it. There was a hulking, shiny pile right next to the queen that looked menacing—an imitation of the shape of a spider—and Kim realized it was the thing's shell. It had shed its skin. What had Julie said? That the spiders were molting? Was that why it seemed so feeble right now? The queen was shivering and shaking, like it was getting ready to . . . Oh, god. It was turning around.

"Uh, guys," Kim said. "I think it knows we're here."

On cue, the smaller spiders started frantically closing in on them. It was such a rapid wave of movement that Kim could hear them. It sounded like a rake scraping pavement, like nails on a chalkboard. It sounded like death.

Hundreds of spiders crashed into her, enough weight that she staggered backward. She saw one of the men who'd come with Cannon try to move backward and trip in his ungainly hazmat suit. He fell hard, crashing through the surface of a glass coffee table, and even before he'd hit the ground, Kim could see spiders rushing through the gash the broken glass had rent in his hazmat suit. The man was screaming, and then Kim heard a whoosh and saw a great blooming burst of fire come out of the nozzle of his flamethrower. As her face mask went dark, she heard the added percussion of gunfire as the men around her pulled their triggers.

So far, the hazmat suit was keeping them away from her, but she had no idea how long that would last. She was completely covered. She could feel the weight of spiders on her back, on her arms, on her legs, could feel their heaviness on the hood of the hazmat suit and as they banged across the glass shield of the face mask. They couldn't seem to get through, but the pinpricks of thousands of spider legs frantically galloping over her body made her feel as though she were in the middle of an ice storm. The weight grew and grew. She could feel her arm muscles start to burn with the effort of keeping her rifle steady. She didn't care how many of those sons-of-bitches crawled on her—she wasn't moving that rifle. Her aim was true, and she knew it.

She pulled the trigger and held it down.

The rifle bucked in her hands, the sewing-machine thump against her shoulder familiar from so many hours on the range.

The only things louder than the gunshots were the searing shrieks that came from the spiders. It was like ten thousand whistles, ten thousand diamonds breaking, and ten thousand drills boring into her skull. She felt her rifle run dry, and she let go so that she could clap her hands over her ears. As she did so, she was unable to stop herself from screaming in an attempt to drown out the sound.

At some point she realized she'd stopped screaming, that the whistling shrieks that had felt like they were tearing out her eardrums had stopped as well. Spiders were no longer weighing her down. Her eyes were scrunched tight, though she didn't remember closing them. Slowly she squinted, letting in the bright sunlight that streamed through the windows. Then she let her eyes open fully.

The queen was shredded meat, her great, bulbous body leaking viscous goo out over the floor. One of her legs twitched oddly, keeping some syncopated rhythm that made Kim feel almost dizzy. She let her hands drop from her ears and turned to look around the room.

There were thousands of spiders littering the floor. They were ankle-deep in most places, knee-deep in some, with odd scattered spots along the carpet that were bare. One of the men took a step and his leg kicked up a movement of spiders. He spun, pointing his rifle down and firing a three-bullet burst.

"Hold fire!" Cannon's voice brooked no dissent. Kim was more than happy for him to take over now.

"Oh my god. The queen. Who shot the queen?" Dr. Guyer turned first one way and then the other.

Kim realized she was shivering. No. Not shivering. She wasn't cold. She was shaking. "I . . ." She tried again. "I did. I'm sorry. It was instinct. The normal spiders didn't seem to care, but it was like she knew we were here. I'm sorry."

"No. No, no, no," Dr. Guyer said, spitting out the words rapidly. "It's brilliant! Don't you see? Look around. Look at this!" She kicked at a mound of spiders on the ground and then took a step and kicked at another pile. It was like watching a child skipping through autumn leaves. "It's like they were just unplugged or something! It's the queen! The queen was the signal. Kill the queen, you kill them all!"

Kim looked around the room again. There was no movement from any of the spiders. She didn't know how to tell if a spider was dead but . . . "Oh, hell. Okay." She reached up and pulled off her mask.

"Kim! What are you doing?" Elroy was right next to her and he grabbed her mask and started to put it back on.

"Stop," she said. She said it calmly. She felt strangely calm all of a sudden.

Elroy hesitated, but then he stepped back and watched as Kim clumsily peeled off one glove and then the other. She waited, but there was no reaction, nothing from the spiders at all, and after a few seconds she started laughing.

And then she stopped. There were three bodies on the ground. The poor guy she'd seen fall through the glass coffee table, his suit sliced to ribbons and spiders flocking to him. He was on his back, but his face mask was a gory blur of red and other things that she didn't want to think about. Over by the room's bar, another body, another one of the men who'd come in with Cannon. There was a red starburst on his chest. Friendly fire, she thought.

But just a few feet from the coffee table. Another body.

Teddie.

She was neatly draped facedown over the arm of the couch, like a coat somebody had put down for a moment. Her camera was still in her hand, but there was a great jagged rip in the leg of her hazmat suit. A shard of glass from the coffee table. Maybe a lamp or something else broken from errant fire. Kim didn't know and she didn't care. She could see the ragged meat of Teddie's leg stripped back to the bone, could see blood pooled in her glass face mask, could see that she was utterly and completely still. And then she looked away. She didn't want to have to look at Teddie's body, didn't want to have to see the way the spiders had savaged her.

She realized that Shotgun was standing next to her, that he was seeing it, too. He reached out and put his arms around her, and Kim let herself collapse into him.

She cried for only a minute, but it left her exhausted. All she wanted to do was sit down somewhere and have a beer.

Cannon's voice pierced her numbness. "Okay. Lance Corporal, I admire your courage in taking off your hazmat gear, but everybody else stay suited up. And I want two and two on each body. Julie? Dr. Yoo? You okay?"

"Yeah," Julie said. "I mean no, not really. I don't think I'll ever be okay after that, but I'm fine. Just twisted my ankle a bit. But I'm good."

"Okay," Cannon said. "Rangers, Marines, two and two. Grab a body. We'll bring them down and leave them in the parking lot for now. Let's get moving. We need to tell the president what we know."

The military men started moving to obey Cannon's order, but Kim noticed that Gordo was staring at the screen of the laptop and looking like he might be sick. She reached out and tapped his wrist. "You okay?"

"No. No, not really. Hey, Melanie."

Melanie didn't answer. She'd sorted through the piles of dead spiders and shoved two of the ones with silver slashes on their backs into a heavy, clear plastic bag. Now she was over by the queen, poking at the monster's bullet-riddled body, seemingly unbothered by the goo and viscera. Julie was limping over, interested.

"Melanie!" Gordo yelled. She looked up this time. "Melanie," he said. "You left Amy with the president?"

"Yeah. She's fine. They're fine. They've got, like, a temporary White House going."

"In New York City?" Gordo asked.

"You bet. Why?"

He held up the laptop. His hands were shaking. "The next closest signal we've got. It's coming from New York."

Moores Airport,
Degrasse, New York

The airport was barely more than a grass field and a small hangar, but it had fuel. Mike did the grunt work under Rex's direction while Leshaun took Annie, Dawson, Fanny, and Carla over to the outhouses behind the hangar. Mike figured he was being paranoid, but he felt more comfortable knowing they had an armed escort.

So far the trip had been easy—easy but wildly uncomfortable, because even though Rex's Skywagon supposedly seated six, they had six plus Annie, as well as survival gear. Rex kept the plane low. Much lower, he said, than he would have if they were flying under normal conditions, but he was worried that the president's no-fly order might still be under enforcement.

"If it's all the same to you, I'd prefer not to be shot out of the sky. Don't want to be eaten by spiders, don't want to go down in a giant ball of fire."

He'd been eating a bag of chips while he said it—which made Mike a little nervous, thinking that it would be good for Rex to keep two hands on the yoke—and he heard Carla mutter something that sounded suspiciously like "But you're not afraid of a heart attack."

The truth was that Rex seemed like a pretty good pilot. Not that Mike really knew what made a good pilot or a bad pilot, but Rex was both methodical and steady. They weren't exactly rushing, but they'd overnighted at their first stop, somewhere in the hinterlands of Michigan, and Mike didn't want to linger. For all that, Rex was no spring chicken.

"You sure you're good?" Mike asked. He had a hand on the fuel hose, although Rex had said it would be a few more minutes at least before Mike needed to do anything.

"Don't look at me like that," Rex said, taking off his ball cap and whacking Mike in the chest with it. "Just because I've got all this gray in my beard doesn't mean I can't hold my own. One more hop, then we'll be as close to off the grid as we can get. Next to being in space, an island off the coast of Maine seems our best bet."

"And it's near Portland?"

"Portland? No. Why on earth would you say that?"

Mike shrugged. "You said it was just off the coast of Maine."

"Maine's a big place, son. No. Up the coast. Kissing the border between Canada and the United States."

Rex shut off the gas and they went through the whole process of cleaning up and readying the plane. By the time they were done, Leshaun was back with the group. Mike had been partners with Leshaun long enough to catch his look.

"What?"

"Natives might be getting restless," he said. "Saw a couple of pickup trucks on the road there, and I think they noticed us going in and out of the outhouses. Might not be the worst idea to get moving."

"Okay. You guys load up. Just let me take a pee."

Rex clapped Leshaun on the shoulder. "Don't forget about me. I've got an old man's bladder."

Mike pursed his lips. "You just got mad at me for insinuating that . . ." He trailed off. In the distance he saw two pickup trucks cruising on the main road toward the turnoff for the airport. "Hey," he called out over his shoulder to the others. "Get in the plane. Rex, if you've got to take a piss, I think you're going to have to do it right here and now."

"Great," Rex said with a harrumph. "Because I need that kind of pressure. Carla!" he yelled. "Fire up the engine for me."

The trucks were only a hundred yards from the hangar by the time Rex was in the pilot's seat and wheeling the plane around. "I'm skipping a few things on the checklist," he called out, "so cross your fingers."

The turf runway was a little bumpy for Mike's taste, but they were in the air before the trucks reached them. He looked out the window, watching the trucks turn around and leave, and then he glanced back at where his daughter and the rest of the group were sitting.

"No harm, no foul," Rex said.

Both he and Mike were quiet for the next ten minutes, and then Mike responded. "Do you think there's any chance that was just an innocent drive-by?"

"Doubt it."

"What the heck is wrong with people?" Mike said.

"Fear. People are afraid."

Mike nodded. He looked out the windows again. They were on the outskirts of the Adirondacks. He wished they were flying higher so he could get a better sense of the land. Down low, all he could see were carpets of trees broken by the occasional glimpse of a lake. He had the sense that it might remind him of northern

Minnesota from a greater height. It made him sad to think that he'd never be back there. His marriage had fallen apart in Minnesota, but he'd also had good years there, and Annie had no memories of ever living anywhere else. He wasn't going to let it get to him. No point looking back. They were some of the lucky ones. He knew that.

"Can't wait to get to this island of yours."

"It's supposed to be beautiful."

"Wait—you've never been there?"

"Nope," Rex said. "We used to fly down to Corpus Christi a couple of times a year to see Carla's parents, but they both passed, and with the cottage on Soot Lake, I wasn't real interested in going anywhere else. Oh, we went to Chicago sometimes, and to New York, and we took our honeymoon in Hawaii, but can't say that I've ever made it to Maine."

"But you're sure we'll be safe there?" He reached out and tapped at one of the dials with a jiggling needle. "What's this?"

Rex glanced down at his instruments and reached out and gave Mike's hand a hard slap. "Keep your hands off that. You're no copilot, buddy." His smile quickly turned serious. "Do you think anybody can really promise anywhere is safe right now? We'll be welcomed. I can tell you that. An old buddy of mine from Vietnam is there. He's good people. He can trace his family line back two or three hundred years on that island. From what he's always said, it's the sort of place where you were either born and bred or you're from away, so I suspect they mostly closed up shop once this hit."

"So why are we—"

"Like I said, he's an old buddy from Vietnam. He owes me one."

White House Manhattan,
New York, New York

"All I'm saying is that I'm married to him," Fred said, "so if he's the hero in all of this, I don't think it's too much to ask that I get some recognition."

Amy took a sip of her beer. Normally she would have been nervous about drinking a beer while walking down the middle of the street in New York City in the afternoon. She wasn't much of a rule breaker. These weren't normal times, however. She was pretty sure the cops had better things to do than write tickets for drinking in public.

Claymore gave a tug at his leash and then led her over to a lamppost. "Okay, buddy. Sure. You haven't peed on that one yet. Seriously, Fred, I swear, he might be the happiest dog in the world."

"To be fair to Claymore, this is all pretty exciting. Lots of new things to smell, lots of people petting him and telling him he's a good dog, and he's had more people food in the last few weeks than— Oh god!"

Amy grimaced as she watched the dog squatting again. "That's why we don't normally let him eat people food." She sighed. "Anyway, I'm sure you're right. Plus he doesn't know he's supposed to be scared. To him, this is all just one great big adventure. I'm sure he misses . . . Fred? Do you think those men are yelling for us?"

They both looked back down the block toward the town house that was functioning as the current White House. Neither she nor Fred had any real standing. They were tolerated only because of their connections to Gordo and Shotgun and that little machine they had made, and it was all a little unsettling. But it also meant there should have been no reason that anybody was looking for them. Except that, it seemed rather clear now, the small group of men in suits running down the steps of the town house and yelling and waving were, in fact, trying to get their attention.

"Well, aren't we popular!" Fred said. He couldn't keep the delight out of his voice. "What do you suppose all that's about?"

Amy gave Claymore's leash a little tug and looked guiltily at the mess the dog had made. She'd come back and clean it up after she found out what the men wanted.

"Inside! Get inside!" the man was screaming, and he was almost even with Amy and Fred by the time they'd worked out what he was saying. He stuttered to a stop and grabbed Amy's arm. "Come on! Run!"

He started to pull her, but she was already running. She spared a look for Fred. Despite all his silliness, he'd been a reasonably decent athlete in high school and had played soccer for two years at Pomona College before deciding he'd had enough. Pomona was a DIII school, but still, even after twenty years, Fred could book it; he was three steps ahead of her before she'd even run ten steps. Claymore, of course, thought all of it was a hoot, and he ran, ears flopping, tail wagging, the whole way.

The Secret Service agents outside the building had their guns drawn and were yelling, and the military men and women were carefully swiveling back and forth with their rifles as Amy ran up the steps behind Fred. As she passed through the door to the town house, one of the men stationed there grabbed her biceps and kept her moving.

"Clear the area! Clear the area!" he shouted, as if Amy was supposed to have any idea what he was talking about.

"Move! Move!" said a woman in a dark suit who stood at the door, waving the agents and troops inside the building.

Somebody, a civilian, pushed rudely past Amy. She didn't fall, but she did have to grab onto a table in the grand entrance. Claymore was wagging his tail and was up on his hind legs, his front legs against the chest of a man wearing body armor and digitalized camouflage. He was carrying a nasty-looking machine gun that looked as if it had been compressed to two-thirds the normal size, but he was very calm and polite as he looked at Amy. "Ma'am, would you mind please getting your dog off me so that I'm free to take action as needed?"

Amy grabbed Claymore's collar, hauling him back down on to all fours. She looked at Fred. "What was that?"

The woman at the door waved the last man in and then hauled the door shut. "Lock it down! Lock it down!"

The men and women in suits and uniforms who had crowded into the entranceway took off, streaming in different directions like so many eager worker bees. It was all a bit overwhelming. Amy realized that despite everything that had just happened, she was still holding her beer. She took a sip. It was very foamy.

Fred held out his hand and obediently she handed him the bottle.

"I have no clue," he said. "But this isn't the most reassuring thing that's ever happened to me."

Approaching Manhattan, New York, New York

The Osprey was positively screaming. Gordo had no clue what the top speed of the aircraft was supposed to be, but it was clear that the pilot was pushing it. He looked at the laptop again. The information they'd been able to gather in Atlantic City meant that he and Shotgun could dial in the reading to a radius of a couple of blocks while they were outside the city. Accuracy would improve as they got closer . . . Okay. There it was. He had it nailed down to a circle of about one hundred yards.

"Where are they—" He stopped, frustrated, and then put the headset back on. He yanked at Melanie's sleeve. "Where are they set up? Where's the temporary White House?"

She had the plastic bag on her lap and had taken one of the silver-slashed spiders out and was staring at it. With her hazmat gear still on, it was clear that she was having trouble manipulating the spider the way she wanted to, but after finishing a lightning debrief with the president, she'd been consumed with staring at it.

"Upper East Side. About a block off Central Park. I think Seventy-Seventh or Seventy-Eighth."

"Just across the park from the American Museum of Natural History?"

"Sure. I don't know. Maybe. I don't really know New York all that well. Is that good?"

"No," Gordo said. Or, rather, he yelled. He realized he was yelling even though he had his headset on, and he tried to calm down. "No, that's not good." He tapped the screen of the laptop with his gloved finger. "That's where the signal's coming from. The museum. It's just across the park."

"Oh. Okay. That's not good," Melanie said, but she was clearly distracted by the spider she was holding. She moved it so Julie could see. "Am I imagining that?"

Julie bent her head to get a closer look and banged her face mask against Melanie's. "Are you kidding?"

"Please," Gordo said, "I know I'm going to regret asking this, but what is it? What do these new spiders have?"

Melanie looked up at him and Gordo recognized the fear on her face. "Teeth," she said. "They've got teeth."

Gordo shrugged. "They all have teeth. Haven't you seen the way they can rip through people? But they don't seem equipped to go through a hazmat suit. As long as we can get to the queen in New York before the spiders decide it's feeding time, we're fine."

"No," Julie said. "We're not fine. Spiders don't have teeth. They use venom to dissolve the flesh of their prey and then drink it."

"Which is why they haven't been able to get through the hazmat suits," Melanie explained. "Their venom is designed to work on organic matter. It melts flesh. It can't get through plastic or rubber or glass. The first-wave and the second-wave Hell Spiders don't have teeth, and they can't get through plastic or rubber or glass. But we've got a new wave."

Gordo shook his head. "Sorry. What?" He glanced out the window. They were losing altitude, and he saw the engines starting to tilt around to put the Osprey into helicopter mode. It was a rather disorienting sight.

"First wave are the black spiders. Second wave are the ones with the red stripes across the back. I figured the queens were the third wave, but, really, the queens are something separate."

Gordo nodded. He realized that Shotgun was nodding along. So was Billy Cannon. Everybody was listening. Cannon held up his hand and spoke. "One minute. Pilot says touchdown in one minute. Right on Central Park West. Get ready to move."

The soldiers all started double-checking their weapons, but Gordo grabbed Melanie's sleeve again. "Okay. First wave, second wave. So these new ones, the ones with the silver slashes on their backs, they're the third wave? And they've got teeth?"

"Right. They've got teeth."

"Okay. Again: So?"

"So," Melanie said, "the first-wave and the second-wave Hell Spiders don't have teeth, and their venom is ineffective against the hazmat suits."

Gordo felt the Osprey hit the ground. He hadn't even unbuckled himself before the military men were boots on the ground. He and Shotgun moved the ST11 carefully. They could build it again if they needed to, but that would take time. And right now what he wanted to do was get to this queen, stomp her out, and then get his wife far away from whatever signals the ST11 said were still out there.

He turned around and looked at the American Museum of Natural History. He watched Kim and her men fan out, watched the men who'd come from New York with the scientists spread out as well. With their hazmat suits and machine guns and flamethrowers, they looked menacing. That queen wasn't going to know what hit—

"Wait a minute." He looked at Melanie. "If they have teeth . . ."

"Yeah," Melanie said. "Seemed like the queen recognized us as a threat, even with the suits on. I think if there are more of the third-wave spiders in there, we might be screwed. You saw what happened in the hotel room. A small hole in the suit is a big problem."

The source of the signal almost leapt off the laptop's screen. There was no question in Gordo's mind that another queen was inside the building. And as he looked up again, he saw thick tendrils of black beginning to stream out of an open window on an upper floor. He pointed it out.

Whatever the spiders had been waiting for, the time had come. They were descending upon New York City.

Kraków, Poland

The queen tasted the acid smell of the night. It was full of hunger. Her little ones brushed past her in endless waves, emerging from the cellar where she had been letting her body recover from its transformation. She could feel more of her little ones emerging throughout the city from attics, from closets, bursting forth from the very bellies of those that served to carry her eggs. The alleyways and the shadows were made darker by the bodies of the little ones going forth. She was hungry. Always hungry.

White House Manhattan, New York, New York

"**W**e've got to get this out there," Steph said. "London. Berlin. Everywhere."

"There's nothing to get out there yet, Steph. We've got what Melanie's telling us, but we don't have the details for this machine they're using. We need to be able to give people something concrete. What we need to do . . ." He spun and looked at Steph. "Broussard."

"What about Broussard?"

"We need to make sure Broussard knows what we've got."

"Manny, I couldn't give a rat's ass about Broussard right now. The guy tried to engineer a coup."

"Look, Steph, when all this is done, Broussard isn't going to come out so well. But right now he's the man who's got his thumb on the US military. We take this machine, this ST11 that we've got, and we pinpoint where the signals are coming from, and we don't need to send in teams in hazmat suits. We send in bombers and jets and just blow them to hell."

The office door banged open and three men in military uniform scrambled into the room. They didn't stop to acknowledge Manny or the president. Not even a hasty salute. Two of them ran to the windows, taking duct tape and loudly ripping it off the roll as they hit every seam. The third dragged a chair to the wall, climbed up, and started sealing off the air vent.

Steph considered for a second. "Fine. Get in touch with him. But you're forgetting, we can't just bomb and rest easy. We're limited to conventional weapons."

Nazca, Peru

They'd spent the night sharing a room in a dingy hotel that was at the edge of town. The hotel was empty, which was a relief. He'd gone into two other hotels but had immediately turned around when he saw the piles of bones and the swarming spiders that seemed to be making sure they hadn't missed a morsel of meat. This hotel didn't seem to have any corpses—at least not in the lobby or in the room they shared—nor did it seem to be infested with spiders. They'd both used the bathroom, and he'd showered, and when he came to bed, Bea had gotten on top of him. The sex was about the same as it had been the entire time they'd been hooking up: better than nothing, but not by a wide margin. In the morning, however, Bea treated him like she hated him.

He'd slept surprisingly late. It was almost eleven. He took another shower, luxuriating in the lukewarm water. By the time he was dressed in the pants and shirt from the day before, his boots laced and his trusty hat in his hand, he was ready to eat. Fortunately, the small dining area in the hotel's restaurant was also free of bones, and he found Bea sitting on a chair, drinking a cup of tea and watching a show on one of those VCR-television combos that would have seemed cool back before Pierre was born. It was a movie he didn't recognize, the dialogue all in Spanish. He greeted her, but she ignored him, so he helped himself to the food in the kitchen. Finally, when he was finished eating, he said, "Well, want to head back to camp?"

She rolled her eyes, but she stood up and walked out onto the street.

The entire walk was like that. It felt interminable. It would have been a lousy walk anyway, what with the death and mayhem and destruction. He understood she was upset, and he did feel bad for her, but he didn't understand how she could possibly be blaming him for anything. They weren't even dating! They'd *never* been dating! It's not like she'd been in love with him and thought of him as some sort of perfect guy and he'd let her down. They'd both been clear from the beginning that they were hooking up because they were stuck in the field together for months and everybody else was already coupled. Heck, she had actually said to him, on more than one occasion, that the only reason she wanted to sleep with him was that she was bored of being alone in her tent, watching reruns of *Modern Family*. He'd joked that she should give *Game of Thrones* a try, but that only earned him a baleful stare.

He would have understood if she was simply upset because she'd seen Dr. Botsford and the other PhD students devoured by spiders. Heck, he would have understood if she was upset for any other reason: because they were thousands of miles from home, because the world appeared to be ending, because there were flesh-eating spiders everywhere, even because all their studying and work on the Nazca Lines and their commitment to getting their doctoral degrees was for naught. But she seemed to be upset over none of those things. What she seemed to be most upset over was the fact that the two of them had somehow survived together.

It was like the world's crappiest miracle, he thought. He knew there had been reports of people being passed over, that the spiders didn't eat absolutely everybody in their path—or, worse, put eggs inside the bodies of everybody in their path. And don't think that Pierre didn't spend a bunch of time in front of a mirror looking for anything approaching a cut or a scrape or a sign that he'd had a spider zip inside him. But the weird, colossal luck of it? That of all the people left behind in that restaurant and on the streets in town, somehow the two of them had been left alone together . . .

Honestly, it was like she was blaming him for the fact that she was still alive.

The walk felt like it lasted forever. For some reason Bea was not only angry at him but also insisted they walk instead of borrowing one of the scooters that had been abandoned on the roadside. Maybe not abandoned, exactly, but it made Pierre feel better to think of it that way.

He did his best to ignore her passive-aggressive grunts and the way she rolled her eyes anytime he said anything, and he took the high road when she made snide comments about how he was either walking too slow or walking too fast; obviously, he couldn't even manage to walk properly as far as she was concerned. He even managed to act like it didn't bother him when she started kicking or stomping on the spiders they passed. Although, of course, *that* scared the crap out of him. What was she thinking? That they were magically immune?

When they got back to their campsite, he sat on one of the field chairs and just stared at the sky for a while, listening to her stomping around and swearing. Which was unusual, since Bea had grown up pretty conservatively.

It felt sort of like giving up to just sit in the chair like that. The spiders, which had thinned out as they left town, started appearing in greater numbers again the closer they got to the campsite; it wasn't like he was wading through them or anything, but they were hard to ignore. Every few minutes one would climb up his leg or come crawling over the arm of the chair and hang out on his arm for a bit. At one point, a spider with a silver slash on its back—he wasn't sure whether he'd seen one of those before, he thought idly—tried to go up under his pant leg, but he brushed it off and tucked his pants into his boots. He kept waiting for the worst—for the spiders to decide that they were ready to eat him now—but at some point, he stopped being afraid and just got bored. Eventually he closed his eyes and must have fallen asleep for a bit. By the time he woke up, the sun had started ducking below the horizon, and his neck was stiff.

Bea was standing directly in front of him, her hands on her hips. She looked even angrier. "I've been thinking about it, and we're done." Without another word, she spun around and stormed off, zipping herself back into her tent. After a few seconds Pierre heard the tinny voices of her playing some sort of show on her laptop.

He reached up and rubbed at the muscles in his neck. There was a part of him that sort of wished the spiders had just gone ahead and eaten him.

American Museum of Natural History, New York, New York

Melanie was glad she'd stayed in shape. She was out of breath, sweating, and terrified, and if she'd been in poorer shape, she wasn't sure she'd have been able to keep control of herself. She glanced over at Julie, who was limping and clearly struggling.

The museum was a maze. It was one of those old-school buildings that had been added onto and connected in such a way that it was easy to feel lost. If they hadn't been in a hurry, it wouldn't have bothered her. She was a nerd at heart, and she would have been more than happy to linger in a cool museum, reading every card and staring at every exhibit. But even as they wove their way deeper and deeper into the museum, Hell Spiders went past them in great floods. They turned left again, Gordo carrying the laptop and pointing the way, and she saw a pile of shed exoskeletons. It looked like a basket of laundry, as if the Hell Spiders had shrugged off their skins and left them for the maid.

Julie saw, too, and she shook her head. Melanie could see her grimacing as she hobbled along.

Suddenly, Gordo halted. Shotgun barely stopped in time to

avoid yanking out the cable that connected the laptop to the box that was the ST11.

"We've got a problem," Gordo said. "Something's wrong."

The Rangers and the Marines were pros. Melanie had to give them that. While she and Julie went over to stand by Shotgun and Gordo and stare at the laptop's screen, the people with the guns and flamethrowers formed a tight circle around them, facing outward and ready for any signs that the spiders' behavior was about to change.

"Are there supposed to be *two* blinking dots?" Melanie asked.

Gordo hit the escape key repeatedly. "No. Something's glitching. Might need to reboot."

"This," Julie muttered, "is why I don't trust self-driving cars."

"Close it out and restart the laptop and I'll have the ST11 cycle through a restart as well," Shotgun said. "Maybe it's a ghost reading. This building is old enough and has enough crap in it that it might have been just an echo or something."

Melanie had the sinking feeling in her stomach that had begun to feel all too familiar. "Don't bother," she said. "I don't think it's a glitch."

Julie and the two men looked at her. Shotgun was the first of them to figure it out. "Oh, great. Two queens."

That, evidently, was enough to make the Rangers and the Marines unprofessional for a few seconds. There was a lot of swearing over the headsets.

"Well," Gordo said, "if it's not glitching, then I think we're about fifty yards away. Turn right at the end of the corridor."

Melanie looked down at the museum map she'd snagged when they ran through one of the rooms. "You're not going to believe this. It's the special exhibition room. And the exhibition? Spiders."

There was another chorus of swearing. Melanie felt like joining in, but she was distracted. Something had changed. It took her a beat to realize what it was. The spiders. Where before there had been a steady file of first-wave and second-wave spiders with the occasional third-wave silver-striped spider thrown in, now it was more heavily tilted toward the third-wave spiders—perhaps half of them now— and they were starting to come closer and closer, as if they were now curious about these hazmat-suited entities among them.

"We better hurry," she said. "And listen, if it's anything like at the hotel, as soon as the queen—or, in this case, queens—recognize that we're a threat, all hell is going to break loose."

She saw Gordo shake his head, and even though he muttered it, she could hear the words picked up through the radio: "Frickin' teeth."

They started moving at a light jog. The Rangers were on point this time, the room wide and open enough for them to go four abreast: two flamethrowers, two machine guns. Beside her, Julie kept up well enough.

"As soon as you identify the queens, frag them," Billy Cannon said. His voice was deep and full of authority, and it somehow made Melanie feel slightly less afraid.

As the first four Rangers approached the corner, it was as if the Hell Spiders had been jolted with electricity. When the men made the turn, the spiders began to close ranks, rushing in from where they'd been moving across the walls, sweeping across the floor in a wave, dropping from the ceiling like black snow. She heard the flare of one of the flamethrowers bursting to life, and the harsh beat of a machine gun, but all of that was overlaid by the sound of first one person screaming and then another.

She felt the pitter-patter of spiders smashing into her hazmat suit, bouncing across her face shield, and then suddenly something much bigger banged into her, and she saw one of the Marines—it was the woman, Kim—rush desperately past her, into the room, toward the queens, her machine gun in firing position.

And then all Melanie could concentrate on was the sudden realization that her fear about the third-wave spiders was right. She could feel the fabric of the hazmat suit splitting open along her arm, felt the unmistakable tactile sensation of a spider's leg touching her flesh.

It was a tearing, sizzling sensation, like a torch held to the nerve endings in her arm, and Melanie began screaming. A cacophony of sounds, of shrieks and gunfire and the hot jet of the flamethrowers. The searing pain on her forearm grew from the size of a grain of rice to a dime to a quarter, and all Melanie hoped for was that it would be quick.

Then, with a suddenness that startled her, it stopped. The spot on her arm throbbed and burned, but it had stopped growing, and she felt the spiders sliding off her hood and her suit, her face mask suddenly clear again as the spiders that had been clinging to it dropped to the ground. She was gasping for air, and frantically, without even thinking about how dumb it was, fumbled with her face mask until she had it off and could pull back the hood to expose her entire head. She gasped in a great gulping lungful of air, the smell an odd mix of smoke and gunpowder and the burned stink of Hell Spiders. She worked her gloves off and then used her hand to tear her sleeve wide open where it had already been gashed by the third-wave spider.

She stared at it with an almost grim curiosity. Where her arm hurt, where it had felt like acid poured on bone, she could see a Hell Spider hanging halfway out of a ragged hole in the skin. Its back had a silver slash on it. She almost expected it to jump as if she were in a horror movie, giving just one more thrash of its body, but it was completely still. Carefully, trying to make sure that no pieces broke off, she pulled it out. It made a sucking sound, like pulling a boot out of mud, and if it hadn't hurt so much, she might have thrown up. As soon as it was out of her skin, however, the pain dialed back to more of a five or six on the pain scale.

She heard the sound of retching and looked over to see Shotgun, his face shield off, throwing up by the wall. A few feet away from him, Gordo was sitting down on the ground and looking at the laptop. They both appeared shaken but fine. Julie was right behind. "You okay?" Melanie asked. Julie nodded, although Melanie wasn't sure she believed her.

Melanie saw that even though several people, including Kim, were standing, there were at least five or six bodies down in the next room. All Rangers. The first ones into the room. They'd been unbelievably brave, she thought. Charging forward, when all she'd wanted to do was run away. They'd given their lives, but it had been worth it, Melanie thought. She could see two queens. They were right next to each other, shredded by machine-gun fire and then both cooked by a flamethrower, flames still dancing off one of their backs. And all around them, the smaller Hell Spiders lay still. Whatever spark of life they'd once had was gone. Kim slowly lowered her machine gun and then glanced over at Melanie. There was no need for machine guns or flamethrowers here, not any-more. The only tool that was needed now was a broom, to sweep up their carcasses and throw them away.

USS *Elsie Downs*, Atlantic Ocean

Broussard sank down heavily in his chair. It was never about power. It was never personal. That's what he had just told the president. It wasn't about her. It wasn't about him. It was about defending the country. And they knew what they needed to do now.

It was time to stand down.

White House Manhattan, New York, New York

Manny tried not to look away while the medic bandaged Melanie's arm. The medic had put in something like sixty stitches to close up the wound where the spider had tried to bore its way into her body, and now, thankfully, he was wrapping it in clean white gauze, so Manny wouldn't have to look at the ragged railway of stitching.

"You'll have a good scar from that," the medic said.

"Thanks." Melanie was seated on the chesterfield in Steph's office. There were men dead, and two of the Rangers and one of the Marines had injuries that were bad enough for them to go to the infirmary on the basement level, but, aside from looking scared and tired and overwhelmed, the rest of the group of men and women who'd gone to Atlantic City and then raced back to run through the American Museum of Natural History seemed like they were in pretty good shape.

The two men who had built the spider-radar machine were at Steph's desk, working on two separate laptops. The tall, skinny one was working on a military model, while the other was doing something to the laptop connected to their machine, the ST11. The tall, skinny one looked up and caught Manny's eye. "We're good," he said. "The program is available for download, and schematics are up. Assuming you can get the word out, people should be able to get their own versions up and running."

"Shotgun, right?"

The man nodded.

"Your husband . . . He's . . ."

Shotgun smiled. "Yeah, I know."

Manny heard the hustle and bustle before Steph came through the door. She didn't waste any time, even going so far as to clap her hands to get the attention of everybody in the room. "We can't screw around on this. Every single minute matters here. If they were in New York, we can't be sure they aren't anywhere else. This is it, people. Melanie"—she turned and pointed to where Manny's ex was sitting on the chesterfield—"how did you say it? Kill the queens; kill them all? We've got a dozen squads formed up and ready to go. All we're waiting on is our targets." She looked now at where Manny was standing, by the desk. "Do we have our locations? How many queens do we have?"

Everybody in the room looked at Manny. He looked at Shotgun. Shotgun looked at the other man, who looked up. "Eighty-seven in North America."

The room exploded in sound. It was like turning on a television that had been left with the volume at full blast, and it took Manny yelling for several seconds to quiet everybody down.

"Are you sure?" he asked. "Eighty-seven? We've got nearly ninety of those queens out there—nearly ninety colonies or broods or whatever you call them of Hell Spiders ready to run rampant?"

"I'm sure," Gordo said. "Sorry. We hooked the ST11 up so it's reading through the US government satellite system. We're picking up everything. What's nuts is, there's a second signal sort of piggybacking on the first. There's the signal coming from each of the queens, and then there's this other, second signal that's being bounced with it. It's like it's using the queens as repeaters."

Manny slid around so he could look at the laptop over the man's shoulder. "A second signal? What do you mean by 'repeaters'? Sorry, what's your name?"

"Gordo. Okay, so, do you have Wi-Fi at home?"

Manny nodded.

"Well, you probably get your Internet through your cable, and wherever that comes into the house, you've got a modem hooked up, and then connected to the modem you've got a Wi-Fi router."

Manny didn't say anything. The truth was that he had no idea how his Internet was set up at home. He was the White House chief of staff: he didn't screw around with setting up the Wi-Fi!

"If you've got a condo or a small house," Gordo continued, "you've probably just got a single router. It's where the Wi-Fi signal comes from. Now, it used to be that if you had a big house, you might not get Wi-Fi in all the nooks and crannies. So you could buy a repeater and plug it in upstairs or in the basement or wherever, and that way you'd have Wi-Fi wherever you wanted. The problem is that the signal strength gets diminished with repeaters. The Wi-Fi's never as good. That's why most people have switched to mesh. But the point is, we've got the signals that are coming from the queens, but with the signal boost through the satellites I'm pretty sure there's another signal riding piggyback."

Manny didn't even bother trying to unpack the comment about mesh. "So the queens are sending out, like, what, two broadcasts? Two sets of commands from each queen?"

"No," Gordo said. "The Wi-Fi analogy holds true. There's a

single source, and all the queens out there are just acting like re-peaters."

Nobody said anything for a few seconds, and then Melanie spoke up. "Gordo."

"Yes?"

"Gordo." Her voice was relatively calm, but there was some-thing in there, a dark tinge that Manny recognized from when they were married. It had never worked out well for him when he heard it in her voice, and yet, miraculously, she stayed calm now. "Cor-rect me if I'm wrong, but it sounds like you're saying that there is one single source that is broadcasting to all the spiders."

"Not broadcasting exactly; more—"

"Gordo. Stop. Where, precisely where, is this coming from?"

He moved his fingers across the trackpad and clicked on a but-ton. "Peru," he said.

"In Nazca?"

"Yeah, how did—"

But Melanie was already on her feet and moving behind the desk to look at the map. So was Steph. It was quite a crowd, Manny and Shotgun and Melanie and Steph all looking over Gordo's shoulder at the laptop's screen.

"Steph," Melanie said, "forget about anything else. Gordo can give you the locations of those eighty-seven queens and you can do whatever you can do, but I need him. I need him and a bunch of people with guns and flamethrowers and hazmat suits, and I need the fastest plane you can give me."

Manny held up his hands. "Whoa. Give me a second here."

"Manny," Melanie said. "Eighty-seven queens. That's how many there are just in the United States. Think how many there are around the world."

"Okay," Manny said. "I'm missing something."

Gordo's eyes were wide-open, and he looked as if he'd just won a million bucks. "Holy crap! It's like a zero-day exploit." He banged Manny on the shoulder with his fist. "It's a hacking term. It means there's a flaw in the operating system you can hack into. It's a zero-day exploit when there's no time to fix it. They can talk to each other, right? But talking to each other is one thing, and having one single spider talking to all of them is another."

"Wait," Manny said. "You're saying that there's, like, what, a queen of the queens? Melanie?"

Melanie looked down and touched the bandage around her arm almost tenderly. "I'm going to Peru. We can put an end to this."

C-17 Globemaster III, Twenty Thousand Feet and Rising

They were wheels-up in less than thirty minutes. Kim was amazed at how fast you could drive through Manhattan during the apocalypse, particularly when paced by police cars and military vehicles. On the tarmac, they stopped just long enough to switch to JLTVs, already loaded up with hazmat kits and flame-throwers and M16s, and then backed the four trucks right up the loading ramp and onto the C-17 Globemaster III.

There were four civilians: Melanie and Julie, plus Gordo and Shotgun and their trusty ST11. The Rangers who hadn't died in Atlantic City or the museum all volunteered, as did Kim. "I want to finish this thing off," she'd said. Billy Cannon had agreed, and they'd cycled in enough fresh Rangers to make the full comple-ment. Sixteen people in all. Four in each JLTV.

The plane took a steep angle into late-afternoon sky, and Kim tried to get comfortable. She suddenly realized that she had no idea what time zone Peru was in. It would be dark, though. She knew that. The C-17 could boogie, but even going close to three-quarters the speed of sound and with a midair refueling, it was going to be another six hours. Still plenty of time for her to get nervous. But in the meantime she closed her eyes. If she'd learned nothing else in the Marines, she'd learned that: Get shut-eye when you could.

Berlin, Germany

Her little ones swirled and pooled around her. She'd been about to send them forth into the night when she felt the sharp disappearance of one of her sisters. It had happened a number of times already, but this one was different. There had been some who had gone from her consciousness, but for those it had been instantaneous disruptions of light and heat. This sister, however, had a moment of clarity before she was torn apart. And then, only a short time later, it happened again.

For the first time she felt fear.

She folded her legs under her and carefully allowed her body to rest on the damp concrete of the sewer tunnel. Her new exoskeleton had hardened, but she didn't wish to cause damage to the eggs she carried. She was still, even as thousands of black and red-striped and silver-slashed little ones swirled and swarmed and skittered over her, moving in the darkness, impatient to be out to feed. She counseled them that it would not be much longer, and she listened.

Her heart beat as one with her sisters, all of them listening to the one singular heartbeat that said to wait, wait, wait. There were still many of her sisters who were recovering from their molts, whose eggs were not quite ready. Soon, soon, soon they would move as one, the heartbeat told her.

She knew it was dark outside these tunnels, but it wouldn't be long before the sun rose again, and by then it would be time.

USS *Elsie Downs*, Atlantic Ocean

The sailors were lined up along the hallways, each one holding a hard salute as he passed. He took his time, acknowledging each and every one of the men and women who'd followed his lead. He wasn't sure what would happen to them, and he owed them at least this much. Nobody knew what would happen in this new world, but he hoped there would be a way forward for the military. As for himself, he didn't care what happened. He'd done what he thought was right. He would stand in front of the president and take full responsibility. There was no walking away from the consequences.

All he could do now was make sure his mistake didn't cost any more lives.

As Broussard walked to the flight deck, he realized he had a grim admiration for President Pilgrim. He'd had her beaten, and she still won. Operation SAFEGUARD had been in his hands, but somehow he'd been outmaneuvered. And even though he understood it meant the end of his career—and almost certainly his life, because he would be tried and found guilty of treason—he didn't regret it. For all he knew, if he hadn't made this move, without the desperation of being chased, the president might still be dithering around with half measures. At least, that's what he told himself.

On the flight deck he chatted briefly with the crew manning the refueling aircraft, then he retreated to a safe distance and watched the plane take off. There was something satisfying about seeing it shrink into the sunset, about knowing that, at least in this one small way, he had made the right decision.

One Mile off the Coast of Maine

Annie was practically bouncing, which would have been fine, but Mike's knees were killing him from being cramped in the Cessna for so long. He'd swapped spots with Carla—she didn't have her pilot's license, but she knew what she was doing more than Mike did, and Rex wanted her up front for the ocean landing—and Annie had insisted on sitting on his lap as they came closer and closer.

"Is that it? Is that it?" She was pointing out the side window at a small, forlorn-looking rock sitting in the ocean.

"No." He laughed and then turned her so that she was looking forward. "Pretty sure that would be a little too small for us. But there, if you look straight ahead, I think that's where we're going. See the harbor? You can see the boats."

He caught Fanny smiling at him, which was nice. They had an amicable relationship that bordered on actual friendship, and it still gave him a warm feeling to know that she thought he was a good dad. It was weird, he thought, to be like this with an ex-wife. They'd gotten along okay since the divorce, with the usual ups and downs, but since everything had fallen apart, he'd spent a lot more time with her and her husband than he would have otherwise. And, at least for the time being, that wasn't going to change. From what Rex said and from what he could see through the cockpit window, the island wasn't much of anything.

They were already low, a few hundred feet above the ocean, so it wasn't a steep descent. Thankfully the water was dead calm. So flat that it looked as though it had been painted on a canvas. That had been Rex's one worry, that the ocean would be heaving, but they had more than enough fuel to turn around and find a place on the mainland. There were at least two airfields close by, but it would have meant finding a car and then a boat to get them to the island. The landing itself felt like nothing. Just a gradual sense that they were slowing down, the ocean seeming to come up until it kissed the pontoons.

Rex kept the propellers spinning, carefully maneuvering the Cessna through the lobster boats moored in the harbor, bringing it near but not up to the pier.

"Uh, folks, I don't mean to be a buzzkill, but we've got a not-so-welcoming party." Leshaun was pointing to a small group standing on the edge of the pier.

They were all armed, a mix of hunting rifles and shotguns, and Mike made out five men and one woman. One of the men was older, near Rex's age, a big man holding a double-barreled shotgun and looking extremely displeased, but the other four and the woman were all closer to his age.

For all that, Rex seemed quite pleased with himself. "No worries," he said. "I know a guy."

Leshaun and Mike looked at each other, and then Leshaun shrugged and mouthed the words *He knows a guy.*

C-17 Globemaster III, Nazca, Peru

"**D**ouble-check your hazmat suits. Make sure every seam is sealed. We know the third-wave Hell Spiders can compromise the integrity of the suits, but they'll keep you safe from the first- and second-wave spiders. Wheels down in ten minutes. Everybody make sure you're strapped in." Cannon had already split them up into the JLTVs, keeping Gordo and Shotgun together with the ST11 in the first vehicle, driven by Kim, but dividing Melanie and Julie into separate trucks. "There is exactly zero extra length on this runway. Our pilot says he's got it under control, but it might get a bit bumpy. As soon as we stop, the crew is going to release the securing straps, drop the ramp, and we're going to hit it. I want the JLTVs at speed as soon as possible. We know there are Hell Spiders on the ground here. Let's not go slow enough to pick up any hitchhikers. Gordo's given us coordinates, so once we're rolling we'll know where we're going, but keep your traps shut in case something comes up and we need to correct course. Questions?"

There were none, and Cannon banged on the hood of the truck that Melanie was in and then hopped into the front passenger seat.

She was behind the driver, so he turned partway and gave her a thumbs-up. "We good, Dr. Guyer?"

"I sure hope so," she said. The truth was, she felt horrible. Her arm ached where the spider had half burrowed into the skin, she was tired, and she was scared.

"You'll be fine," Cannon said. "Okay, crew, one more time. We get as close as we can in the JLTVs. First preference is to identify the target from a distance and call in a strike. We've got two Super Hornets with air-to-surface weapons inbound, and they'll be circling by the time we're on-site. But we need to see the target. No guessing. If we can't stay at a distance and call in the cavalry, next preference is to engage using the mounted .50-cals. And if that doesn't work, well, I hope you guys are ready to toast some spiders."

Melanie could hear the Rangers respond with a hearty cheer, but she knew that if they got to vote for it, she was picking door number one.

"Gordo," she said, once the cheering died down. "Still looking good on location?"

"It's on the screen like a bonfire in the dark," he said. "This is it. No question. Each mile the signal's stronger and stronger. And . . . Okay. You're not going to believe this."

"Try me."

"Overlaying the signal with the maps. It's out on the Nazca Lines, about seven or eight hundred meters off the road. Want to take one guess which of the Nazca Lines the ST11 is telling us the signal's coming from?"

"You've *got* to be kidding me."

"Well, unless you're thinking it's the monkey or something other than the spider, no, I'm not kidding you."

There was a little bit of nervous chatter for the next five minutes, and then Cannon had them check their hazmat suits one last time, each person going over their own setup and then checking the person next to him or her. After that, it was just the bounce and screech of the plane's tires hitting tarmac. Because the JLTVs had been backed into the plane, Melanie felt herself pushed deeper into her seat as the pilot jammed the engines into reverse. She'd never experienced such an abrupt landing. It was over too quickly for Melanie to panic, but she was glad she couldn't see the shortness of the runway. According to the information they had, the airport outside Nazca was designed for the sort of small planes that Melanie had ridden in years ago, with Manny, when they'd come here as tourists. It wasn't the sort of airport that handled military transport aircraft.

She could still feel the plane moving when crew members started scurrying to unsecure the JLTVs. Melanie figured they could have fit at least one more inside the belly of the C-17, but she also figured that if their small crew couldn't get the job done, adding one more truck wouldn't have helped. She was in the second vehicle, behind the one driven by Kim that carried Shotgun and Gordo and the ST11. Although the view was obscured, she could see the rear hatch opening to the inky darkness of Peru.

The first JLTV lurched forward, and then Melanie's followed. She couldn't stop herself from turning around to make sure the other two vehicles were still close behind. As she straightened up again to look ahead, the truck lurched and bumped, wheels on the ground in Peru. The driver floored it, and the JLTV's wheels bit down, thrusting the armored vehicle forward. It was almost completely dark out, which confused Melanie for a moment. It was an airport. It should have been lit up. But then she caught a glimpse of a skittering dark mass and the baseball-size bodies held aloft by eight legs, and she realized that of course it made sense that the airport was dark. There was nobody left to turn on the lights.

Nazca, Peru

Kim had caught a couple of hours of sleep on the plane, and she'd spent most of the rest of the time staring at the map. Cannon had put her in the position of lead driver, and she didn't want to make any false moves. Everybody seemed clear that speed was their friend. The idea of having to stop and figure out where they were, or of getting stuck and having to back out of some dead-end alley, was not appealing. The spiders in the casino and hotel in Atlantic City seemed not to have even noticed them, but the museum had not been an experience she enjoyed. It was hard to argue against the notion that the spiders seemed to be learning, and since the ones with silver slashes on their backs could evidently chew their way through the hazmat suits . . .

Grimly she pushed her foot down, picking up speed. The roads were in better shape than she had expected, and she hit top speed as soon as they were out of the airport and on the main drag. According to Gordo, it was eighteen miles along roads from the airport, and from there the signal was about twenty-five hundred feet out into the dirt. Thankfully, though there were dead cars and trucks in their way, they were spread out far enough that she could either drive on the wrong side of the road or, in some places where the wide dirt shoulder wasn't encroached by buildings, kick up dust for a few seconds before getting back onto the hardtop. She made sure to check her mirror regularly; the other three JLTVs kept pace. They had to head into the town of Nazca and then back out, and once they were out on the high-desert highway, it was smooth sailing. Thankfully, they were moving fast enough that the bodies stripped down to bone on the side of the road were barely caught in the sweep of the headlights before she passed them by. It meant the corpses were almost removed of their menace. Almost.

"Gordo?"

"Still going strong, Kim. Signal's holding steady."

Even if she hadn't asked, she would have been pretty sure. By the airport, there had been a few spiders, and in town she'd seen clusters and, in places where the light pooled, dark shadows that betrayed themselves with their alien movement. Out here, however, even with just the beams of her headlights, she could see that there were more and more. One flew up and hit the windshield with a loud splat, leaking guts all over the glass. Kim turned on the wipers. It left a thick, nasty smear.

The Ranger sitting in the passenger seat was carrying one of the homemade flamethrowers. He shook his head. "Gross."

"Gordo, how close?" Cannon asked over the headset.

"Maybe four miles."

"Okay. Let's do this. I want eyes on the target before I call in an air strike. Can't risk being wrong on this."

Nobody responded to Cannon.

Kim kept her fingers wrapped around the steering wheel. Three miles out, and then two, and the spiders were thick enough that she had to concentrate to make sure she stayed on the road. They obscured the boundaries between the blacktop and the dirt.

The thrum of the truck's tires on asphalt turned into something else, like driving in snow. A wet, crunching crush of spiders under rubber.

Gordo leaned forward to tap Kim on the shoulder. "Another mile." Then he remembered that he was wearing a headset under his hazmat suit and that everybody was on the same frequency. "Hey, guys, be ready. In about forty-five seconds we're going to pass a viewing tower on the left. Not like a real tower. More ramshackle. Once we pass that, one-tenth of a mile and then a hard left out onto the dirt. From there . . . Hell, let's just see what we find."

Another spider bounced up and into the windshield, but with a bang this time. Kim could feel her heart jackhammering in her chest and she almost swerved off the road when she heard the scream through the headset.

"It's in my suit! It's in my suit!"

"Jackson, just—"

"My leg!"

"Keep driving!" Cannon's voice cut above the yelling, and Kim didn't let off the gas. Jackson was one of the Rangers in the third JLTV. The one that had Julie Yoo in it.

The truck was eating up the road, moving as fast as it could go, but it didn't seem fast enough as she heard screaming and yelling.

"Oh, Jesus!" She yanked her right hand off the wheel to swat at her left. A spider had just run across her wrist; she'd felt it through the hazmat suit before she'd seen it. Okay. Okay. All-black first-wave spider. "We've got hitchhikers."

She saw the tower in the headlights: maybe three flights of stairs, but in the glow from her headlights, she could see that the structure seemed to writhe and move, the second skin of spiders making it seem alive.

"Left! Left!" Gordo yelled.

His voice was almost lost in the yelling and screaming that was still coming from the third truck, but then the noise stopped and was replaced with Julie's voice. "I think we're good. Taping up Jackson's suit with duct tape. Looks like we're clean otherwise." She sounded shaky to Kim, but that seemed reasonable enough, since Kim felt shaky herself.

She slowly turned the wheel and hit the brakes so that she didn't lose control, but she was still doing thirty miles an hour as she angled off the asphalt and out into the dirt. Or at least she was pretty sure it was dirt. The entire landscape was a tangled nightmare of spiders, their black bodies and legs both reflecting the headlamps and seeming to absorb all light at the same time. "Which way?"

Shotgun answered. "Left about ten degrees. You've got this, Kim. Keep driving. It's out there." His voice was surprisingly calm, and it was enough to settle her down a bit.

And then she could see the spiders starting to roil and shake, the black mass covering the ground beginning to gather and move, shifting in waves. It was as if—

Kim yelled it as soon as she realized what was happening. "She knows we're coming!"

"Don't stop!" Cannon shouted. "All the way in, eyes on, and then we engage. The only way out is through. Let's end it!"

Kim could feel sweat curling down the back of her neck, her bones jostling with each bounce of the truck across the uneven ground. Ahead of her, the shifting swarm rose up, turning into a wall of spiders that was now at least as high as her bumper. She hit the accelerator harder, ticking her speed up even as she could hear the Hell Spiders pinging and bouncing off the truck like hail.

"Two hundred feet!"

There was a burst of screaming over the radio again, garbled voices, and this time Kim had no clue who it was. She risked a glance in the rearview mirror and saw that the headlights of one of the JLTVs were moving away at an angle, the driver obviously no longer in control.

"One hundred!"

"Oh my god!"

Ahead of her, it was like a growing tidal wave. Fifty feet in front of her, the Hell Spiders seemed to be pulling back on themselves. They streamed away from her, building up five, ten, fifteen feet high, leaving the high-desert dirt uncovered. "I'm stopping," she yelled, and slammed on the brakes. She got jerked back by her seat belt and then undid it so she could scramble up to the .50-cal, cursing about the way the hazmat suit slowed her down. The Ranger who'd been sitting next to her came sliding out through the passenger door, the flamethrower sparking before he even had his boots on the ground. Behind her, the other two JLTVs rocked to hard stops, their doors swinging open, great glorious arcs of flame spitting out from them as well.

She had enough presence of mind to realize that the only saving grace was that instead of continuing to try to overwhelm them, the Hell Spiders had pulled back to surround and protect whatever was behind the living curtain.

"Circle around the point vehicle!" Cannon yelled. "Keep them back!"

As the men with flamethrowers took their positions, fanning their fire back and forth, the wave of Hell Spiders suddenly came crashing toward them with a sound loud enough to carry over the guzzling hiss of the flamethrowers. It was the worst sound Kim had ever heard. She steadied herself and grabbed the trigger, swinging the .50-cal to bear on the greatest concentrations of spiders.

And as the spiders began to rush toward them, the curtain parted and she saw it.

The queen.

Barely fifty feet away. It was the same size as the one she'd seen in Atlantic City, like a keg balanced on broken broomsticks, except that was where the similarity ended. This queen was stunning. Her legs were covered in thick, matted black hairs that were the color of the night sky in summer, and her exoskeleton shimmered, so black that it was almost blue.

She could see the onrushing spiders immolated by the wrath of the flamethrowers, but there were too many of them. The first Ranger was overrun and fell.

She steadied herself, concentrated, and pulled the trigger. As she did, she realized she was screaming, "Eat this!"

She felt the gun coughing, the sound more a physical experience than something she could hear. She held the trigger down. The Browning could spit out five hundred rounds a minute, and she intended to keep squeezing forever.

It was the most glorious thing she'd ever seen in her entire life.

The queen danced miserably, her body jouncing as it was torn to shreds by the .50-cal. Kim kept firing, tracking the queen's body as it moved, turning the spider into nothing more than a piece of liquid meat.

Finally she let go of the trigger. The heavy thump of the .50-cal was replaced with the hurricane of the flamethrowers, but then those went off one by one.

It wasn't quiet. Even with the hood of the hazmat suit making it difficult to hear, the sound of hundreds of thousands of Hell Spider carcasses sliding and settling was overwhelming, like that of a freight train or an ambulance. But there was no mistaking the fact that they were lifeless. Just corpses succumbing to gravity.

The next thing Kim heard was the sound of cheering.

Nazca, Peru

Melanie stood next to what was left of the queen. Even destroyed, the queen was a beautiful monster.

She was holding her face shield in one hand and had her hazmat suit peeled down with the arms tied around her waist. There had been a rip near her hip, but unless her adrenaline was pumping too hard for her to feel it, she was pretty sure she was unscathed. This time. Her arm still hurt and she could feel it throbbing under the bandages. Still, it felt good to be standing there in the night sky, the cool desert air drying the sweat.

It felt good to be alive.

"Dr. Guyer," Cannon said. He glanced at the destroyed remnants of the giant Hell Spider. "I'm sorry, but we've got to move. We've got several men who need medical attention." He didn't say anything about the truck full of men that had veered off course, or the other three men who were beyond the need for help. "We're going to be able to do a lot more for them back at the plane."

Melanie nodded.

They heard yelling from where the three remaining JLTVs were parked. A jolt of ice ran through her body, but then she realized it wasn't the sound of panic. The yelling was excitement. She jogged over with Cannon.

"Sir! You're not wearing your headset."

"Sorry, son. What did I miss?"

"Reports in from Berlin, Boston, uh, heck, a couple of other places. It's like we cut the cord! The spiders are just done. Turned off, sir. All of them!"

Cannon nodded and looked at Melanie. For the first time she thought he looked his age, and she realized he must be as tired as she was. But at least in that moment she felt wildly wide-awake.

"Dr. Guyer. Melanie. I know we don't have all the information, but—" Cannon stopped.

"What does it mean? That's what you were going to ask, right?" Melanie couldn't stop herself from grinning. "It means we did it."

She started to laugh. "We won."

Nazca, Peru

Shotgun grunted every time the truck jostled his leg, which meant he was constantly grunting. They still had to travel several hundred feet before they could turn back onto the relatively well-paved road, and even though Kim was driving slowly, it was a bouncy ride.

Gordo tried to hold Shotgun's leg as steady as he could. He'd cut away the hazmat suit so he could dress Shotgun's wound, which was pretty gruesome. The Hell Spiders had done a real number on his calf and ankle.

For all that, his friend had an extraordinarily broad smile plastered on his face.

Nazca, Peru

One of the Rangers had recovered the errant JLTV, driving it over so they could load the additional dead bodies inside. They weren't leaving anyone, living or dead, behind. Kim was thankful that she got to drive the living.

She was also thankful when she finally got her wheels off the dirt and back on the highway. Shotgun had been given painkillers already, but they clearly hadn't kicked in yet. It would be good to get him back to the airfield. Shotgun wasn't the most badly injured man, but he needed more than just a field dressing.

Next to Kim, Julie Yoo sat looking stunned.

"You okay?" Kim asked.

"Honestly? Yeah. I mean, I'm sort of numb, but not in a bad way. I'd like a glass of wine. And maybe a Xanax or something."

Kim laughed. She brought the truck up to about forty miles per hour. She wanted to get to the plane as soon as possible, but the road was littered with dead Hell Spiders, and she didn't want to risk an accident. With only her headlights to lead the way, she was more concerned with . . .

"Hey, Julie? Am I imagining things, or is there a pair of headlights coming toward us?"

"I see them, too."

Kim slowed down as the headlights came closer and closer. By the time the pickup truck pulled alongside them, driver's-side window to driver's-side window, she'd stopped.

"Hi there," Kim said. She honestly couldn't think of what else to say.

"Oh my god, I am so glad to see you. And you're American!" The guy driving was a couple of years older than Kim, maybe mid-twenties. A woman with a sour look on her face sat in the passenger's seat.

Kim felt Julie's hand on her leg as she leaned over. "Pierre?"

"Julie?" The man's eyes opened so wide that Kim was afraid they were going to pop out of his head. "Julie? What on earth are you doing here?"

His passenger let out a harsh, barking laugh. "Of course," she said. "Why not?"

The man, Pierre, glanced at the woman, clearly rattled. But then he looked past Kim right at Julie, and with a sort of puppy-dog earnestness he blurted out, "I love you! I mean, I'm sorry, I know this isn't the time or the place, but there's been so much happening, and I keep thinking about you, and even before any of this I kept thinking about you, and I have to tell you I love you. I've been in love with you forever, and—"

"Pierre." Julie had to say his name two more times to get him to stop. Kim took a second to glance in the rearview mirror. She saw the lights of the two other JLTVs approaching.

"Julie," Kim said, "we've got to go. We need to get Shotgun medical attention."

"Right." Julie leaned farther over so that she could put her hand on the windowsill—almost like she was reaching out to try to hold Pierre's hand. Almost, but not quite. "Pierre, this isn't the time or the place. But if you want to follow us, I'm pretty sure you can hitch a ride to the US."

"Seriously, we've got to go," Kim said. She shrugged. "Sorry." By then the lights of the trailing JLTVs were almost upon them, so she started driving again. In the rearview mirror she saw the pickup truck turn around and start trailing them.

She and Julie were quiet until they hit the outskirts of the city, and then Kim said, "He loves you?"

"I guess," Julie said.

"And you dated in college?"

"Sort of."

"So . . . ?"

"Yeah."

And then they were quiet again until they reached the airfield.

EPILOGUE

Stornoway, Isle of Lewis, Outer Hebrides, Scotland

He'd wanted to go to Edinburgh. Somewhere with a major hospital, but Thuy had refused. It was a low-risk pregnancy, she said, and the Western Isles Hospital in Stornoway was more than well equipped to handle a simple childbirth. Besides, she'd said, she was *working* there. How was it going to look if she went somewhere else?

The other truth was that the medical systems were completely overwhelmed, not just in Edinburgh, but everywhere. It was worse in the big cities like Edinburgh and all around the globe, however, and not just medical. There had been reports of food riots in Toronto the previous week, and in parts of the world where winters were even harsher, infrastructure failures loomed large. For the most part, however, travel was back to normal. Well, not normal—nothing would ever be back to normal—but it was possible to travel. Which probably played a big role in Thuy's insistence as well, because it meant that her family had been able to get to Stornoway. The first thing he and Thuy did after S-Day—Spider Day, the day of victory, but everybody just called it S-Day, like D-Day—was get married. Her family had to miss that, but they sure weren't going to miss the birth, too.

They were all out there, in the waiting room, sitting with his grandfather: Thuy's mom, dad, her brother, his boyfriend, and his boyfriend's dog. Aonghas had no idea how they'd managed to persuade the hospital staff to allow the dog inside.

He leaned over and kissed Thuy on the forehead. She was sweaty and flushed, and to his mind she'd never looked more beautiful. And then he leaned over and kissed their daughter, who was mewling and pink. If he was being totally honest, she was kind of squishy; but she was also perfect in every way, and staring at her button nose made him want to start crying all over again.

"Bring them in?" he asked.

Thuy smiled, so he opened the door and her family rushed in, chattering and oohing and aahing, and it was all he could do not to laugh as they crowded him out. His grandfather, beaming, waited patiently.

"Do you want to hold her?" he asked his grandfather.

"In time, in time, Aonghas. Let Thuy's parents have their turn."

They were quiet for a minute, standing together, grandson and grandfather, and Aonghas felt an almost physical weight for how much he loved the man next to him.

Padruig spoke quietly, so that only Aonghas could hear. "Does she have a name yet?"

The question genuinely surprised Aonghas. "Of course," he said. "She's named after her."

"Ah. After your mother. Of course."

"No," Aonghas said. He realized he was about to start crying again, but he tried to hold it together. "After my grandmother. Your wife. Ealasaid. We were going to name her after you if she had been a boy, but she's a girl, so it's Ealasaid."

Watching his grandfather's face was like watching a wall crumble slowly into the sea. His lips started to tremble and then break, and then great big tears rolled down his craggy face.

It was a good way to ring in the New Year.

Oxford, Mississippi

Santiago knew that others had suffered worse, but still, it hurt.

They'd held a funeral just after Thanksgiving for Juliet. It had broken his heart, but he understood that her time had simply run out. She'd lived longer than the doctors had promised at her birth, and he had thought of every extra minute as a gift.

He'd taken the rest of that day off to mourn with his wife and Oscar and Mrs. Fine. The work crews went six days a week, and he was a foreman, but even so, his men were surprised when he was back the following morning. He told them there was too much to do, but the truth was that he was afraid to stay home. Work was solace for him, for his wife—she was a manager of a farm work crew—and even for Oscar, who had returned to school in October, when the doors reopened. The government had picked Oxford as a resettlement site, but perhaps only half of the homes were occupied. It was enough, however, to mean that there was work to do, that there were ways to keep occupied in the wake of Juliet's death. Even Mrs. Fine worked, sitting at the register even though gas was so rationed that they pumped only on weekends and the shelves of the store were barer than they were full.

They were sad, but he was also happy, because he knew they had done everything possible and that Juliet had lived as full a life as she could have. What more could he have asked from God?

And then, only a few days after Christmas, with New Year's Eve approaching, Mrs. Fine had not come down to breakfast. He'd known in his heart before he began to climb the stairs.

He dug the grave himself. He could have used a backhoe, but he wanted to honor her with his work. The day was overcast, but it was warm enough that he worked up a sweat. He stopped a few times for water, to eat a sandwich that his wife had packed for him. He had plenty of time. Even with the new world that lay before them, the work crews had New Year's Day off. He would finish digging, go home, shower, and change into his one suit—he had not expected to wear it again so soon—and they could lay Mrs. Fine to rest.

And once that was done, he thought, he would find another piece of granite as he had done for Juliet. On Juliet's, he'd chiseled her name, her birth and death dates, and just the first three words of the song he used to sing to her: *La linda manita*. His work was rough, but it was as fine as he was capable of. His wife agreed that Juliet's headstone needed nothing other than her name, the dates, and those three words.

As he dug, he knew that the granite above Mrs. Fine's grave would have only a single word: *Abuela*.

Burlington, Vermont

Gordo waved the Geiger counter over the load. Every few weeks they'd get something that contained a contaminated item from the red zones. It didn't matter how dire the warnings were; scavengers always thought it was worth the risk. Even though almost everything got screened before it made its way to Vermont, Gordo thought it was a smart precaution, so the town council decided to add the redundancy. Since the town council consisted, in its entirety, of Gordo, Shotgun, and Amy, it wasn't like he'd needed to make much of an argument. So far he hadn't found anything that was hot, but back in September several dozen people in Philadelphia had died from radiation poisoning after a screwup. Better safe than sorry.

The radiation detector didn't let out a single beep, so Gordo cleared the load. "I'm done for the day," he said to his assistant, Wendy. She was only sixteen—a kid, really—but she was a quick learner, and these days sixteen was old enough to earn your place.

"Want me to finish logging everything?" she asked, but he could tell she didn't really want to. He kept long hours, and it was

unusual that he'd knock off before seven. He was sure she liked
the idea of seeing her boyfriend.

"No worries. We can pick up where we left off in the morning."

He spent a few minutes straightening papers and shutting
down his computer, and then he did a quick round to make sure
the warehouse was sealed up. They were fortunate to live in an
area that had access to a lot of natural resources, so there wasn't the
same kind of pilferage that was a problem in some of the resettlement areas, but it didn't hurt to be careful. Burlington had been extremely lucky, and they'd suffered casualties of only approximately
twenty percent of the population, but that meant the area's needs
were higher, too. Most of Gordo's time was spent as a glorified
stockkeeper. He entered the code to set the alarm, checked to
make sure he had the monitor in his pocket—he'd get an alert if
the alarm went off—locked up, said good night to the two guards
coming on for the night shift, and started walking home.

He could have driven, since he rated a car and triple gas rations,
but they lived only a few blocks from the warehouse. He liked the
walk. He felt lucky to be able to enjoy walking, particularly after
what had happened to Shotgun. The man didn't complain about
it, but Gordo was pretty sure Shotgun's leg still ached where the
spiders had torn it up. As nasty as it looked on the outside, there'd
been a lot of damage inside to muscles and nerves and tendons.
Shotgun was able to get around okay with a cane now, but he
would always be gimpy.

It had been a mild winter so far, thankfully, and the streets were
bare. It was mild enough that Gordo didn't bother zipping up his
jacket. He walked quickly, ready to get home. He and Amy had
taken a gingerbread-style cottage that was only a few doors down
from a Victorian that Shotgun and Fred shared with an older cou-

ple. Gordo and Amy's house had two small bedrooms—one for them and one that Gordo used as an office—but the living area had been renovated sometime recently. It was an open space, with the kitchen and dining room and living room all one single room.

He was still five or six houses away when he heard Claymore barking and saw the dog running toward him.

"Hey, boy!" Gordo bent down, bracing himself, but as always Claymore skidded to a halt instead of crashing into him. The chocolate Lab was whining and wagging his tail so hard that Gordo was afraid the dog was going to knock himself over. He laughed and gave Claymore a heavy scratching on his chest and behind his ears. "Come on, buddy. I wasn't gone that long."

Claymore ran ahead the rest of the way, disappearing into the yard behind the house. Gordo bounced up the steps and pulled the door open.

"Hey. Smells good."

Amy was standing in the kitchen with Fred. She was still dressed from teaching—she had been installed as an English teacher at one of the middle schools despite her protests that being a technical writer wasn't proper training, and she'd surprised herself by really enjoying the work—but she had on a dark-blue apron over her dress. Fred was wearing what he wore every day: loafers, slacks, a button-down, and a bow tie. On top, he'd thrown a white apron with the word *GrillMaster!* spelled out in red letters.

"Don't let the apron fool you," Fred said. "We're having pasta."

Of all of them, Fred might have adjusted the quickest. Despite complaining about having to survive Vermont and the attendant winters, he'd found a natural fit; at the referendum meeting the week after they arrived—the same one that had elected Amy, Shotgun, and Gordo to the three council seats—those in attendance had voted overwhelmingly to appoint a director of activities.

The thought was that the post-S-Day world was going to be hard enough. It didn't have to be joyless. Amy immediately nominated Fred, and he was elected by general acclaim. It was the job he was born to do. Burlington had already been one of those vibrant college towns, and Fred was like the magic elixir to bring things back to normal and then some. While he'd always been good at throwing a party, it turned out that he also had a knack for getting other people to throw parties, and the fact that almost everything was rationed didn't seem to stop him.

Gordo hung up his coat and came over to give Amy a kiss. "Hey," he said. "Wine! What's the special occasion?"

Amy kissed him. "We've got guests."

Gordo smirked. "I'm not sure having Shotgun and Fred over counts as a special occasion."

As he spoke, he felt a gust of cool air and turned to see Shotgun limp through the door. And then, to his surprise, following right behind were Kim and a stocky young man who looked to be close to her age.

The next few minutes were a hubbub of hugs and introductions. The boy was Kim's boyfriend, nineteen or twenty, the same age as Kim, and evidently also a Marine, and Amy herded them all to the table.

"I'm only here overnight," Kim said once they were all seated. Claymore had come in the door with them. He'd been attached to Kim's hip the entire time. He was standing next to her, his head on her lap. "Technically, I'm here on business." Gordo passed her the basket of bread. She took a piece, ripped off half, and promptly handed the other half to Claymore.

"Business? Come on, Kim. Are we really supposed to believe you're here on business? We all know the only reason you came up to Burlington was so that you could see Claymore," Gordo said, and they all laughed. "Seriously. What business, exactly, does Lance Corporal Kim Bock have in Burlington?"

Kim's boyfriend nearly choked on his bread. Shotgun casually handed the kid a glass of water.

The boy took a sip and then put the glass down. "Sorry. Just, well, that was funny."

Gordo looked at him. "What?" Then he looked at Kim. "What did I say?"

Kim shrugged. "Well, I'm not wearing my uniform, so it's hard to tell, but I'm not a lance corporal anymore."

The boy coughed. Or maybe he laughed. Gordo couldn't tell.

"Congratulations, Kim," Amy said. She lifted her wineglass. "I know you're not technically old enough to drink, but I think this deserves a toast. To . . . well, what are you now if you're not a lance corporal? What's your rank?"

Kim hesitated, and then she lifted her glass. "Major general, actually."

Gordo couldn't figure out what was funnier: the way Kim's boyfriend blushed, the fact that neither Fred nor Amy seemed to understand what Kim's new rank meant, or the fact that the announcement made Shotgun spit out his wine. Either way, he had to laugh.

Shotgun shook his head. "Well, that's impressive." He put his arm around Fred. "That means she's a, what, two-star general?"

"Two very shiny stars," Kim said. She opened her hands up in a gesture of innocence. "It's pretty crazy. The armed forces don't work like that. The Marines don't work like that. But, well, I'm basically Cannon's bird dog, and between him and the president a lot of rules got broken."

They talked of her promotion for a while, of all the ways in which Cannon and the president bucked tradition and rewrote the laws to make it happen, and of the steep learning curve Kim was facing in her new job. And then she spent a while asking them about their new lives in Burlington. The entire time she never once stopped petting Claymore. After a while she pushed her plate a few inches away and wiped at her mouth with her napkin.

"The thing is," she said, "I really am here on business."

Fred let out a gasp. His voice shook as he spoke. "They're back?"

"Oh, gosh, no!" Kim used her free hand to touch Fred's hand. "I'm sorry. No. Honestly, I don't think we're ever going to feel completely safe, but since Nazca, since S-Day, we've been clear. Not even the hint of a whisper. I mean, yeah, every few days somebody has a scare and we have to check something out, but no. No more spiders. That's the thing, though. That's the special project. We've been devoting so many resources toward recovery, but maybe we need to put more resources into making sure nothing like this ever happens again. That's why I'm here."

"The answer is no," Amy said.

It surprised Gordo. It surprised everybody. He looked at his wife. She had a stern look on her face. He recognized it, because he'd visited her classroom one day and saw her whip it on when a few boys were acting up. It was a face that brooked no disagreement.

"Sorry?" Kim said.

"No. And I'm sorry, Kim, but I know why you're here. The president or Cannon or somebody wants Shotgun and Gordo to come to Washington to work on this project, and I understand that it's important, but the answer is no." She shook her head. "We've only been here for a few months, but we're settled. We're happy here. This is our home now. We're not going. Whatever it is, they can work on it here."

Kim looked at Amy for a few seconds. It was interesting for Gordo to watch. No matter how young Kim was, there was a strength to her that had been forged in the fight. Whatever the normal way of going about it was, she'd earned those two stars.

"Shotgun?" she said. "Gordo? Fred? Does Amy speak for all of you?"

One by one they nodded, because Amy was right. This *did* feel like home. Even if LA hadn't been nuked and radiation wasn't an issue, they'd never really thought about returning to the bunker out in Desperation, California. They'd lived there for years, but it had never been anything other than a place to live. No. Burlington was *home*.

Kim gave it a few beats and then showed her teeth in a genuine smile. "I told her you'd say that. But you know how the president is. Don't worry about it. I took care of it before I even came inside. Fred, Amy, don't take this the wrong way, but the president wasn't asking for you two, just Shotgun and Gordo. And if you don't want to go to Washington, that's okay." She looked first at Gordo and then leaned forward so she could turn and see Shotgun. "I'll walk you guys over to your new workshop in the morning, okay? We can talk through the project then. I've got a broad outline, priorities, requests, and some suggestions, but mostly we're going to be leaving it up to you two to figure things out."

"Uh, Kim?" Shotgun said. "Not to be a hassle, but I've got a job. Two jobs, really. I'm also on the town council."

"Not anymore. I told you, I took care of it. You've been reassigned. Both of you. You're full-time on Special Projects now." She winked. "We might be a bit diminished, but the US military can still get stuff done."

Despite himself, Gordo felt excited. Being a glorified shopkeeper wasn't exactly fulfilling. And judging by the expression on Shotgun's face, he wasn't disappointed either.

"Tell you what, Kim," Shotgun said. "How about instead of waiting until the morning, we head over there right after dinner?" He suddenly stopped and turned to Fred. "Sorry. Is that okay, honey?"

Fred shook his head. "Boys," he said, and although it was clear he was trying to have the word come out in a huff, he couldn't hide his smile either.

Gordo felt Amy give a gentle squeeze to his thigh, and across the table he heard Claymore let out a soft groan of pleasure as Kim scratched right behind the dog's ear.

It was a good night to be alive.

Washington, DC

M anny felt like he was going to throw up.

They were alone, just the two of them, in the Treaty Room. Bush and Obama had each used the Treaty Room as a private study, but the two presidents who followed them had preferred different spaces. When Steph took office, she'd had it redecorated. It was a private space, and one of the few places Manny knew they'd be alone.

Which didn't make it feel any less excruciating that she was just standing there, staring at him.

He couldn't take the silence.

"I know it's only been a couple of months since you and George decided to split, and it's only been a month since the divorce became official. But I feel like maybe I've been waiting my entire adult life for this, and we've wasted so much time, and—"

"Manny." She said his name quietly, but it was loud enough to get him to shut his mouth. "Manny. Sweetie. You're babbling."

"I'm nervous," he said. "And this is hurting my knees." It *was* hurting. Getting down on one knee was a much younger man's game.

"Then why don't you stand up, you great big fool," Steph said, "and kiss me."

He hesitated. "Is that a yes? Because you didn't say yes."

She reached out, took his hand, and helped him to his feet. And then, instead of waiting for him to kiss her, she kissed him, and in that kiss was the answer he'd been hoping for.

Loosewood Island, Maine

The wind was up over the water. Mike could taste the salt of the ocean spray. He could understand how it might not be for everybody, but he'd fallen in love with the island from the jump. It had been easy to fall in love when they first got there, just as the summer was bringing the long days and the hot sun that stood in such contrast to the frigid water. But even now, in the winter, Mike thought that sometimes everything just had a way of working out.

Well, almost everything. He'd stayed up well past midnight celebrating New Year's Eve the night before, and because it was a special occasion, there was plenty of booze at the party. He was out of the habit of drinking, and he'd been feeling kind of rough all day. The cold, wet air was good, though. It woke him up. He still wasn't convinced the island needed a full-time lawman, but he didn't have any other skills that he could think of, so he didn't mind the job. Besides, the truth was that it didn't really matter what job he did; people were always going to think of him as Mr. Melanie Guyer.

He'd been as surprised as anybody when she tracked him

down. She'd come to the island with her graduate student—now colleague—Julie Yoo, and a bodyguard complement of something like twenty flamethrower-toting Army Rangers. The Rangers were gone by the end of August, but both Julie and Melanie stayed behind. He was more surprised than anybody that he had embarked upon a second marriage before Halloween. And yet, not once had he had any reservations.

He had no idea that marriage could be so *easy*. He'd said as much to Fanny at Thanksgiving when the two of them were washing dishes. She laughed and told him that was how marriage was *supposed* to be, and the fact that he was so surprised said everything about why their own marriage had failed. That had been a good night, their two families and friends meshed together: Fanny doing most of the cooking, Dawson carving the turkey, Leshaun bringing over brussels sprouts and a pecan pie, Rex and Carla pleased as punch with themselves just to be there, Annie running around like a maniac and then falling asleep curled up on the rug like a dog after dinner, and Julie Yoo, thankfully, agreeing *not* to bring anything over, since it was universally agreed that she was a horrible cook. The whole night, every time Mike looked at Melanie, he couldn't understand his luck. Sometimes the universe just conspired to make you happy despite yourself.

They all got together like that once or twice a week, and it was always somewhat raucous. More so now that Fanny had given birth. Baby Rex. Which of course had made both Rex and Carla cry, which had made Fanny and Dawson cry, which . . . well, there was a lot of happy crying surrounding that. So now dinners meant Rex and Carla, baby Rex and Annie and Fanny and Dawson, Leshaun, Julie, and Mike and Melanie. Housing was at a bit of a premium on the island—there'd been an influx of people after S-Day—but Melanie and Julie's status afforded them some benefits, including a quick-built lab inside an empty storefront. The government had promised to break ground on a new building in the spring, with state-of-the-art equipment and enough lab space for Melanie's research group to grow.

He opened the door to their apartment. It was empty. Melanie must have still been at the lab. He checked his watch. He was, for once, early. He had an hour before she was going to get home. Quickly he locked his gun in the safe, changed out of his sheriff's getup into civilian clothes, and scribbled Melanie a quick note in case she got home before he was back. He thought for a second about seeing if Leshaun was free and wanted to join him, but decided not to stop in. At the end of the party the night before, Leshaun and Julie had been less than subtle about the fact that they were leaving together—according to Melanie, that had been going on for a couple of weeks—and Mike didn't want to drop in unannounced. Julie had dated a hangdog guy named Pierre for a couple of months—evidently she'd known him from college and then actually stumbled upon him while she was in Peru—but that had ended early in the fall, and Mike thought Leshaun and Julie seemed like they might be a great match. It made him happy to think of his partner partnered up.

He grabbed the kite and went outside. It was only a couple hundred yards from his and Melanie's place to the small clapboard house where Fanny and Dawson lived.

He knocked, and Fanny opened the door looking slightly frazzled. "Hey," she said. "Sorry. Rex just fell asleep. I cannot even tell you how lucky we were with Annie. That kid was an angel when she was a baby."

"You want to drop him and Annie off for an hour or two tonight? You and Rich can go out and do something like grown-ups for a bit."

"Rain check? Rich has to work late tonight."

"You know, if you'd told me a year ago that the world might end because of an ancient breed of flesh-eating spiders, I might have believed that. But if you'd told me that the world was *almost* going to end because of an ancient breed of flesh-eating spiders and that, when it didn't end, we'd all end up on an island off the coast of Maine and your husband would still be working as a defense lawyer? That," he said, "might have seemed like a stretch."

Fanny chuckled. "It kills you, doesn't it?"

"What?"

"That you like him so much."

"Yeah. A little," Mike said. "But it makes me happy to see you so happy."

"That's sweet, Mike." She stepped in close and gave him a kiss on the cheek.

"Ew," Annie yelled as she ran up to them. "Gross."

Fanny put her finger to her lips. "Rex is sleeping."

"Sorry, Mom," Annie said. She lowered her voice, but she didn't really look sorry. She looked excited. She spun in almost a full circle trying to get her coat on. "Is that it?" She snatched the kite from under his arm.

"Yep," Mike said. "Melanie put in her last requisition for lab equipment. I'm sure somewhere in Washington there's a clerk right now who's scratching his head and trying to figure out why Melanie needed a high-performance box kite with Spectra line. What do you think about that, kid?" he said, tousling her hair with his hand.

"You're weird, Dad."

Mike feigned being shot in the heart, and Fanny pushed the two of them out the door. He told her he'd have Annie back in an hour, but she said not to worry about it. Anytime before dinner.

The wind was coming steady now, and as they walked to the promontory, Annie talked his ear off. She told him about what her new best friends, a twin brother and sister, had gotten for Christmas; how Rex squeaked like a mouse while he was eating; how, if Leshaun and Julie got married—apparently, Mike thought, everybody but him knew about *that*—she wanted to be a flower girl again as she'd been for Mike and Melanie's wedding; and how Dawson was teaching her to juggle.

They held hands, and he noticed that she'd grown again. It seemed to happen in spurts. He'd see her one day, and the next she was simply taller. She was still his little girl, however, and he was happy to listen to her, to ask questions, to just be with her.

On the promontory, they assembled the kite and then tied the line. For a moment, holding the line made him feel nervous. It took a moment to process what was bothering him: something about the shape of the box kite and the Spectra line made him think of the pictures he'd seen of the queens and the cobwebbed corpses that had been found in the aftermath of S-Day. He could feel his breath catch in his throat and his heart rate start to jack up, but then he calmed himself. It wasn't true. They were gone. Melanie was clear about that. They were safe.

He didn't say anything, and Annie didn't seem to notice. She was too excited.

That's what he wanted for her. He wanted her to be a normal kid. As normal as any kid was going to be in this new world. He wanted her to be happy and to grow up and to have a life of her own. As he helped her launch the kite and watched her play the line out, he was struck with a sudden feeling of warmth and joy.

He'd done everything that needed doing. How close had they come to dying? What miracles had enabled him to get his family out of Minneapolis before the spiders reached the city, before it was wiped from the face of the earth? And with Leshaun's help he'd made sure that the kinds of men who preyed on the weak didn't find another victim. And then there was the gift of flight so freely given by Rex and Carla . . .

He stood there and watched Annie run back and forth, laughing, her eyes only on the kite. Beyond her, he could see the rolling sea and where the ocean met the sky, the great open waters that seemed to go on forever. The world was wide-open, but there was nowhere he needed to go anymore: everything he could ever want was right here, on this island.

The kite rose higher and higher, the line spooling out, and he could hear Annie laughing. He wanted to call his daughter back to him, to pull her into his arms and lift her up and hold her and tell her over and over again that he loved her, but he didn't do that. This made him just as happy. It was good to watch her run.

In some ways everything had changed, but in the most important way nothing had changed at all: He was still her father. He was still there to keep her feet safely on the ground. He was still there to help her soar.

ACKNOWLEDGMENTS

Thank you to my literary agent, Bill Clegg, and all the fine folks at the Clegg Agency, as well as to my screen agent, Anna DeRoy, at WME. Thank you to Emily Bestler, Lara Jones, and David Brown, at Emily Bestler Books/Atria; Anne Collins, at Penguin Random House Canada; and Marcus Gipps, at Gollancz.

Sabine, don't worry, I didn't forget about you.